THE CONW
BOUR KII

By Simon McCleave

A DI Ruth Hunter Crime Thriller

Book 9

Your FREE book is waiting for you now!

Get your FREE copy of the prequel to
the DI Ruth Hunter Series NOW
http://www.simonmccleave.com/vip-email-club
and join my VIP Email Club

*For Simon, Rachel, Jack,
Louie and Minnie x*

Note to the reader:

ALTHOUGH THE COVER of this book shows the title as the Anglicised 'The Conway Harbour Killings', I have opted to use the correct Welsh spelling of the town, Conwy, throughout the story. Apologies for offence caused to my Welsh readers.

PROLOGUE

SUNDAY 13th September

Stepping out of the shower, Geoff turned and looked at himself in the mirror. He wrapped a towel around his waist and gazed at his reflection. *Not bad at all,* he thought to himself. He was in pretty good shape for forty-eight. Flat stomach, defined chest and muscular arms, he still worked out at the gym he owned, and played veterans' rugby at the weekend. When he saw some of the other men his age at his gym or down at the rugby club, with their beer bellies and man boobs, he couldn't help but feel a little smug. Didn't they have any pride or self-respect? They lacked the kind of focus and discipline needed to look as good as he did. And Geoff enjoyed flirting with the gaggle of MILFs that congregated every weekend to watch their sons play rugby. Not only had Geoff won a couple of caps playing for Wales, he was now Conwy Rugby Club's chief coach which effectively made him God in the eyes of the teenage boys that he trained twice a week. It also made him very attractive to the bored middle-aged mums of Conwy. Geoff had been using that to his advantage for years now.

As he leaned towards the mirror and dried himself, he felt the familiar but excruciating pain in his lower back. The codeine he had taken a few hours ago must be wearing off. Opening the cabinet, he took another two tablets. He knew that taking 250mg of codeine a day was dangerous, but it was

6

the only way he could function. Years of playing rugby had taken their toll on his lower spine and it was irreparably damaged. Geoff had sought out several chiropractors in recent months, which had eased the pain a little – but not enough to quit the codeine. There was a nagging feeling somewhere in his mind that he was addicted to them, but it wasn't something he was willing to face right now.

Turning his right shoulder, he glanced at the large, red Welsh dragon tattoo which had the words *Cymru Am Byth* across the top – it meant *Wales Forever*. He'd had it done in his 20s before every other Tom, Dick and Harry decided tattoos were fashionable. Splashing cold water on his face, he looked back into the mirror and decided that he'd wait until the morning to have a shave. He met his eyes in the reflection. Even though he still had a post-coital buzz, he wasn't sure how comfortable he was looking at himself directly in the eye. It was a distinctly uncomfortable experience.

Stepping out onto the soft fawn bedroom carpet, he went over to close the curtains. The light of the day had faded to the darkness of evening. From where he stood, the black Medieval turrets of Conwy Castle cut across the horizon, and beyond that, Conwy Harbour. It was only the bloody English that spelt it Conway. The town's name derived from the old Welsh words, *cyn*, which meant chief, and *gwy*, which meant water.

Geoff had lived all his life in Conwy. His father had moved there in the 60s to work as a PE teacher in one of the local schools. His taid and nain, Welsh for grandfather and grandmother, once owned a huge sheep farm on the northern edges of Snowdonia close to the small village of Caerhun, on the west bank of the River Conwy. He had spent endless summer holidays there, helping his taid on the farm and swimming in nearby lakes. However, such halcyon memories would always be scarred by a fateful afternoon in the June of 1982 when his eight-year-old cousin, Reece, had drowned. He and Reece had spent that blazing hot afternoon jumping off the old wooden pier into Llyn Anafon on the lower slopes of the Carneddau mountains. Their family had fished for brown trout in the lake for generations, and the day before, he and Reece had spotted otters on the banks to the east.

Their taid had often told them about the time a German Heinkel He-111 bomber had been shot down over Snowdonia in April 1941. The pilot had tried to land the plane on the surface of Llyn Anafon, but he had lost control and it had crashed and sunk to the bottom of the lake. Their taid said that only one of the German crew members survived. The rear gunner, a man named Kurt Schlender, escaped the plane as it sunk, swam to the shore and walked down the valley to seek help at a farm in Cydgoed. After the war, Schlender went to live in Canada and in the 1960s, he returned to the area with his family to show them the lake and introduce them to the family who had helped him.

Excited by their taid's enthralling story, Geoff and Reece had often dreamed of diving to the bottom of the lake, finding the wreckage of the Heinkel bomber and returning to the surface with German medals or a Luger pistol. However, on that day, Reece had dived in too close to the bank and became entangled in thick weeds and plants. He couldn't escape and died. Geoff nearly drowned trying to rescue his cousin for over twenty minutes before raising the alarm. It had taken another hour before Reece's body had been found and cut free. Although he had never admitted it, Geoff had never really got over his fear of swimming anywhere outdoors.

A gust of wind from outside broke his train of thought as it rattled the open window and blew and billowed the curtains.

As he looked outside into the black sky, Geoff could see it was starting to rain. Droplets of water began to patter noisily on the painted wood of the window sill. *What ridiculous colour was it again?* he wondered to himself in annoyance. His wife, Claire, had chosen overpriced paint called 'Oval Room Blue.' He thought it was something to do with The White House, but apparently it referred to a formal 18th century style of room instead. *What a load of bollocks.*

The sound of creaking from the stairs grabbed his attention.

He listened for a second. The house was over two hundred year old and, as he used to joke, it creaked and groaned like a pensioner. He wondered if his wife Claire had come back from her business trip early. She would have shouted up if she had, but then again he'd been in the shower.

He got the distinct impression that someone was in the house. It was making him feel uneasy.

'Hello!' he shouted.

Nothing.

Turning to pull the curtains, he looked down into the street to check that Claire's car wasn't outside. It wasn't. *Phew.*

There was another noise from the staircase.

'Hello?' he said, this time more uncertainly.

Nothing.

There were a few seconds as he froze, listening intently. His pulse had started to quicken. He wasn't a man that was easily spooked but he sensed that he wasn't alone.

Suddenly, there was movement from the landing. It startled him.

Bloody hell!

Geoff glanced up to see a figure appear at the doorway.

It frightened him.

'What are you doing here?' he asked as his stomach tightened. Their appearance and facial expression made him feel uneasy.

As the figure approached, Geoff was occupied looking at their face and didn't see the knife coming at him. It plunged into the right-hand side of his stomach. The sickening sound of metal entering flesh.

'Jesus!' he gasped.

For a moment, he felt nothing but shock. *How can this be happening?* And then a white hot, searing pain from the stab wound. He was unsteady on his legs. Aiming a punch at the figure, he missed, and the knife came again. It seared through the flesh at the top of his right arm until it hit bone.

'What ... are you doing?' he yelled as his voice faltered in terror.

Now dazed, Geoff backed away. Was this really happening? His disbelief was escalating to fear. He put his hands up defensively. 'Stop ...'

Going into survival mode, Geoff ran at his assailant, pushing them onto the bed. He ran as best he could onto the landing and headed for the narrow wooden staircase. It didn't feel real. His heart was thumping hard in his chest.

Stumbling down the staircase, Geoff lost his footing, fell down the last flight and landed heavily on the floor. His head was swimming. Hearing the sound of the figure starting down the stairs after him, he scrambled to his feet. The blood from his stomach wound was dripping heavily down his leg and onto the floor.

He panicked as he headed for the front door. *If I can just get outside, I can escape.* He tried the door. It was locked. *Where is the key?* The spare key was hanging on a hook in the kitchen.

Please God, don't let me die!

Staggering along the hallway, he went into the kitchen and over to the back door. Twisting the handle, he felt the door open.

Thank God!

There was a sudden piercing pain in between his shoulder blades. He had been stabbed in the back. It took his breath away.

'Ahhh!' he wheezed as his body seemed to lock in agony.

With his head now spinning and dizzy, he turned around only to see the knife coming at him again. The figure gritted their teeth as they thrust once more.

Frantically he reached out to grab the knife. The blade pierced his hand and came out the other side. Screaming in pain, his pulse thumped noisily in his ear. He was losing consciousness.

Don't pass out. Whatever you do, don't pass out!

His assailant had a wild look on their face as they stabbed at him again.

Geoff's legs went from under him and he collapsed to the floor. *I'm not going to die. I refuse to die!*

He used his hands to crawl across the floor. The blood from his hand smeared over the tiles.

His vision blurred and lost clarity. Fighting to draw breath and stay conscious, he clawed at the floor like a dying animal in slow motion.

It was no use.

He stopped clawing.

Everything went black.

CHAPTER 1

31 HOURS EARLIER

Saturday 12th September

As the wind picked up, Detective Inspector Ruth Hunter of the North Wales Police gazed up at the sun, took a deep joyful breath and spun around in utter delight. She looked at the cobbled road of Pont Neuf, the oldest bridge over the River Seine. It was a far cry from the desolate countryside of Snowdonia that she now called home.

Sarah gestured for Ruth to pose for a photograph. 'You can smile, you know?'

'I don't know why we can't take a selfie,' Ruth grumbled as she perched on the beautiful ornate black lamppost and tried to recreate Gene Kelly's pose from *Singin' in the Rain*.

'I want a photo of you on your own,' Sarah laughed. 'But not like that.'

Ruth pulled a face and giggled. 'Oh, that's charming.'

Nearby, tourists inspected an ornate plaque a few feet away that explained in French that construction of the bridge had begun in 1578 during the reign of Henry III, and was completed under Henry IV in 1607. It was so exciting to be wandering around the French capital with all its history and culture.

Ruth couldn't believe that at last she and Sarah had been reunited. It was a search that had lasted over seven years. In fact, Ruth had to keep pinching herself to make sure that she wasn't dreaming. *Please God, don't let me wake up.*

Sarah gestured. 'Lean back against the side of the bridge and look happy.'

'I am happy, you plank!'

Looking around, Ruth took in the beautiful views of Paris, a city that dated back over two thousand years. The Pont Neuf was split into two parts, with one section going from the left bank of the River Seine onto the Île de la Cité island. The second stretch went over onto the right bank by the Musée du Louvre. Sarah groaned that the Mona Lisa had been a big disappointment, complaining that it had taken an hour to get near to something that she described as '... tiny and miserable looking.'

Ruth didn't think she had ever been as happy as at that very moment.

As Sarah took the photograph with her iPhone, Ruth noticed two men looking over at them and talking. They had shaved heads, dark stubble, and black bomber jackets. If she was going to make a guess, she would have said they were Eastern European. As they talked, she made eye contact with one of them and began to feel uneasy. Maybe being a copper for thirty years had made her paranoid, but she wasn't going to start taking chances.

Striding over to Sarah, Ruth grabbed her arm and said in a singsong voice, 'Come on, I need a sit down, a ciggie and an enormous glass of vin rouge.'

'Vin rouge?' Sarah hit her playfully. 'You never told me you were bilingual.'

With her eye on the two men who still seemed to be watching them, Ruth laughed. 'Bilingual, bisexual, I've got it all going on, darling!'

Sarah frowned and asked quietly, 'Who are you looking at?'

'No one,' Ruth said, endeavouring to sound cheerful. She didn't want to send Sarah into a panic. 'Come on. Let's keep going.'

The men turned and followed them.

Sarah grimaced. 'You're acting really weird.'

'Am I?'

'Well, weirder than your normal weirdness.' Sarah grabbed her hand. 'I can't believe we're here together in Paris!'

'I know, it's perfect, isn't it?' Ruth said, but she couldn't help glancing back. The men were now only twenty yards behind and one of them was talking into a mobile phone.

'I think we're being followed,' Ruth said in a virtual whisper.

'What? Are you kidding?' Sarah asked, and immediately looked behind. 'Shit! They don't look very friendly. I'm sure I recognise one of them.'

'Maybe we should run?'

'What? Really?'

The two men were speeding up.

'If fact, I definitely think we should run.'

'When?'

'Now,' Ruth said, pulling Sarah by the hand as they both began to sprint.

Ruth looked back. She was alarmed to see the men were running too. They were being chased.

Shit! Who the hell are they?

As they weaved in and out of the tourists, Ruth looked ahead to see how best to make their escape. Passing the gigantic statue of Henry IV sitting on a horse, they sidestepped a man selling balloons.

'What do they want?' Sarah yelled breathlessly.

'I don't know,' Ruth panted. 'And I don't want to find out.'

Their feet clattered on the cobbled stones of the road as they stepped off the pavement to avoid a large school party. The end of the bridge was only fifty yards away.

Ruth's lungs were burning as she scanned the road along the embankment, desperately looking for a police car. Glancing back, she saw the men had disappeared. Her eyes roamed across the bridge and the tourists behind them, but they were gone. *That's weird!*

Slowing down to a fast walk, Ruth glanced at Sarah. 'Where the hell have they gone?'

'I don't know,' Sarah shrugged as she squinted back at where they had just come from. 'How can they have vanished into thin air?'

'I don't know. Let's get into a taxi and get out of here,' Ruth said with a sense of urgency.

They stopped for a second at the end of the bridge to get their breath back.

Ruth shook her head. 'Did we just imagine that?'

'I don't think so ...' With her chest still heaving, Sarah looked at her. 'No, they were definitely chasing us, weren't they?'

Suddenly, a black Mercedes van pulled up onto the pavement with a screech about ten yards from where they were standing. A couple of pedestrians were startled and backed away.

The panelled door crashed open and two men in black balaclavas jumped out, ran to Sarah, grabbed her by the arms and shoulders and dragged her towards the van.

'Oh my God!' Ruth yelled, going to help her.

'Ruth!' Sarah screamed, but she was completely overpowered. 'Help!'

Ruth frantically grabbed one of the men around the throat. He turned, punched her square on the jaw and Ruth stumbled back in a daze.

'Helps us! Please!' Sarah screamed at the crowds of people. No one reacted.

Before she could clear her head and do anything else, Ruth watched helplessly as they pushed Sarah into the back of the van. The panelled door slammed shut, and the van sped away down a side road and out of sight.

'No!' Ruth cried at the top of her voice.

Blinking her eyes open, Ruth gasped for breath. Her heart was thumping in her chest. She felt the weight of the duvet on top of her. As she opened her eyes fully, she took a deep breath and then glanced around her dark bedroom.

Letting out an audible sigh of frustration, Ruth sat up in bed and ran her hands through her untidy hair.

'Jesus Christ!' she mumbled under her breath.

The nightmares about Sarah had become an almost nightly occurrence.

Throwing the duvet off in exasperation, she knew that only a coffee and a ciggie would make her feel better.

This is getting ridiculous!

It had been four weeks since Ruth had seen her missing partner, Sarah Goddard, on a FaceTime call to an elite escort agency in Paris for a fleeting few seconds and said 'Hello'. Before Sarah had responded to the call, the screen had gone blank – but not before Ruth had heard what she thought was Sarah scream.

The emotional impact of seeing Sarah had been immense and overwhelming. Ruth hadn't seen or heard from her for over seven years. No one had. The date was etched on Ruth's mind like the chiselled date on a tombstone. *5ᵗʰ November 2013*. It was the day that Sarah boarded the 8.05am commuter train from Crystal Palace station to London Victoria but never arrived. She had vanished. No contact, no note, no idea where she had gone. As a copper, Ruth had made sure the CCTV footage from that day had been scoured. Every station on that line had been searched. There had been television appeals and articles in the press. There had been sightings of Sarah from all around the world. Ruth had followed women she thought looked like Sarah. But she had simply disappeared off the face of the earth.

Ruth sat up and swung her legs over the side of the bed. She stared down at the carpet for a while. Her whole body still carried the tension from her dream.

What day is it? she thought trying to focus on the day ahead. *Saturday*. It should have been a leisurely day but she and Nick had to go and take a statement from a witness.

Getting up, she padded through the kitchen. The wooden floor was cold underneath her feet. As she clicked the kettle, the growing noise of the boiling water was a welcome relief against the uncomfortable silence of the house. Daylight from outside came in through the kitchen window and the open blind created a striped pattern on the stone floor. The light seemed to be colourless.

Taking her coffee to the bathroom, Ruth undressed and turned on the shower, waiting for it to warm up. She reached for the plastic radio in the form of a leaping pink salmon, that was attached by suckers to the mosaic wall. It had been a present from Sian and they had howled with laughter at its sheer tackiness. *Blinding Lights* by The Weeknd was playing. She loved The Weeknd! The catchy melody of the upbeat music began to take her out of herself.

She stepped into the shower, closed the door and let the sprays of hot water hit her face as she tried to wash away the edgy tension in her body.

OPENING HIS EYES FOR a moment, Detective Sergeant Nick Evans peered at the woman sleeping next to him. Seeing the tresses of dark hair that lay across the pillow, he remembered it was DC Georgie Wild. With his heart racing in a panic, Nick tried to play back the events of the previous evening. This wasn't good. *What the bloody hell happened?* he wondered. He didn't even drink these days, so he couldn't have blacked out from alcohol. *Oh God, this is not good.* Georgie Wild was a work colleague and Nick had a partner, Amanda, and a young daughter Megan.

You dickhead, Nick, what have you done? he thought, feeling sick with anxiety.

Nick blinked rapidly as he became more awake. *Was that a dream? And am I now awake?* He was still feeling full of anxiety.

Looking again at the tresses of hair on the pillow next to him, he saw they were now blonde.

Amanda stirred, rolled over and looked at him.

Thank you, God.

'Are you all right?' she asked in a sleepy voice. 'You look really weird.'

'Just a dream,' Nick said as his anxiety dissipated.

'Nightmare?'

'Sort of,' he replied with a guilty shrug.

Amanda reached out with her hand and touched his face. 'Hey, happy birthday!'

It's not my birthday. What's she talking about?

Nick smiled then as he remembered it was the fourth anniversary of his last drink and therefore his fourth Alcoholics Anonymous birthday. 'Oh yeah. I don't know how that's happened.'

Amanda grinned. 'It's brilliant. I'm so proud of you.'

'Not bad for a smelly old alchy.' Nick leant over and kissed her.

'I bought you a cake.'

He laughed. 'How many candles would you need?'

Amanda rolled her eyes. 'Four candles. Very good.'

They were referring to the lines from a classic BBC comedy sketch where a customer goes into a hardware shop for *fork handles* only to be handed *four candles*, resulting in a lot of amusing confusion.

Nick glanced at his watch – it was 8am. 'Ruth's picking me up in half an hour.'

'Eh? It's a Saturday.'

'I thought I told you?'

'No, you didn't,' Amanda said grumpily.

'We've got to get a statement from someone before they leave the country,' Nick explained. 'I'll only be gone a couple of hours. Promise.' He leant in and kissed her gently on the mouth.

'Are you kissing me just to pacify me?' she asked, arching an eyebrow.

'Yes, of course.'

'How's Ruth doing? I haven't seen her since that horrible FaceTime thing with Sarah.'

Nick shrugged. 'I think part of her is relieved. A couple of months ago, it was a fair assumption that Sarah was dead. Now she's seen Sarah on CCTV and then on FaceTime.'

'Yeah, but that then throws up the question of what the bloody hell has Sarah been doing for the past seven years, doesn't it?'

Nick nodded. 'Of course. And part of me thinks that's somehow worse.'

'Worse than being murdered?'

'In some ways. It means that Sarah chose to just disappear. How does that make Ruth feel?'

'What if she was taken against her will?' Amanda asked.

'I've seen the CCTV from outside The Dorchester Hotel. She didn't look like she was doing anything against her will.'

'Maybe she was on drugs? Or maybe she's being black-mailed to do what she's doing?'

Nick nodded. 'Ruth said she thought she heard some kind of scream when the FaceTime call cut out, but she wasn't sure.'

'God, that's horrible.'

Nick got out of bed and headed for the shower.

'Nick?'

He turned back to look at her.

'Yeah?'

'Make sure you look after her, eh?'

'Ruth?'

Amanda nodded. 'Yeah.'

Nick frowned. 'She's my boss.'

'She still needs looking after,' Amanda said with a shrug.

'Yeah, I know.' Nick smiled and then gestured to the bathroom. 'Want to join me?'

'Not after you told me you pee in the shower.'

'That was once, and it was ages ago. Come on, it's my birthday.'

Amanda rolled her eyes and laughed as she got out of bed. 'All right. But I'm not washing your willy.'

'We haven't got enough soap to do that,' Nick quipped.

'In your dreams, Sergeant Evans. I've seen bigger acorns out on the lawn.'

CHAPTER 2

IT WAS A CHILLY SATURDAY afternoon and Zoe Ellroy stamped her feet on the cold ground, trying to get warm. Autumn had truly arrived, and the summer felt like a distant memory. Zoe had just turned forty-six but with dyed black hair and a nose stud, she wasn't going to allow herself to look mumsy like most of the middle-aged women standing beside the rugby pitch.

Glancing across at a huddle of muddy teenage rugby players, she picked out her son, Louie. Short, muscular, with scruffy blonde hair, he looked older than most of the others even though he had only just turned seventeen. Watching him give a rousing team talk filled her heart with joy. He was Conwy Rugby Club's U-18s fullback and star player. He had already represented North Wales and there was now talk that he might be called up into the squad for Wales U-18s. The only thing against him was his volatile temper. Louie's family were very proud of him. They had Geoff Williams, Conwy Rugby's ex-pro and handsome coach, to thank. Taking Louie under his wing from the age of ten, Geoff had guided him to become one of the best players the club had ever produced. Zoe had made it no secret that she had a crush on Geoff.

'I don't know how you do this every week,' said a voice from behind. Zoe turned to see her daughter, Rhian, shivering.

Zoe rolled her eyes. 'I told you to put a decent coat on.'

'Can I go and sit in the car?'

'No.' Zoe pulled a face. 'They haven't started yet. Come on, you hardly ever watch Louie play these days. He'll be gutted if you sod off to the car.'

'I'm sure he won't even notice, Mum ... I'll give it ten minutes.'

Rhian was Zoe's twenty-one-year-old daughter. She was attractive, with thick dark hair and chestnut eyes. It was a family joke that the parental/child roles had been reversed. Rhian was the sensible one and would scold Zoe on her latest tattoo, for getting drunk, or for being too loud or inappropriate. Rhian had just finished a degree in Chiropractic Therapy in South Wales and was now working at a local practice. She had moved back home to save up enough money to buy a house with her long-term boyfriend, Jason. Zoe had told her that she was far too young though. Zoe wanted her daughter to travel the world and live life to the full before settling down. However, Rhian was an adult and she needed to let her make her own mistakes.

The other issue was that Zoe, and her husband Neil, weren't fans of Jason. He was a bit rough and ready for their liking and they wished Rhian had met someone at university rather than continuing to see Jason. But her daughter insisted that she loved him and they were going to build a life together.

Zoe spotted Geoff Williams on the opposite side of the pitch and pointed to him. 'There's Geoff. I wondered where he'd got to.'

Geoff was often talked about at home as he had been such an integral part of Louie's future in rugby.

'I know, Mum. I have seen and met him before,' Rhian said, sounding distinctly disinterested. 'You act like he's a bloody popstar.'

Zoe smirked. 'He could take me for a bit of personal coaching any day.'

Rhian's eyes widened. 'Mum!'

Zoe laughed and shrugged. 'What? Your dad knows I've got a soft spot for Geoff.'

'Yeah, and it pisses him off. He doesn't even like Geoff. Dad's just nice to him because of Louie,' Rhian groaned.

Zoe raised her shoulders. 'Yeah, but you've got to admit, he's pretty fit.'

'For an old man,' Rhian joked, shaking her head.

'Bloody hell, Rhian,' Zoe protested. 'The man's only two years older than me!'

Rhian grinned. 'Your point being?'

'You cheeky sod!'

Rhian rolled her eyes. 'You're meant to be a happily married woman.'

'I am. No harm looking, is there? Not your type then?'

'No, of course not. I'm not looking for a father substitute!'

Zoe laughed as she turned to watch the two rugby teams face each other in preparation for kick off.

'What are you two cackling about?' asked Neil Ellroy, Zoe's husband and Rhian's father, who was approaching. He was short and skinny with a balding head that had been shaved.

Zoe saw Rhian instantly bristle. Neil and his daughter didn't really get along and nothing Zoe did seemed to be able to mend their relationship. Even though it was hard to admit, she knew that Neil had some kind of resentment towards their adopted daughter.

Without acknowledging her father, Rhian looked at Zoe and said, 'I'm going to the car, Mum.'

As Rhian marched away, Neil rolled his eyes. 'Oh, something I said.'

'Maybe if you didn't treat her like a second-class citizen, things would be a bit easier,' Zoe suggested.

Neil ignored her comment and pointed over to a man in a tracksuit on the opposite side of the pitch. 'That's the scout from the WRU, love.' It stood for Welsh Rugby Union.

Knowing that there was a scout watching Louie made Zoe feel nervous. 'Christ. I hope he has a good game. I'd love him to play for Wales.'

'The trials are in two weeks' time,' Neil said.

'If he gets selected,' Zoe said anxiously.

Neil put a reassuring hand on her shoulder. 'Don't worry, he'll have a good game. And Geoff will put a good word in for him - that counts for a lot.'

Zoe gave a wry smile. 'Bloody hell, Neil. You're a two-faced sod. You spend all your time slagging that man off, but now you think he can help Louie you think he's all right.'

Neil pulled a face. 'I wouldn't go that far. The man's still a prick in my book.'

An opposition player kicked the ball long and high into Conwy's half. Steadying himself, Louie watched the ball and prepared to catch it.

'Go on, son,' Neil yelled from the touchline.

As Louie took the ball expertly into his chest, an enormous boy clattered him with a dangerously high tackle. Louie crumpled to the floor in a heap.

There were gasps and angry shouts from the touchline.

'Oh my God!' Zoe gasped in a terrified voice. She had seen a local rugby player who had been paralysed from the waist down after a neck tackle. He sometimes came to watch games in his wheelchair and it broke her heart to see him like that. Sometimes she wondered why she had ever allowed Louie to play rugby.

'For fuck's sake! You can't do that!' Neil shouted.

Getting slowly to his feet, Louie shook his head and steadied himself as the referee came over to give a penalty and talk to the other boy.

Zoe sighed. 'Thank God. I thought he'd broken Louie's neck.'

Louie and the boy who had tackled him began to fight. At first, they squared up to each other, pushing and shoving. Then, out of nowhere, Louie threw a punch that cracked against the other player's jaw. It poleaxed him and he crumpled to the floor in a heap and didn't move.

'Bloody hell!' Neil exclaimed.

The referee immediately brandished a red card and sent Louie off.

As Louie stormed over to the touchline, Geoff said something and Louie shoved him before marching away.

Zoe looked at Neil. 'You'd better go and talk to him and calm him down.'

Neil frowned. 'I thought he'd stopped acting like a total psycho on the rugby pitch.'

Zoe shook her head and glanced apprehensively over at the WRU scout. 'So did I.'

CHAPTER 3

SUNDAY 15th September

Wrapped in a blanket, Ruth took a deep drag of her cigarette and blew out a bluish stream of smoke into the air. Looking out at the North Wales countryside that stretched away, she could see that the leaves had darkened a little. Autumn was here. The air smelled different and the colour of the sky was less vibrant.

The bells from St Dunawd's Church in Bangor-on-Dee chimed to signal the Sunday morning service. If Ruth craned her neck, she could just about see the 18th century church's bell tower. Her thoughts turned to Sian. She had loved the autumn and claimed it was her favourite season. She said it was an excuse to unpack her cosy jumpers and scarves, cook stew, and drink heavy red wine. Thinking of Sian in her favourite rust jumper, Ruth felt a tear come to her eye. It had only been six months since her on-off partner Sian had been killed in a police operation at Solace Farm. There were still mornings when Ruth woke and was convinced Sian was lying next to her in bed or pottering around in the kitchen. And in those precious few seconds of deceptive normality, the darkness of her grief was replaced by a wonderful but cruel lightness. The expectation that Sian was going to appear any second with two cups of tea, followed by the stark, overwhelming and terrible realisation that it was never going to happen again.

'You know that only grannies sit in the garden with tartan blankets wrapped around them?' said a voice. It was her daughter, Ella.

Turning around to look at her, Ruth gave her a sarcastic grin. 'It's bloody cold, you cheeky sod.'

Ella held up a bottle of wine. 'Fancy a drink?'

'Always,' Ruth said with a smile.

How could her beautiful little girl be only days away from turning twenty-five? It seemed like it was only yesterday that she had pushed her on the swings on Clapham Common, bought her ice-creams, or picked her up from nursery. Ella was the one thing in life that Ruth felt she had got right.

'Here you go, Grandma,' Ella joked, putting the glasses of wine down on the garden table.

Ruth took a swig from the glass. 'I won't be a grandma until you procreate, and that doesn't look like it's going to happen anytime soon,' she said.

'Oh, my God. Now that I've got a boyfriend, you're not going to be one of those mums that guilt-trips their daughter into having a baby, are you?' Ella groaned.

'Far from it. I'll encourage you to travel and live life to the full before you do that,' Ruth explained.

'You think you were too young when you had me?' Ella asked, sounding a little concerned.

'Probably. But you're the best thing I ever did with my life.'

Ella seemed awkward – she didn't like flattery. She put her glass of wine down and asked, 'Have you heard back from the French police yet?'

Ruth shook her head. 'Not yet. It's in the hands of the Police Nationale, and they're meant to be liaising with Interpol and then the Met. So, as you can imagine, it's a bureaucratic nightmare.'

'Don't worry, Mum. I'm sure they'll track her down.'

Ruth looked at her, shook her head and said quietly, 'I saw her ... I actually saw her. And I was just so close to talking to her. And now she's vanished again.'

Ella put a reassuring hand on her shoulder. 'Hey, at least you know she's alive, and all those years searching for her weren't wasted. The best way to look at it is that you're closer now to finding out what happened than ever before. That has to be a positive.'

Ruth gave her a wry smile. 'How did you get to be so wise? You don't get that from me, and you definitely don't get it from your dad.'

Ella shrugged and then grinned. 'I just look at how you and dad deal with things ... and then do the opposite.'

Ruth laughed. 'Bloody cheek. Now pour me some more wine.'

PUSHING MEGAN IN HER pushchair through St Stephen's Park in the middle of Llancastell, Nick found a bench close to the playground and sat down. He had bought a takeaway latte. For a moment, he got a glimpse of himself and the life he now had. It was Sunday morning and he was sitting with a coffee, his daughter asleep in the pushchair. He didn't have a hangover, and there was no guilt or shame from the night before. In the old days, he would have been drunk by now. He'd have woken on a Sunday as a complete wreck and had a few ciders just to take the hangover away. Thank God for AA and sobriety.

With a sense of well-being, he sat back and took in the view. There was a boys' football game over in the far corner of the park and he could hear the odd shout or cheer for a goal. He had left Amanda at home to sleep. She was three months pregnant and it seemed to have knocked her for six. It wasn't a surprise. She had suffered from severe fatigue when she was pregnant with Megan.

He spotted an attractive woman jogging towards him down the central pathway. She was wearing a white baseball cap and he couldn't help admiring her figure as she got closer.

Try not to stare, mate. She'll think you're some kind of perv, he said to himself and turned away towards the playground. He would take Megan on the little swings if she woke up soon.

'Nick?' asked a female voice.

Looking up, he realised it was the woman he had watched jogging. She peered down at him and smiled. It was Georgie.

Oh shit!

His pulse quickened.

'Georgie. I didn't see you there,' he said. Technically, he was lying.

With her chest heaving, Georgie tried to get her breath and pointed to the bench. 'Mind if I sit down?'

'No, of course not. I can give you CPR if you need it,' he joked.

'Ha, ha. I might need oxygen though!' Georgie gave him a sarcastic smile. 'Had a girls' night out last night. I was trying to run it off, but I actually feel worse.'

Nick laughed. 'Yeah, my solution to that was to get back on the sauce. And I don't recommend that slippery slope.'

'Oh, yeah. I forgot you don't drink,' Georgie said as her breathing returned to normal. 'Must be nice to wake up every Sunday with a clear head.'

'Definitely.'

'No Alison?' Georgie asked.

'It's Amanda,' Nick replied, aware that Georgie got her name wrong every time she said it.

'Oh, God, sorry. Amanda.'

'I brought Megan out so Amanda could sleep in,' Nick explained.

Georgie grinned. 'You wouldn't think it, but you're quite a catch aren't you, Nick?'

'I can't work out if that's a compliment?'

Georgie leant forward as Megan woke gently and opened her eyes. 'Ah, she's beautiful, isn't she? Hello, Megan.'

'Yeah. I promised to take her on the swings before we go back.'

Megan blinked and smiled.

'Aww, she's got your eyes,' Georgie said.

Nick smiled. 'That's what everyone says.'

Georgie looked at him. 'Lucky her. They're your best feature.'

Nick felt his pulse quicken. 'Right.'

Georgie got up and gave him a grin. 'Right, I'd better get back. Long hot bubble bath might do the trick. See you tomorrow, Sarge.'

Nick watched her as she jogged away.

ZOE TOOK A PILE OF plates from the table and chucked them into the dishwasher. She wasn't one of those uptight people who were fastidious about how a dishwasher needed to be stacked. Life was way too short for that. The family had just finished their usual Sunday brunch – eggs, bacon, mushrooms, sausages and, most importantly, Welsh black pudding from the local butchers.

Rhian was sitting at the table trying to avoid helping to clear up, which wasn't unusual. Instead, she was staring at her phone.

As Zoe approached to wipe down the table, Rhian turned to look at her. 'I need to ask you something.'

Zoe shrugged. 'Okay.'

'But I don't want to piss you off.'

Zoe laughed. 'I'm sure you're not going to piss me off. What is it?'

'I'm thinking of trying to track down my birth mother, but I want to know what you think?'

'Erm ... I think that's great.' Zoe gave a half smile. Even though she had always told Rhian she would support her if she wanted to find her birth mother, the thought also scared her. She feared her relationship with Rhian would change. 'I said to let me know if you feel that's what you want to do.'

Rhian pulled a face. 'Doesn't it make you feel weird?'

Zoe took a few seconds. She wasn't sure how honest she should be. 'Maybe a little bit. But it's not about me, it's about you.' Zoe went over and put her hand reassuringly on her daughter's shoulder. 'I'm happy you want to do it. Honestly.'

'There seem to be a few companies out there who will help me get hold of my adoption records.'

'What's brought all this on?' Zoe asked with a smile.

'I don't know really,' Rhian said. 'You told me about my birth mother ages ago didn't you?'

Zoe nodded. 'Yeah. The agency told us her name was Lisa. She was seventeen, a single mum, and had been a heroin addict - but not during the pregnancy.'

'She was from Liverpool, wasn't she?' Rhian asked.

Zoe nodded. 'From the sound of it, she'd had a really hard life. But that was a long time ago, love.'

Rhian frowned. 'Sometimes I worry that if I did try and track her down, I'd find out that she was dead or something horrible.'

'I guess that might happen,' Zoe said. 'But it might be better to know something like that, rather than worry about it. She might be perfectly happy and married with kids.'

'Then I think how difficult it must have been to give me up,' Rhian said. Zoe could see she was lost in thought.

'I don't think it's a decision she would have taken lightly,' Zoe reassured her.

'But then I think it would have been easier if she had just had an abortion,' Rhian said. 'And then I just wouldn't be here would I?'

'Hey, don't worry about that,' Zoe gave her a hug. 'You *are* here and that's all that matters.'

'I don't know how people do it, do you?' Rhian asked.

'You mean, have an abortion?'

'Yeah,' Rhian nodded. 'I don't know how anyone thinks that's okay.'

'It's hard to judge unless you're in someone else's shoes, love,' Zoe shrugged. 'You sure you're okay?'

'Yeah. I just know that once I've found her, there's no going back. And that's a bit scary,' Rhian explained and then pointed to her phone. 'I'm going to send this company a message.'

'Good for you,' Zoe said as she went across the kitchen and put Louie's breakfast in the warming part of the oven. Then she looked over to where her daughter sat. She loved the very bones of her. She was a smart, funny and accomplished young woman. They had adopted Rhian when she was only two weeks old. She and Neil couldn't seem to conceive. Of course, when Zoe had fallen pregnant with Louie four years later she and Neil were gobsmacked. Louie was a medical miracle.

'I can't believe you make Louie all that food and then put it in there for when he gets up. He's so spoilt,' Rhian joked. 'I'm sure you never did that for me when I was his age.'

Zoe rolled her eyes. Rhian seemed to be convinced that Louie was their favourite, even though she had done everything in her power to treat them exactly the same. The fact that Louie was her biological child meant that she had to be extra vigilant to be fair. Neil found it harder to hide his preference for Louie and it had been a long source of conflict within the family. He always denied any favouritism, but Zoe knew it hurt Rhian intensely.

'I'm sure I did.'

'Where is golden-balls, anyway?' Rhian asked.

'Still in bed. I think he's still sulking after yesterday,' Zoe explained.

'Yeah, well he really lost the plot,' Rhian said. 'At least we know he's not perfect.'

'I think the pressure of having that Welsh scout watching must have got to him,' Zoe said, but she knew that Louie's explosive rage was ruining his chances of making a career in rugby.

Neil came into the kitchen looking annoyed. 'I found Geoff skulking around outside. He came to see if Louie was all right.'

'Louie owes him a bloody apology!' Zoe tutted. 'Where is he?'

'Taking off his shoes. Said he doesn't want our carpets to get ruined.'

Zoe knew that Neil wouldn't be overjoyed that Geoff had popped in but he would never say anything.

'Bloody hell. I think that ship's sailed,' Zoe said, and saw that Rhian had answered her phone and was getting up. 'Where are you off to?'

Rhian pointed to the phone. 'It's Jason. I'm going to the garden because the wi-fi in this house is crap.'

'Are you not going to say hello to Geoff?' Zoe asked.

Rhian frowned sarcastically. 'It's all right, thanks. I don't really know him.'

Just as Rhian went out onto the patio, Geoff entered the room with his usual winning smile. 'Morning everyone.'

He really is very charismatic, Zoe thought, hoping that she didn't look too bedraggled. She would have spruced herself up if she'd known that he was popping in.

Zoe gestured to the table. 'Come and sit down.'

'Thanks. I'm not staying long. I just wanted to check on Louie after yesterday,' Geoff said pulling up a chair.

Zoe could see that Neil was doing little to hide his indifference to Geoff.

Right on cue, a shaggy-haired, bleary-eyed Louie wandered into the kitchen. When he saw Geoff sitting there, his eyes widened.

Geoff laughed. 'Talk of the devil.'

'Morning ...' said Zoe as she glanced at the clock on the wall. It was 11.55am. '... just about. Geoff came to see how you're doing.'

He looked over at Louie with a wry smile. 'How you doing, sunshine?'

Louie shrugged awkwardly and grunted, 'Yeah, all right.'

'Eloquent as ever,' Neil said, rolling his eyes.

'I know it was a bad tackle yesterday, mate,' Geoff said. 'But you've got to keep your cool in a situation like that. We've talked about it before.'

'What did the scout say?' Zoe asked.

Geoff pulled a face. 'He didn't get to see Louie play. There was no way he could invite him to the trials.'

Louie let out an audible sigh. 'Bloody hell!'

Zoe smiled. 'Couldn't you put a word in for him?'

Geoff looked at Zoe and Neil. 'I'm going to be honest with you guys. I can't recommend him for trials if he's going to do what he did yesterday.'

Louie glared at him. 'Oh, thanks very much.'

Neil couldn't hide his disappointment. 'I know it wasn't a one-off but you've told me how talented you think Louie is.'

Geoff shrugged. 'Talent's no good without discipline and control on the pitch.'

Zoe could see that Neil was getting agitated.

'Come on. Give him a second chance,' Neil said.

'I can't at the moment. It's my reputation at stake. I'm sorry.'

'No, you're not sorry!' Louie growled. 'You're a pompous wanker!'

'Louie!' Zoe exclaimed as Louie stormed out of the kitchen.

Getting up from the table, Geoff seemed a little embarrassed.

'I'm really sorry,' Zoe said.

Neil fixed Geoff with a stare. 'I can't believe you're not going to give Louie his shot.'

There were a few awkward seconds, and then Geoff pointed to the door. 'I'll see myself out. Thanks for the coffee, Zoe.'

As he disappeared, Neil glared at Zoe.

'What?' Zoe asked.

'I told you he was a prick!'

Zoe shrugged. 'I can see Geoff's point of view though.'

Neil snorted as he got up from the table. 'Well that's not a big surprise, is it?'

CHAPTER 4

EVEN THOUGH IT WAS a Sunday, the shift rota meant that both Ruth and Nick were working in Llancastell CID. Having been out to take a statement from an eyewitness in a robbery, they were making their way back across town. The mid-afternoon traffic was thinning out.

'Is the grumpy little lady any better?' Ruth asked. Nick had mentioned that Megan had caught a cold and was particularly grisly and moany.

Nick pulled a face. 'You know. Still bossy, pedantic and uber tidy ...'

Ruth snorted. 'Did you just use the word 'uber', Nick?'

Nick smiled. 'Possibly.'

'God, you've changed from that monosyllabic, slightly neanderthal Welshman I met a few years ago,' Ruth joked.

'That's sobriety for you,' Nick said. 'So, Amanda is her usual self. Luckily, Megan is now on the road to recovery so the helmet and body armour can come off.'

Ruth laughed. 'I was asking about *Megan*, you twit!'

Nick grinned. 'Yeah, I know.' He then reached over and checked the Tetra radio system. 'It's been so quiet in CID in the past few weeks, I'm starting to think this thing isn't working.'

'Oh my God,' Ruth tutted. 'You said the Q word.'

'What?'

'It was always police folklore in the Met. If you said things are *quiet*, then something major always happened,' Ruth explained.

Nick shrugged. 'Good. I'm bored when I'm not busy.'

'You're unbelievable,' Ruth said, as she rolled her eyes. 'I bet the residents of Llancastell are glad to know that you're praying for some terrible crime to happen because you're a bit bored.'

'That's not what I meant.'

From out of nowhere, a white jeep sped past and then tore down a side road.

Ruth frowned. 'Where's the bloody fire?'

'Ah, at last. A bit of action,' Nick said as he snapped on the blues and twos, put his foot down, and followed the car.

Ruth shook her head. 'You must be really bored if you're chasing traffic offences.'

'Zero tolerance to all crime, Boss.'

A few seconds later, they spotted the jeep up ahead. Without indicating, it screeched right and down another side road.

'You know who drives white jeeps, don't you?' Nick asked rhetorically.

Ruth shrugged. 'Hairdressers, footballers?'

'Well, yeah. I was going to say drug dealers.'

'I thought they drove black Range Rovers?' Ruth asked.

'Only in *Line of Duty*.'

Turning hard right, they gazed ahead, but the jeep had disappeared.

Ruth frowned as she scanned the road in front. 'Where the bloody hell did they disappear to?'

Nick pointed to a line of parked cars. 'There.'

The jeep had parked over by the pavement and Nick pulled up behind.

As they climbed out of their car and approached the jeep, the sound of AJ Tracey's *Ladbroke Grove* was thundering from the vehicle's stereo.

They reached the driver's door and the young woman inside buzzed down the window. She was wearing thick eye make-up, fake tan, and had her blonde hair pulled back into a ponytail.

'Hello?' she said with a slightly inane grin.

Oh God, what have we got here? Ruth thought.

Getting out his warrant card, Nick peered down at her. 'Could you turn off the ignition and radio please?'

'Oh shit!' The woman smiled sheepishly as she turned off the engine and lowered the volume. 'How can I help?'

'Do you know why we've followed you down here?' Nick asked.

The woman gave him a flirty grin. 'Don't I recognise you from Tinder?'

Ruth stifled a laugh – *Wow, she's got balls.*

'Just answer the question please, Miss.'

'Louise,' she said, fluttering her eyelashes at Nick. 'Was I doing something wrong then, officer?'

Nick glanced over at Ruth as if to say, *Is she for real?*

'Speeding and driving erratically,' Nick replied.

She giggled. 'Sorry? What's driving erotically?'

Nick looked into the car. 'And you're not wearing a seatbelt.'

Louise pointed to her chest. 'I've just had my tits done, and it's really sore when I wear a seatbelt.'

Ruth bit her lip to stop herself from laughing. She could hear that the young woman was slurring her words.

'I'm not sure that's a valid excuse.' Nick raised an eyebrow. 'Have you been drinking today?'

'Not that much,' Louise said.

Nick reached down and opened the driver's door. 'Can you get out of the vehicle, please?'

'Bloody hell!' Louise was offended. 'I'm really late for my nephew's christening. Can't you just give me a ticket and let me go?'

'If you could get out of the vehicle please,' Ruth said sternly.

Louise gave Nick a disparaging look. 'What's her problem?'

'I believe you are over the legal alcohol limit to be in charge of a vehicle. So, I need to get a uniformed patrol here to administer a roadside breathalyser test,' Nick explained. 'Do you understand what I've just told you?'

She got out of the car and looked at Nick. 'You're very handsome, do you know that? I love men with beards.'

As Louise tottered over to the pavement, Ruth could see that she was completely hammered. In fact, it seemed like she was going to topple over at any point.

Oh my God, how was she even driving?

Walking back to their car, Nick opened the rear door and gestured to Louise. 'Why don't you sit in here until the uniformed patrol arrives, eh?'

Louise staggered over and cackled. 'You want me to get in the back of the car with you? Jesus, you don't hang about, mate.'

Nick looked over at Ruth and rolled his eyes. 'Come on. Just get in.'

Louise then pointed over to Ruth and giggled. 'Hey, does your mum know you're on Tinder?'

Bloody cheek!

Louise stumbled and fell into the car, and Nick closed the door behind her.

Ruth bristled. 'Don't you dare say anything.'

Nick shrugged. 'What?'

Ruth gave him a sarcastic smile. 'This is all your bloody fault, you do know that?'

'What? How can this be my fault?'

'You said the Q word. You cursed us, and now look what we're dealing with,' Ruth said gesturing to Louise who had just left a lipstick kiss mark on the window.

IT WAS DARK AND RAINING heavily as Zoe arrived home with Jack, the family's pet labrador. She towelled off Jack's wet legs and paws and then watched him head for the water bowl. They must have walked a good three miles and Zoe's legs felt heavy from the effort, but in an agreeable way.

For once, the kitchen was as she left it an hour or two earlier. Clean and tidy. Neil had texted her to say he was checking a few things at the nearby housing development that his company was building. Rhian had gone to see her boyfriend, Jason, and might well stay the night at his house. That just left Louie.

Zoe poured herself a glass of white wine from the bottle she and Neil had opened the night before. She went out of the kitchen and into the hallway that was in darkness. She clicked on a small table lamp.

'Louie? Are you in?' she yelled up the stairs.

Nothing.

He could be asleep, listening to music, or just ignoring her. She would go and check on him in a minute.

Wandering back into the kitchen, she picked up the TV remote and put on *Antiques Roadshow*. It was a suitably relaxing and comforting way of spending time on a Sunday night.

As she sat down at the kitchen table, Zoe thought to herself how nice it was to have peace and quiet in the house for once. She gazed at the television screen, and her mind turned to Louie. She was worried by what she had witnessed the day before on the rugby pitch. It wasn't the first time that Louie had lost his temper in a game and been sent off for violent conduct. And his reaction earlier that day to Geoff had been totally unacceptable. Maybe it was just all the testosterone running around his body.

The noise of the front door broke her train of thought.

Must be Neil coming back, she thought to herself.

As she watched the hooded figure coming down the hallway towards her, she could tell that it wasn't Neil.

'Louie?' she asked, getting up from the table.

As Louie came into the kitchen, she could see he was in a dark tracksuit and he was soaking. He had AirPods in his ears.

'Did you get caught in the rain?' she asked him as he took the AirPods from his ears and nodded.

He had a very peculiar expression on his face, which immediately worried her.

'Are you all right? Do you want me to get you some water?'

'Yes, please,' Louie mumbled as he sat down at the kitchen table.

Going to the tap, Zoe looked at him. 'You don't normally go running at this time.'

'Does it matter?' Louie grumbled.

'Have you overdone it?'

'Probably.'

As she handed him the glass of water, she noticed that he was shivering. 'Are you cold?'

It hadn't been chilly when she had walked Jack – in fact it was a fairly warm autumnal evening. But she could see Louie was shaking as he lifted the glass to his mouth. 'Are you all right, darling? You're shaking.'

'Yes, Mum. Bloody hell. I ran five miles. Of course I'm shaking!' he snapped at her.

Louie stood up and pulled off his sweatshirt. 'All right if I get this washed?'

Zoe pointed upstairs. 'If you pop your wet clothes in the washing basket when you have a shower, I'll get them washed for you tomorrow.'

Louie was now taking off his tracksuit trousers. 'Can't I just put them on to wash now?'

What's the rush with washing the clothes? she wondered.

Zoe shrugged. 'Pop them in the machine then.'

There was something about his behaviour that was making her feel uneasy. He had only washed his own clothes once or twice before. She knew her son, and he was hiding something from her.

Wandering past her, Louie headed into the hallway and up the stairs to have a shower.

A few seconds later, the front door opened. This time it was Neil. He took off his wet boots and raincoat.

As he walked down the hallway, Zoe could see that his shaved hair was wet.

'Cup of tea?' she asked with a smile.

'Something stronger,' he said, blowing out his cheeks. 'I'm bloody soaking.'

Zoe poured him a glass of wine, and watched as he went over to the sink to wash his hands. As she joined him, she could see that he had a large, bloody gash running from the knuckle of the forefinger towards the base of his thumb.

'Jesus Christ, Neil. How did you manage to do that?' she asked.

'Someone's kicked down one of the mesh fences at the site. Don't know if it was someone trying to steal something or just kids messing about. I tried to put it back and did this.'

Zoe went into the laundry room and over to the medicine cabinet. She pulled out a box and found a bandage and some antiseptic cream. Looking down at the floor, she noticed that Louie had dumped his wet tracksuit beside the washing machine rather than put it inside.

'Bloody hell, Louie,' she muttered under her breath.

Bending down, she scooped up his sweatshirt and shoved it into the empty washing machine. She then picked up his tracksuit bottoms. As she was putting them into the washer, something at the bottom of the trouser legs caught her eye. A dark substance had splattered on the material. At first, she thought it was mud – but it wasn't the right colour. Smudging it with her finger, she saw that the specks of whatever it was were a dark ruddy brown.

With a slightly uncomfortable feeling, she screwed them up, put them into the machine, added a washing powder tablet and turned the machine on.

Still lost in thought about Louie's strange behaviour when he had returned from the run, Zoe went back to the kitchen.

'Here you go, love,' she said, going over to the sink and unscrewing the top from the antiseptic.

Neil looked at her. 'You okay?'

Zoe shrugged. 'Yeah, fine. Do I not look okay?'

'Not really. You look away with the fairies.'

'It's nothing. Long day,' she replied with a smile. 'Now come on. Let's get that dry and I'll put some cream and a bandage on it. It looks nasty.'

CHAPTER 5

MONDAY 14th September

It was nearly 7am by the time Claire Williams pulled up outside her house. It was her favourite time of day to look out at Conwy from where she lived with her husband Geoff. The sun was rising above the horizon and the early morning clouds were stained in hues of orange that then scattered over the bay.

Claire got out of her car and went to get the suitcase from her boot. She had spent the weekend at a dreary sales conference in Liverpool. The only saving grace had been the food and drink on company expenses, and a drunken snog in the hotel lift with Rupert Phillips, the sales rep from Aberdeen. Rupert had suggested that she go with him to his room to see the great view he had of the Albert Docks. Claire explained she was a married woman, although she didn't use the adjective *happily*. She had no desire to see Rupert with no clothes on. In fact, the thought made her feel a little queasy. Plus, she had someone else waiting in her room for her and she didn't think a threesome with Rupert was on the agenda.

She and Geoff had been married for nearly ten years. However, she got the feeling that they both felt their marriage had run its course. Even though she was convinced that Geoff had had several affairs, she could never prove it. And while he was busy having an affair, or coaching the local rugby team, he was out of the way and she could do what she wanted. It also meant that he no longer pestered her for a dull, passionless shag in the missionary position, which was what their sporadic sex life had consisted of for years. Geoff was a fucking narcissist who believed his own press.

She was forty-five and there was a whole kinky, sexually gratifying world out there for her to explore. Claire was aware that Geoff's latest affair, which she thought had probably started a few months ago, was making him happy and energised. Maybe this time he had met someone he wanted to leave her for? She really didn't care. They would sell the house and she would move on with her life.

Walking up the drive, Claire let out a sigh. It had been an early start and a long drive. Her boss, Nigel, had allowed the sales team to work from home that afternoon. She couldn't wait to get in, have a hot shower, and sleep for a couple of hours.

She opened the front door. The lights on the ground floor were all still on.

That's weird. Why's Geoff left all the lights on?

Claire wheeled her suitcase through the front door and hung up her coat. Her eyes felt heavy from the long weekend and early morning drive.

As she went to the foot of the stairs, she spotted something on the cream hall carpet. At first, she thought it was chocolate.

Or is that red wine? What the hell has Geoff been doing while I've been away?

As she headed down the hallway towards the kitchen, she spotted more stains on the carpet. Her stomach tensed as she wondered if what she was looking at were actually blood stains.

What the hell has happened here?

She entered the kitchen and saw a crumpled heap over by the back door. For a second, she thought it was washing. Then she realised it was a body.

Oh, my God! Geoff!

She felt sick and began to shake.

Walking over cautiously, she saw Geoff's body lying face up by the back door. His naked stomach and towel were soaked with blood.

'Oh my God, no! Geoff? Geoff?' she screamed as her entire body shook. She leant down and touched his neck and his face.

They were stone cold.

He was dead.

CHAPTER 6

RUTH AND NICK PULLED up outside the property belonging to Geoff and Claire Williams on Bay Road in Conwy. There were already two uniformed patrol cars and a SOCO van parked outside. A tall uniformed officer was just finishing taping off an area around the house. Some neighbours had come out onto the street to see what was going on.

Ruth approached the officer and flashed her warrant card. 'DI Ruth Hunter and DS Nick Evans, Llancastell CID. What have we got, Constable?'

Putting the roll of blue and white tape on the pavement, the constable fished his notebook from his top pocket. 'Victim is a Geoff Williams. His wife, Claire, entered the property at seven this morning and found her husband lying dead on the kitchen floor.'

'What do we know about the victim?' Nick asked.

'He was forty-eight. Ran a sportswear company and a local gym. Ex-pro rugby player,' the constable explained.

Nick frowned. 'Geoff Williams? I know his name.'

'Think you know him from when you played rugby?' Ruth asked.

'Maybe. I think he played for Wales.'

Ruth looked back to the constable. 'Any idea of cause of death?'

'Yes, ma'am,' he said. 'From what I could see, the victim was stabbed once upstairs in the bedroom and then again in the kitchen. There's a trail of blood across the landing, down the stairs and along the hallway.'

Wow, he's keen, Ruth thought.

'Any sign of the murder weapon?' Nick asked.

'No, sir. I only had a quick look around and then let the SOCOs get on with it.'

Ruth nodded. 'Anyone else live in the house? Kids?'

The constable shook his head. 'No, ma'am. It's just the two of them.'

'Where's Mrs Williams now?' she asked.

'She's with my colleague, PC Abbott. They're in the conservatory at the back of the house. You can access it from the garden if you don't want to go through the house. Obviously, Mrs Williams is very shaken up,' he explained.

Ruth nodded. 'Can you start a scene log for me? And can you get some preliminary statements from the neighbours either side? Tell them that they need to stay put until me or DS Evans has spoken to them. They're not to go anywhere. If the press arrive, I want them kept at a distance too.'

'Yes, ma'am.'

'You said that Mrs Williams entered the property at seven this morning. Where had she been?' Nick asked.

'A sales conference over in Liverpool. She drove back this morning.'

'Thank you Constable.'

Ruth looked at Nick as they made their way to the open front door. 'That's an early start.'

Nick nodded. 'She must have left Liverpool before six then.'

A SOCO approached and handed them each a full forensic suit and mask.

'Thank you,' Ruth said as she began to pull on the Tyvek suit with its distinctive chemical smell. *God, I hate these things.*

'Who's the lead SOCO today?' Nick asked as he pushed his arms into the suit.

'Tony Amis,' the SOCO replied.

Ruth had worked with Amis several times since she'd arrived in North Wales. He was thorough, and even though he seemed jovial, she had seen that he didn't suffer fools at a crime scene.

Pulling the elastic around her ears to secure her surgical face mask, she got a waft of rubber from the purple gloves she had just snapped on.

As Nick gestured for her to go into the house first, a couple of SOCOs made their way from the premises carrying evidence bags.

'Good morning, DI Hunter,' boomed a distinctly public school voice. It was Amis. He gave them both a salute. She could see his milky white skin and bushy ginger eyebrows from behind his mask.

'Morning, Tony,' Ruth replied as she followed him across the aluminium stepping plates. She could see the familiar dark stains of blood on the carpet. 'Any idea of time of death yet?'

'Quick guess would be yesterday evening or night. I would have said well before midnight. We'll know more after the postmortem.'

Casting her eyes around the ground floor, Ruth noticed the sparse and slightly sterile nature of the home. Framed black-and-white photographs of desolate Snowdonia landscapes lined the wall that led down to what she assumed was the kitchen.

As they arrived at the kitchen, Ruth saw a SOCO taking photographs of a body that lay on the floor by the back door. The man was naked from the waist up with a long towel wrapped around his middle. There were dark patches of congealed blood across his stomach, his shoulder, and the towel. A large Welsh tattoo on the top of his right shoulder was visible under the smears of blood.

'What does that say?' Ruth asked as she indicated the tattoo's inscription.

'Wales Forever. I guess it's to do with rugby, given his background. Looks like he was trying to escape,' Nick said, pointing to where the body was positioned by the back door that was open by about six inches.

Ruth nodded as she glanced around the modern kitchen. 'Any signs of forced entry, Tony?'

Amis shook his head. 'No. Nothing to suggest a break-in. Laptops and jewellery are all still here. No sign that this was a robbery.'

Nick gestured to the ceiling. 'You think the attack started upstairs?'

'Definitely. The blood trail leads from the bedroom, down the stairs, and ends here,' Amis explained. 'There are deep stab wounds to the stomach and shoulder, which I think happened in the bedroom. The wounds to the victim's back and hands happened where he fell here.'

'Okay.' Ruth pointed back towards the stairs. 'Let's go and have a look, shall we?'

'Yes, Boss,' Nick said as they moved across the stepping plates.

There were a few framed family photographs on the wall beside the staircase. As they didn't have children, Ruth assumed they were possibly nephews and nieces. There was also a large photograph of a man playing rugby – it had to be Geoff Williams.

Nick nodded towards the photograph. 'I recognise him.'

'He's too old for you to have played rugby against, isn't he?'

'Maybe. I'm sure I've seen him at Llancastell nick. We had him in for something.'

'It'll come up on his PNC check,' Ruth said, wondering whether this had anything to do with his death.

They reached the landing and headed right, following the stepping plates to what looked like the main bedroom. It was neat and tidy but lacking in character. In fact, Ruth thought it was decorated like the bedroom you might find in a business hotel chain.

There was a door open on the far side that she could see led to an en-suite bathroom.

Glancing around the room and noting the yellow plastic markers that signified bloodstains on the carpet, she tried to piece together what could have happened. 'Our victim was about to have a shower, or had just had one. He came out into the bedroom with a towel around him and was stabbed just over there.'

Nick nodded as he made his way to the en-suite bathroom. 'Yeah, there's no blood inside the bathroom, Boss.' He searched through the bathroom cabinet.

Ruth continued, 'We've got no signs of a break-in, so how did our attacker get in?'

'Maybe he knew them? Or maybe they had a key?' Nick suggested.

'He might have left the door unlocked. It still amazes me that people in North Wales still leave front doors unlocked for any Tom, Dick or Harry to come wandering in.'

'Spoken like a true Londoner,' Nick said with a smile. He then showed her a blister pack of pills. 'One of them was on anti-depressants.'

Ruth gestured downstairs. 'Let's speak to the victim's wife.' Ruth knew that two thirds of all murders are committed by partners, or former partners. Therefore, any investigation into a murder in a domestic setting like this has to start with that hypothesis.

'We need to check her alibi. I'll contact the hotel in Liverpool,' Nick said as they walked back down the landing to the stairs.

'Let's get an ANPR check and see if we can see where and when she actually drove back from Liverpool,' Ruth said, thinking out loud. 'We need a family liaison officer. And Mrs Williams will need to stay somewhere else for the next day or so while forensics are here.'

Nick nodded. 'Yes, Boss. I'll talk to the neighbours before we go and see if they saw or heard anything. They might have heard her arriving home.'

Ruth and Nick went outside and took off their forensic suits. It was never a good idea to interview anyone dressed like that if you wanted to put them at ease. They then made their way down the side of the house to a large well-kept back garden, and spotted the open doors to a conservatory. Claire Williams was sitting inside with a female uniformed officer.

Ruth smiled. 'Thank you, Constable. We'll take it from here.'

The female officer nodded, got up and left.

Claire held a tissue and her face was blotchy and red from where she had been crying.

'It's Claire, isn't it?' Ruth asked gently as she and Nick sat down on a large sofa.

Claire gave a slight nod, but she seemed shell-shocked.

'I'm so sorry for your loss,' Ruth said with compassion. 'I'm Detective Inspector Ruth Hunter and this is my colleague, Detective Sergeant Nick Evans. Would it be okay if we asked you a few questions?'

She stared at them blankly. 'Yes.'

Nick took out his notepad and pen. 'We understand you had been in Liverpool for the weekend?'

'Yes,' she said, her voice faltering. 'It was a sales conference for the company I work for.'

'Could you tell us what you did and where you were last night?' Ruth asked.

Claire took a few seconds to compose herself. 'We all had dinner at the hotel. Some of us stayed in the bar for a bit. And then I went to bed.'

Ruth looked carefully at her. Was she lying to them? Had she in fact travelled back to North Wales? Had she discovered

something in Geoff's life that she wanted to confront him
with? Had things escalated and got out of control?

Nick glanced up from his pad. 'What time did you go up
to your room?'

'Ten. Something like that.'

She seemed very nervous when she said that.

'And what did you do then?' Ruth asked.

'I had a shower, went to bed and watched the television.
And then I went to sleep,' Claire explained in a cautious tone.

*Ruth's instinct was that Claire was lying about something.
She wasn't sure what it was.*

Nick nodded. 'And what time did you leave the hotel this
morning?'

'Just before six.'

'And you drove straight back here?' Ruth asked. 'Or did
you stop along the way?'

'I stopped for petrol just past Chester,' Claire explained.

'You don't happen to know where you stopped for petrol,
do you?' Nick asked.

Claire shook her head. 'No. But I have the receipt so I
could tell you from that, if that's helpful?'

She seems very confident about that.

Ruth gave her a kind smile. 'Yeah, that would be useful.'

'And when you got home, you came straight into the
house?'

'Yes.'

'And could you tell us what happened then?'

Claire took a deep breath. 'The lights were on downstairs.'

'And that was unusual?'

'Yes.'

Claire pursed her lips as a tear rolled down her face. 'Then I saw something on the carpet. It was ... blood. And so I followed it down to the kitchen. And that's ... when I saw Geoff.'

Closing her eyes, Claire sobbed and dabbed her face with the tissue.

Ruth leant forward. 'Thank you, Claire. I know how difficult this must be for you ... Did you call 999 straight away?'

Claire nodded. 'Yes.'

'At the moment, we can't find signs of a break-in. Would the front door to your house usually be locked?' Nick asked.

'Yes,' she replied, her voice ragged. 'We had a burglary a few years ago at our last house, so Geoff's very security conscious.'

'Does anyone except for you and your husband have a key to the house?' Nick enquired.

Claire nodded. 'Myra Davies, our neighbour. Just in case we get locked out or there's an emergency.'

'And you get on well with Mrs Davies?' Ruth asked.

'Oh yeah. She's in her seventies. Sometimes she comes over for a cup of tea.'

'Is there anyone you can think of that might want to harm Geoff?' Nick asked.

Claire shook her head tearfully. 'No. I was sitting thinking about it before you came in. I just don't understand who would want to do this to him.'

Ruth was beginning to think that Claire was genuinely telling them the truth. At least, that was her initial instinct based on the past few minutes.

'Any arguments at work?'

'No. Nothing. It doesn't make any sense.'

Nick looked over at her. 'When was the last time you spoke to your husband?'

'Saturday night. About eight, I think,' Claire said.

'Did he mention anything that was out of the ordinary?'

Claire shook her head. 'No, not really.'

'Do you know if he was planning on seeing anyone yesterday?' Ruth asked.

Claire thought for a second and then nodded almost imperceptibly. 'There was something actually, but I don't think it's anything.'

'Go on. Anything, however small, might help us,' Ruth said softly.

'Geoff said something had happened at the U-18s rugby match. A boy, Louie Ellroy, got sent off. I think he and Geoff had a row or something, so he was going to pop around and see Louie. He's got a soft spot for him.'

Ruth's ears pricked up at that comment. Geoff was a man in his late 40s who had *a soft spot* for a teenage boy. Was it something they needed to look at?

'Geoff was going to Louie's parents' home to talk to him on Sunday?' Nick asked to clarify.

Claire nodded. 'That's what he said.'

'He didn't mention that he was going anywhere else?'

'No. He was looking forward to a beer and binge watching something on Netflix.'

'You said he's got a soft spot for Louie? What did you mean by that?' Ruth asked.

'He's always said that Louie Ellroy is a naturally gifted rugby player. He's always supported him. I think he saw Louie as the son he never had,' Claire explained. 'Geoff sounded a bit upset that they'd fallen out.'

Ruth nodded and thought they should pay a visit to Louie Ellroy's family for starters.

CHAPTER 7

THE ELLROYS LIVED IN a small detached farmhouse on the outskirts of Conwy. Dating from the late 1800s, it was built from grey stone with a black slate roof. The windows and front door had been recently painted in a fashionable bay green, and the front garden was neat and tidy, with an array of stylish wooden flower boxes and hanging baskets.

Nick and Ruth pulled up on the drive. Although they had run through all the things that needed to be checked for the investigation, they hadn't had time to really dissect what Claire Williams had told them.

'What did you think of the wife?' Ruth asked.

Nick shrugged. 'She seemed genuinely upset. But we know how often it's a partner that's involved. If she's lying about being in Liverpool, or when she came home, that's going to be a big red flag.'

'What about Geoff Williams' relationship with Louie Ellroy?' It was the one thing Claire had told them that had made Ruth a little uneasy.

'Yeah,' Nick responded. 'I did wonder about that. A forty-eight-year-old rugby coach and a seventeen-year-old boy who he treats like a son. After the Sheldon Inquiry, that stuff always rings alarm bells.'

The Sheldon Inquiry had been set up to investigate allegations of historic child sexual abuse in UK football clubs. These investigations had sent shock waves through the football community, with several football coaches being jailed and nearly nine hundred victims coming forward.

Ruth rang the doorbell, then stood back and waited. A dog barked from somewhere inside and then the door opened. A woman in her 40s, with dyed black hair and a nose ring, gave them a quizzical look. 'Can I help?'

Ruth and Nick flashed their warrant cards. 'We're from Llancastell CID and we're looking for a Louie Ellroy? We understand that he lives here.'

The woman nodded. 'Yes. I'm his mum. Do you want to come in?'

'Thank you,' Ruth said as she and Nick entered. 'Is he in?'

'He's still in bed, I'm afraid. Teenage boys ...' Zoe said, and then her face darkened a little. 'Is this about Geoff Williams?'

Ruth nodded. 'Yes. We're investigating his death.'

Zoe shook her head and looked upset. 'I couldn't believe when I heard it on the news. He was here yesterday, sitting in our kitchen and ... Sorry.' She wiped a tear from her face. 'Come through.'

Ruth and Nick followed her down the hallway and into the large farmhouse-style kitchen. 'Please sit down. Can I make you a tea or a coffee?'

'We're fine thanks,' Ruth said as she and Nick sat at the large oak table. The kitchen was a mixture of the traditional farmhouse style - Aga cooker and a Welsh dresser, with a modern fancy-looking coffee machine and a flat screen television mounted to the wall.

Nick took out his notebook and pen.

'Did you know Geoff well? Ruth asked.

Zoe leaned against the kitchen counter. 'Yes. He's been Louie's rugby coach for seven years. But we know him socially too.'

Nick glanced up from his notebook. 'And is it just the three of you here?'

Zoe shook her head. 'I have a daughter, Rhian. She's twenty-one.'

'Is Rhian here?' Ruth asked.

'No. She was at her boyfriend Jason's last night. And I assume that she's at work today.'

'Could you tell us where she works?'

'At the Conwy Therapy Clinic. She's a chiropractor there.'

Ruth nodded with a kind smile. 'So, Geoff came to this house yesterday?'

'Yes.'

'What time would you say that was?' Nick asked.

'About twelve, I guess.'

'Could you tell us what happened when he was here?'

'Neil, that's my husband, invited him in. He had come to see if Louie was all right after what happened at the game on Saturday.'

Ruth looked at her. 'We understand that Louie and Geoff had some kind of argument?'

'Yes. A boy from the other team neck-tackled Louie. It was very dangerous. Louie reacted, punched him, and was sent off,' Zoe explained. 'Geoff tried to talk to Louie and calm him down. I think he shoved Geoff. That was it.'

'Was it unusual for Louie to react like that?' Nick asked.

Zoe paused in thought for a second. 'Not really. He's got a bit of a temper, but he's not normally that angry.'

'Geoff and Louie had a short row after the game, and he came to see if Louie was okay. How did that go?' Ruth asked.

'Not very well. There had been a Welsh Rugby scout at the game. They were supposed to be watching Louie to see if he'd be invited to the trials for the Wales U-18s.'

'Except he got sent off,' Nick said.

'Yeah. But Geoff knows a lot of the people at the WRU. We thought he might put a word in for Louie to see if they would give him a trial anyway.'

'But he wouldn't?'

'No. He said he couldn't do that. Not after Louie had punched another player.'

Ruth raised an eyebrow. 'And how did Louie react?'

'He was upset. And disappointed.'

'What about you and your husband? How did you feel about Geoff's decision?' Ruth asked.

'I said it was fair enough. I could see Geoff's point of view, it's his reputation. But Neil was pretty pissed off with him.'

Ruth processed this for a moment. Both Neil and Louie had been angry with Geoff only six hours before he was murdered. But was their resentment about the rugby trials really a motive to go and kill someone?

She allowed a few seconds of silence before asking, 'Could you tell us where you were last night, Zoe?'

Zoe's brow clenched, as if she wasn't sure why she was being asked the question. 'I was here.'

'All night?'

Zoe thought for a second. 'I took the dog out for a walk.'

'What time was that?'

'About sixish, I guess.'

Nick nodded. 'And how long were you out for?'

'An hour, maybe a bit longer,' Zoe replied.

'Was everyone in the house when you got home?' Ruth asked.

'No.' Zoe shook her head. 'Louie got back just after me. He'd been for a run. And then Neil came in a few minutes later.'

'Where had your husband been?' Nick asked.

'Just checking a broken fence on a housing development his company is running,' Zoe said as she went over to look at a piece of paper beside the phone.

'How long was he out of the house for?' Ruth asked.

'An hour and a half at a guess,' Zoe said with a shrug. 'You'll have to ask him.'

'And what about Louie? How long did he run for?'

'Just under an hour normally. He went out while I was walking the dog.'

'Could we have a chat with Louie now?' Ruth asked.

Zoe frowned and gestured to the piece of paper in her hand. 'He's left me a note. He's gone out on his bike.'

Something from Zoe's reaction made Ruth think there was something unusual about this.

'Does he often go out on his bike?' Ruth asked.

Zoe glanced up at the clock on the wall. 'Christ, not this early. He doesn't get up until lunchtime in the holidays. I don't even know if he's heard about what's happened to Geoff.'

Ruth noticed Zoe's expression. Although she was trying to hide it, Zoe seemed unduly concerned by Louie's disappearance. Was he really out on his bike? He was a seventeen-year-old boy so why was she so worried? Was there something far darker about Louie's absence from the family home that was actually troubling her?

IT WAS MID-AFTERNOON and Incident Room One was now buzzing with chatter, excitement, and the odd boom of laughter. Murders were still pretty rare in North Wales, so the anticipation of a homicide investigation was palpable. There were around a dozen CID officers, mostly male and middle-aged. Ruth came out of her office and spotted Nick talking to the *new girl on the block*, DC Georgina Wild, or Georgie as she was known. Ruth could see she was attractive in a slightly obvious way. She certainly wasn't Ruth's type. However, she was worried that Georgie was Nick's type. In recent months, she had got an uneasy feeling about their growing friendship. As Nick spotted Ruth coming out of her office, he made his excuses and walked across IR1. It was exactly that kind of thing that made her worry. She would keep an eye on it. Workplace affairs, or *going over the side* as it was known in police slang, were common in the force. Ruth had reasoned that it was because of the high-octane and dangerous nature of the job. Those who weren't police officers, *the civilians*, didn't understand what it was like.

Clutching her files, Ruth made her way to the front of the room as she focused on the new investigation. 'Good afternoon, everyone. If we can get going please.'

CID had already set up a large investigation scene board. At the centre was a holiday photo of Geoff Williams, pint of Guinness in hand and wearing a British Lions' rugby shirt, looking directly at the camera, carefree and smiling. Geoff's details were written in blue marker to one side. His name and address, date of birth, plus the time and location of his death.

Ruth walked over to the whiteboard and pointed to the photo. 'Okay. I don't know if you've had a chance to see this, but this is Geoff Williams, our victim. This was a brutal attack on a defenceless man in his own home. And I want you to look really hard at the photo because it should be important to all of us that we get justice for Geoff and his family. He worked in the community, and had given a lot of his time coaching kids to play rugby. He deserves our best work, and I want us to be meticulous in everything we do.' Ruth was calm. 'Okay, what have we got so far, Nick?'

'Boss. Geoff Williams, aged forty-eight. Former rugby player. He owned a local gym and sportswear company. As you said, Geoff was heavily involved as a rugby coach at the local Conwy Rugby Club, working with boys at all levels. His wife, Claire Williams, returned from a work conference in Liverpool to their home in Conwy at seven this morning. Geoff had been stabbed whilst in the bedroom and then again when he reached the kitchen where he died. We have an FLO with Claire now and she has gone to a local hotel until SOCOs have finished their forensic examination of the house.'

'Thanks, Nick.' Ruth nodded. 'So, we need initial statements from the neighbours. When was the last time they saw Geoff? Did they see him leaving or returning home yesterday at any point and, if so, when? Did they see anyone else coming or going? Or anyone else around the property or in the vicinity? Did they hear or see Claire Williams arriving home as she claims to have done at seven this morning?'

A young bearded officer, Detective Sergeant Daniel French, looked over. 'Boss, I've spoken to the council. CCTV coverage in that area is virtually non-existent. Our best bet is to talk to Traffic and see if we can spot vehicles in the area yesterday evening. The nearest set of lights with a camera is Talbot Street, which is half a mile away.'

'Thanks, Dan. I'd like an ANPR check too. I want to make sure that Geoff Williams visited the Ellroy's home at the time that Zoe Ellroy claims.'

DS Dan French had recently passed his Sergeants' Exam and was now an acting DS in CID until further notice. Ruth liked French's calm and intuitive approach to police work. She had high hopes for him within the CID team.

Ruth pointed to the photograph of Geoff. 'Our victim was seen having an altercation with Louie Ellroy after he was sent off in a game on Saturday. When Geoff visited the family home on Sunday, he said that he wouldn't be able to recommend Louie for trials for the national Welsh U-18s. Zoe said that both her son and husband were angry. It's a long stretch for that to be a motive for murder but, at the moment, it's the only thing we've got of any significance in Geoff's life in the days leading up to the attack. I need someone to get separate statements from Neil and Louie Ellroy. And split them up to see if we get any discrepancies between the two. At the moment, I want us to assume the killer targeted Geoff Williams rather than this being a random crime. Let's see if we can build up a pattern of the victim's life. The answer will be somewhere in his lifestyle. Bank accounts or any money worries? His mobile phone records. Computer history. Social media. Any medical problems? Disputes with staff at his gym or sportswear company?' Scanning the room, Ruth saw that Georgie was trying to catch her eye. 'What have you got, Georgie?'

'Initial forensic report from SOCOs,' Georgie said pointing to a printout. 'There was no sign of the murder weapon at the crime scene. There is a large Sabatier kitchen knife missing from the wooden knife block in the kitchen.'

'Thanks Georgie. I guess the PM will tell us if our victim was stabbed by a kitchen knife.'

'No signs of a break-in or disturbance. We do, however, have a partial trainer print with a trace of blood.' Georgie raised an eyebrow. 'Forensics think it's a UK size 5, which I'm guessing is a woman's size.'

'Size 5?' Ruth's eyes widened. 'Could be a woman's shoe. Or it could be a child or teenager.'

AS ZOE SCANNED THE TV channels, she stopped when she saw BBC Wales News. A serious-faced female presenter appeared behind the news desk. Dressed in a grey trouser suit, she read from an autocue as the dramatic news music played.

'A massive police hunt is underway in North Wales to find the killer of Geoff Williams, a well-known rugby coach in the Conwy area. Mr Williams' body was found at his home early this morning, with police saying that he had been brutally attacked. They are appealing for any witnesses who may have seen anything suspicious. Tributes, flowers, and cards have been arriving at the Conwy Rugby Club ground, for a man who had played and coached there for over thirty years.'

Muting the volume, Zoe tried to get her head around the fact that Geoff had been killed. It just didn't feel real to her. *Who would want to harm Geoff?* she wondered to herself. She took a deep breath and blinked away a tear.

Looking up, she saw the front door open and Neil come in. He seemed preoccupied, but that wasn't surprising given the events of the last twenty-four hours.

'Everything okay?' Zoe asked as Neil came into the kitchen, even though she knew it was a slightly inane question.

'Have you seen Rhian?' he asked with a frown.

Zoe shrugged. 'No. Not since she left yesterday. I did text her. Why?'

Neil leant against the work surface. 'The clinic called me about five minutes ago. Rhian didn't turn up for work. She just sent a text saying she wasn't feeling well. They rang me to see if she was okay.'

'That's weird. She was all right last night,' Zoe said, but there was something that bothered her about what Neil had said. 'And you know what Rhian's like. She would have made a phone call to say she was unwell. I don't think she would have sent a text?'

'I suppose so,' Neil said with a shrug. 'I'm sure she's fine. Jason would have called us if there was anything to worry about.'

Zoe knew that Neil was probably right, but Geoff's murder had made her jittery and anxious. 'I'm going to call Jason just to check.'

Neil nodded as he went over to grab himself a beer from the fridge.

'Since when do you drink on a Monday lunchtime?' Zoe took out her phone and dialled Jason.

Neil frowned at her and muttered. 'It's not really your average Monday, is it Zoe?'

Even though she knew he had a point, Neil didn't need to have taken that tone with her. Her mobile phone connected to Jason's. It rang four times and then switched to his voicemail. 'Jason? It's Zoe, Rhian's mum. Apparently she was off work sick today. I have texted her but she hasn't replied. Can you get her to give me a ring when you pick up this message, please? Thanks.'

As she put her phone back down on the counter, she saw Neil giving her *a look* as he swigged his beer.

'What?' she asked with a frown.

'Rhian's twenty-one. She's just off work ill. Christ, she spent three years in South Wales on her own and we only heard from her once a week if we were lucky. Leave the girl alone,' Neil snapped.

Who crawled up his bloody arse? Zoe thought, wondering why Neil seemed so hostile since he walked through the door.

'Neil, can I remind you that a friend of ours was found murdered this morning,' Zoe growled. 'It's okay for me to check that our daughter's all right.'

There was an awkward silence between them that was broken as Louie shuffled in. 'Are you two arguing again?'

'It's just a difference of opinion, love.' Zoe tried to give him a hug. 'Are you okay? This thing with Geoff has been a shock for all of us, hasn't it?'

Louie glared at her. 'This thing with Geoff? He was stabbed to death, Mum!'

'Okay, I'm sorry,' Zoe held up her hands defensively and then found herself feeling teary at the thought of what had happened. 'I just can't believe it.'

Louie grabbed a carton of chocolate milk from the fridge, took two bananas from the fruit bowl, and went silently out of the kitchen and up to his room.

Taking a tissue, Zoe dabbed her eyes and then spotted Neil looking at her again. 'What now, Neil? I know you didn't like Geoff much, but I did. I'm allowed to be bloody upset.'

'It's not that,' Neil said with a perplexed look. 'Did you know Geoff had been stabbed to death?'

Zoe wondered what Neil was getting at. 'No. The police said it was a murder, but I didn't know he'd been stabbed.'

'Neither did I.'

'So what, Neil? What difference does that make?' Zoe snapped at him.

'I listened to the news on the way home. It wasn't mentioned.'

And then she realised why Neil was talking about it.

'Yeah, I've watched the BBC News,' Zoe said, gesturing to the television. 'It's not been mentioned.'

'Then how did Louie know Geoff had been stabbed to death? If me and you don't know, how the bloody hell does he know?'

CHAPTER 8

SITTING ON HER SOFA, Ruth grabbed the laptop, opened it and waited for it to whirr into action. She was using most evenings at the moment to work on her quest to find Sarah. It had been several weeks since she had found CCTV footage of Sarah with a Russian billionaire, Sergei Saratov, entering The Dorchester Hotel in London in 2015. It proved, for the first time, that Sarah hadn't been attacked or murdered on the train from Crystal Palace in November 2013. However, it posed a whole new set of questions. Saratov had been implicated in the trafficking of sex workers to luxury hotels in the exclusive Swiss ski resort of Verbier. Ruth had no idea what Sarah's relationship to Saratov was, but the CCTV footage seemed to imply that Sarah wasn't being held against her will. With the help of Met Missing Persons Officer Stephen Flaherty, Ruth eventually tracked Sarah down to an elite escort agency, Global Escorts, in Paris. And that was where Ruth had her first glimpse of Sarah in over seven years during a FaceTime call. Before Sarah had replied to Ruth, there had been a scream, and the call ended. Despite endless tracking by Ruth and then the Met Police Missing Persons Unit, the number couldn't be traced and the website had been closed down.

So, all Ruth knew was that Sarah was alive and had been in Paris about a month ago. She was now waiting for Interpol and the Paris police to find whoever had been running the escort agency. Once she had an address, Ruth knew she would travel to Paris herself.

Having spotted an email from Stephen Flaherty sent an hour ago, she was keen to see if there had been any developments in the case. But before she had time to open the email, her phone rang. Strangely, it was Stephen Flaherty calling her.

'Stephen,' Ruth said, answering the call. Her pulse always quickened whenever she saw he had emailed or called. It was the eternal hope that there had been a major breakthrough in the ongoing search for Sarah.

'If you haven't read my email, don't bother. There have been some significant developments in Paris since then,' Stephen explained.

Ruth felt her mouth go dry. 'What developments?'

'The Paris police have raided a property in Montmartre. It looks like it was set up for escorts with luxury apartments above. I've been dealing with an officer, Frederic Giresse, who works for ... my French isn't very good. Something like officers contre la criminalité organisée.'

'Basically our version of the National Crime Agency?'

'Yes.'

'What did they find?' Ruth asked feeling anxious, but now realising that Sarah hadn't been rescued.

'I need to send over a passport photograph to your phone,' Stephen said.

A moment later, Ruth's phone buzzed. She opened the attachment and saw the photo of a woman. Even though she seemed to be wearing a black, Myrabed wig, she could see it was Sarah staring back at her.

'Yeah, that's Sarah,' Ruth said in a virtual whisper.

'You're sure?'

'Yes. What's the significance?' Ruth asked. Her mind was racing as to what Stephen was about to tell her and what had been found in Paris.

'This photograph is in the passport of a woman called Amandine Thiney. It was found, along with twelve other women's passports, at the property in Montmartre. It looks like someone tipped them off about the planned raid. They fled in a hurry and left their passports behind,' Stephen explained. 'And that's good for us.'

Ruth wondered what he meant. 'Why do you say that?'

'We have Sarah's UK passport. You gave it to us seven years ago when she disappeared. She can't get a replacement without us being alerted. Clearly, she has been travelling on a false passport as Amandine Thiney. However, we now have that passport too.'

The penny dropped.

'Which means Sarah is stuck in France because she no longer has a passport to travel with,' Ruth said, thinking out loud.

'Exactly,' Stephen replied.

CHAPTER 9

TUESDAY 15th September

It was 8am and Ruth had been in her office in IR1 for over an hour and a half. As she glanced out of her window, she gazed over at the mishmash of architecture that defined Llancastell. Was she going to stay in the North Wales Police force until she could retire in about four or five years' time? Would she then choose to live out her retirement on the edges of Snowdonia? Even though these questions had journeyed through her mind before, she knew that until she could find Sarah it was impossible to plan anything in her future. Could she even dare think Sarah might be in her future? Who could say? Six months ago, Ruth was ninety percent convinced that Sarah was dead and buried in a hole somewhere.

Trying to get her head back into the case, she looked at the paperwork in front of her. She had been sifting through reports and emails and could see that a traffic ANPR report and CCTV had confirmed the timings of Geoff Williams' journey to and from the Ellroy's house at midday on Sunday.

'Boss, we're ready for you,' said a voice which startled her. It was DC James Garrow.

'Oh, right. Thanks Jim,' Ruth said, getting her head back into SIO mode. She grabbed her files and headed out to take the CID briefing on Day 2 of the investigation. 'Okay, guys. If you can listen up, I'd like to get going on this quickly please

...' The room quietened, as it always did when she began. She assumed it was a sign that she had the respect of her team. 'As most of you know, in a case like this my philosophy is for us to operate a TIE investigation. So, we're going to trace, investigate, and eliminate as many people connected to Geoff Williams as we can in the next forty-eight hours. Dan and Georgie, I want you to go and talk to Louie and Neil Ellroy this morning. Nick and I will talk to Geoff's business partner, Lynn Jones. What else have we got?'

Garrow looked over. 'Tech boys have got Geoff's mobile phone and laptop. They'll have something for us first thing tomorrow.'

Ruth nodded. 'Thanks, Jim. Can we hurry that along? I want to see who called him or who Geoff spoke to on Sunday afternoon or evening? And can we make sure we check the phone records for the landline at that address too?'

'Yes, Boss.'

Nick raised his pen. 'I'm still trying to track down Myra Davies, the neighbour who has a spare set of keys to the Williams' home.'

'Okay, let me know when you've spoken to her. Any word on the PM?' Ruth asked the assembled team.

Georgie nodded. 'Preliminary PM is this afternoon, Boss.'

'Okay,' Ruth said as she went over to the board and thought out loud. 'Geoff Williams went out at midday on Sunday to talk to the Ellroy family. He told them he wasn't prepared to help Louie Ellroy get a trial for the Wales U-18 team because of his temper. As far as we know, no one then heard or saw him until his wife Claire returned at seven the following morning. In that time, someone had come into the house and stabbed

Geoff repeatedly as he came out of the shower and then again downstairs. There was no break-in and no robbery. That means that Geoff was targeted by this person. Claire Williams told us that he was security conscious and would have kept the doors to the house locked. Does that mean that he let whoever killed him into the house?'

'There is a problem with that though, Boss,' Nick said with a frown. 'Why do you let someone you know into your home and then go and have a shower?'

Georgie raised an eyebrow. 'You might do if you've just had sex with them.'

Ruth nodded. 'If Geoff is having an affair, then that could make sense. He has sex, goes into the shower, and this person then stabs him to death. Why?'

Having walked over to a printer, French grabbed a print-out. 'Boss. This is the PNC check on the Ellroy family.'

'Anything of interest?' Ruth asked.

French nodded at her. 'Louie Ellroy has been convicted of ABH and assault in the last two years. He got a hefty fine and a six-month suspended sentence from Mold Magistrates' Court.'

ZOE PARKED HER CAR on the street, got out, and glanced over at the small house that Jason, Rhian's boyfriend, shared with his brother Tom. She had received a call this morning from the Conwy Therapy Clinic to say that Rhian had texted again to say she was still too unwell to come into work. Having called her phone twice with no answer, Zoe had panicked. It was completely out of character for her daughter to go off radar like this. She had called Jason's phone twice too, but it had gone to voicemail each time.

Zoe walked down the untidy garden path and rang the doorbell. Her stomach was knotted. What if something had happened to both Jason and Rhian? Why hadn't either of them returned her calls or at least sent a text?

As the wind picked up, Zoe could smell the sea – the coast was only two minutes away. It reminded her of her childhood. She had grown up in Conwy, but it had been far from idyllic.

She rang the doorbell again and stood back. Taking a deep breath, she tried to convince herself that there was a perfectly good explanation for Rhian not going to work and not being in contact.

Straining to hear, Zoe wasn't sure if there was the sound of movement from inside the house. The sudden caw of gulls swooping overhead startled her.

I don't understand where Rhian could be? If she was so ill that she couldn't come to the door, surely Jason would have told me?

Finally, the locks of the door clunked, and Jason peered out at her. He looked terrible. Unshaven, pale and tired.

'Jason?' Zoe said, shocked to see him looking like that.

Jason gazed at her with disdain. 'What do you want, Zoe?'

Zoe frowned. 'I want to see Rhian.'

Jason squinted in the daylight. 'What are you talking about? She's not here.'

'I don't understand.'

'Why would she be here?'

'Because she left us on Sunday saying that she was coming here.'

Jason frowned. 'Eh? I'm completely lost here.'

'Her work told us that she texted them yesterday and then again today to say she's too ill to go in. She's not answering her phone or my texts,' Zoe burbled, realising that she was speaking quickly and sounding slightly hysterical. 'And you didn't get back to me.'

'I'm still really confused,' Jason said in utter bewilderment. 'Why the hell would Rhian say she's coming here?'

'You're her boyfriend, Jason,' Zoe said with a growing sense of unease. 'She comes over here all the time.'

'No, she doesn't.' Jason furrowed his brow.

'Yes, she does.'

'We're not going out anymore. We split up about four months ago, so I don't know what the hell is going on or what you're talking about.'

For a moment, Zoe thought she had misheard him. Then an overwhelming sinking feeling and sense of panic set in. 'I don't understand. She comes here two or three times a week.'

'No.' Jason shook his head. 'Not anymore, she doesn't.'

'Where is she going then?' Zoe asked, thinking out loud.

Jason snorted. 'No idea. She told me four months ago that she wasn't sure that she wanted us to move in together anymore. She wanted a break. When I asked her if she wanted to have a break or actually split up, she admitted that it was over.'

'Oh my God. I'm so confused. She didn't tell me any of that,' Zoe said, her mind now racing as to what Rhian had been doing and with whom. 'When was the last time you saw her?'

'When she came to collect her things, which was a few days later. I haven't seen her since. That was months ago.'

Zoe took a deep breath. The news had rocked her. She was feeling sick with anxiety. 'Have you any idea where she might be?'

Jason shook his head. 'I'm really sorry. I haven't got a clue.'

'Did you think there was someone else?' Zoe asked.

'Yes.' Jason nodded. 'I knew something was wrong.'

'If there was someone else, have you got any idea who it might be?'

'No. And I don't want to know,' Jason said with a flash of anger. 'And Rhian wouldn't tell me in case me and Tom went round to beat him up.'

Zoe's heart was thumping and she couldn't think clearly. 'I don't know what to do.'

Jason looked at her. 'If you're really worried, why don't you call the police?'

CHAPTER 10

'I DIDN'T HAVE A FIGHT with Geoff!' Louie protested.

French and Georgie had been interviewing Louie Ellroy in the family's garden for about five minutes.

Georgie was surprised at Louie's arrogance. She couldn't work out if it was an act to compensate for a weakness, or if he really believed that the world revolved around him. Maybe that was just teenage boys?

French was taking notes as they went. 'Could you tell us exactly what happened then, Louie?' he asked.

Louie crossed his muscular legs. He was wearing shorts and a replica Welsh Rugby top. 'Geoff told me I was an idiot for getting sent off. So, I pushed him ...'

Georgie raised an eyebrow. 'You didn't think you were an idiot for getting sent off?'

'Yeah,' Louie huffed. 'But this kid had nearly taken my head off. I reacted and punched him.'

'Sounds like you were angry with yourself?' French suggested. 'Especially as there was a Welsh Rugby scout there to watch you.'

Louie shrugged. 'I suppose so.'

'What happened between you and Geoff after that?' Georgie asked.

'Nothing. Geoff spoke to my dad, and we went home.' Louie sat forward and picked at the wood on the table. 'That's it.'

I don't think he's made eye contact with either of us since we got here, Georgie thought.

'Could you tell us the next time you saw Geoff after that?' French asked.

'Sunday.'

'Could you tell us what happened?'

Louie rolled his eyes. 'I came in. Geoff was sitting in my kitchen. He told us he wasn't going to put a word in for me with the WRU to get me a trial for the U-18s.'

'How did that make you feel?' Georgie asked.

Louie scowled. 'I dunno.'

'Angry?' she suggested.

'Yeah.' Louie shrugged. 'I didn't know why Geoff was being such a dick about it. He's always telling me how good I am at rugby, but then he's not gonna talk to the WRU! What's that about?'

French looked over. 'So, you were furious with him for not helping you out?'

Louie glared at him. 'I didn't bloody kill him, if that's what you think. It's only rugby.'

French checked the notes in his notebook. 'And we understand you went out for a run on Sunday evening?'

'Yeah.'

'What time was that?'

'About six or half six.'

'And how long were you out running for?'

'Forty minutes. I try and get five miles done,' Louie explained.

French raised an eyebrow. 'Five miles in forty minutes. That's pretty quick. Where did you go?'

Louie pushed his hand through his blonde hair. 'I dunno.'

'You don't know?' Georgie said in disbelief.

'I've got three different runs I go on. They're all about five miles. I can't remember which one I did on Sunday ... maybe down along the harbour front.'

'Okay. We're going to need you to give us details of all three runs that you might have been on, Louie. Is that okay?' she asked.

Louie shrugged. 'Yeah, okay.'

French stopped writing. 'Have you ever been in trouble with the police, Louie?'

Louie shook his head. 'No.'

Georgie glanced at French – *Why is he lying to us?*

'We've seen your police record, Louie. Do you want to tell us about that?' Georgie asked.

'Oh, that!' Louie said, squirming in his chair. 'That was self-defence. There was three of them.'

'ABH is a serious offence, Louie,' she responded stiffly.

'I hit him with a chair because he kept coming for me. Not my fault it knocked him out,' he said forcefully.

Georgie waited for a few seconds and then asked, 'Can you think of anyone who might want to harm Geoff?'

Louie looked decidedly uncomfortable. 'No, of course not.'

'How did your dad react to Geoff's unwillingness to talk to the Welsh Rugby Union on your behalf?'

'He was really pissed off,' Louie grunted. 'But that's not really a surprise.'

Georgie and French exchanged a look – that was a loaded answer.

'What do you mean by that?' Georgie asked in a non-committal way.

'Dad can't stand Geoff. I've heard him and Mum rowing about it before. Geoff and Mum carry on like a pair of bloody teenagers. Mum really flirts with Geoff and he just encourages it. Dad pretends to laugh it off sometimes, but other times he just explodes.'

'You've seen your dad get angry about it?' French asked.

'Of course!' Louie exclaimed. 'He told me once that he'd swing for the pair of them if they didn't stop.'

RUTH AND NICK WERE in the office of GW Gym in the middle of Conwy with Lynn Jones, Geoff's business partner. Lynn was middle-aged, slim, with dark hair pulled back off her face. The office was neat with posters for various protein supplements and gym equipment lining the walls.

'Everyone is in shock,' Lynn said. She was clearly upset. 'We closed the gym yesterday. I just keep expecting him to walk through that door with a big grin and a silly joke. And then I realise ...' Lynn blinked as she took a deep breath.

'I'm sorry. This must be very difficult for you,' Ruth said in her usual gentle tone.

'It doesn't feel real.' Lynn dabbed her eyes with a tissue.

Nick clicked his pen and flipped open his notepad. 'When was the last time you saw Geoff?'

Lynn thought for a few seconds. 'Friday afternoon. We take it in turns to leave early and it was Geoff's turn. He left here about 3pm.'

'And how did he seem?' Ruth asked.

Lynn looked at her. 'You know, I don't think I've seen him happier. He was talking about the rugby game at the club the next day. He said that he had the house to himself because Claire was away. He made some joke about being able to wear, watch, eat and drink whatever he wanted for once.'

'And for our records, where were you on Sunday evening Lynn?'

'I was at home.'

'Can anyone verify that?'

'No, no. I live on my own,' Lynn replied. 'Does that matter?'

'Not at the moment,' Ruth said with a reassuring smile. 'Do you know Geoff's wife, Claire?'

Lynn scratched her neck and hesitated. 'Yeah. Not well though.'

What's she not telling us? Ruth wondered.

Ruth gave her a kind smile to disguise the awkward question. 'What do you think of Claire?'

'She's all right,' Lynn shrugged. 'Not my cup of tea. Bit cold and a bit … snobby. But she's English, you know?'

I'm English, thank you very much, Ruth thought to herself in amusement.

'Did Geoff ever talk about Claire?' Nick asked. 'Do you know if they were happy together?'

'They seemed fine. Geoff would moan about her little habits. I got the feeling that she liked things 'just so'. But he made a joke about it. Mrs Bloody Right Angles, that's what he called her sometimes. Claire liked everything to be neat and at right angles. Christ, she'd have a bloody shock if she came to my house.'

Lynn stopped and Ruth could see that the reality of what had happened had dawned on her again. 'Sorry, I didn't mean to witter on ...'

Ruth smiled at her. 'That's fine. It's good for us to have as clear a picture of Geoff as we can get. You've been very useful so far.'

'Have I?' Lynn asked. 'I usually talk too much.'

Nick looked over. 'You're Geoff's business partner, is that right?'

'Yes. We have a sportswear company and this gym,' Lynn explained.

'And you own half each?' Ruth asked.

Lynn shook her head. 'No. It's a seventy/thirty split.'

'Which way?' Nick enquired.

'Oh, right. Geoff owned seventy percent. I inherited some money about ten years ago. I'd helped Geoff run the sportswear company for years. He asked if I wanted to invest in the company and in opening a new gym. And I said yes.'

'And how are things financially for the business?' Nick continued.

'Fine. I'm not going to buy a yacht or anything, but we do all right. I earn a lot more than I used to.'

'You're glad that you made the investment?' Ruth asked to clarify.

'Yes, very much so.'

'As this is a murder case, Lynn, we will be looking through all Geoff's finances, and that will include the company accounts,' Nick stated.

'Oh okay. Of course.'

'Are you married, Lynn?' Ruth asked.

'Widowed actually,' she replied with a slightly awkward tone. 'My husband died in a boating accident just over ten years ago.'

'I'm sorry to hear that,' Ruth said quietly.

'If we can just go back to last Friday,' Nick said. 'Did anything out of the ordinary happen during that day? Something that Geoff said or did that wasn't usual?'

'Nope. It was just a normal Friday,' Lynn said with a shrug.

Ruth nodded as she caught her eye. 'Anything, however small you might think it is, could help us. Did Geoff go out anywhere or did he have an argument with someone?'

At that moment, Ruth spotted that something had occurred to Lynn.

Lynn pulled a face. 'Actually, yes. It's embarrassing if I'm honest.'

Nick gave her a wry smile. 'Don't worry Lynn, we've heard some pretty weird things over the years.'

Lynn pointed to the far side of the office. 'Someone called Geoff on the phone here.'

'That doesn't sound out of the ordinary.'

'No, it's just that he was arguing with whoever had called him.' Lynn gave a forced smile. 'And I couldn't help but try to hear what it was about. I thought it must be Claire.'

'What were they arguing about?'

'I don't know. But it wasn't Claire.'

Ruth frowned. 'How do you know?'

'Geoff called her Zoe at one point. I assumed it was one of the mums from the rugby club.'

'Why do you say that?' Nick asked.

'Geoff's a big hit with the mums down there. They all fancy him. I think it's caused problems with some of the dads. But that's just gossip,' Lynn explained.

Ruth exchanged a look with Nick – *that sounds interesting.*

HAVING FINISHED THEIR preliminary interview with Louie, French and Georgie were now talking to Neil. Georgie hadn't taken a liking to him. He seemed to be overcompensating for something, which made him a bit spiky and somewhat of a know-it-all.

'First things first, could you tell us your shoe size please?' French asked.

Neil gave them a smug smile. 'Ten.'

'Louie said that he takes a size nine shoe. Is that correct?'

'Yes,' Neil said with a shrug. 'Why would he lie about that?'

French ignored him and flicked through his notebook. 'In an earlier statement, you said you were out at a building site on Sunday evening?'

Neil nodded. 'That's right.'

French read from his notes. 'From about 6pm to about 7.30pm. Is that right?'

'At a guess. I don't know exactly.'

'And you went to mend a fence at the Shore Lane building site, which is a housing development that you're running?'

'Yes.'

Georgie looked over at him. 'Anyone see you there, Mr Ellroy?'

'Nope,' he answered with a wry smile. 'It was a Sunday.'

French waited for a few seconds. 'How would you describe your relationship with Geoff?'

'Not much to tell,' came the reply. 'He's been Louie's rugby coach for years.'

'Ever see him socially?' Georgie asked, probing further.

Neil nodded. 'I see him down the pub, especially when Wales are playing.'

'So, you're friends?' French asked.

'No. I wouldn't go that far,' Neil said, with a slightly pompous snort. 'If I'm honest, Geoff was a bit full of himself. I stuck to talking to him about Louie and how his rugby was progressing.'

'Did you ever have cross words?' Georgie asked.

Neil shook his head. 'Not really. It wasn't like that. I was always civil to him, he just wasn't someone who I thought of as a friend.'

'And how did Louie feel about Geoff?' French asked.

Neil gave a wry smile. 'Geoff was his hero. He walked on bloody water as far as Louie was concerned. I mean, Geoff had played rugby for Wales. I couldn't compete with that.'

Compete? That's a strange word to use, Georgie thought.

'And how did that make you feel?' Georgie asked in a throwaway tone intended to disguise the intent of the question. It was a technique that she had seen Ruth use to great effect many times.

Neil thought for a few seconds. 'Feel? I'm not sure what you're getting at?'

And now he's getting defensive.

Georgie smiled at him. 'Oh, it's just that you said that you couldn't compete with Geoff.'

Neil shrugged. 'I'm Louie's dad. By definition, I'm not very cool. And that's not helped by having an ex-international rugby player taking a close interest in my son.'

Something about the way Neil had said *close interest* bothered Georgie.

'So, Louie and Geoff were very close?' she asked.

'You could say that,' Geoff said ironically. 'Like peas in a pod, they were.'

'And you didn't find that strange?' French asked.

'Hang on a sec,' Neil snapped. 'I know what you lot are like. I didn't mean anything weird was going on. Bloody hell!'

'This is a murder investigation, Mr Ellroy,' Georgie said calmly. 'Therefore, we have to explore every avenue open to us.'

Neil gave an audible huff. 'If you knew Geoff, you would know that nothing like that could happen.'

'Why do you say that?' French asked.

Neil hesitated for a moment. 'I don't want to speak ill of the dead, but Geoff had a reputation as a ladies' man.'

Georgie frowned. 'Even though he was married?'

'I don't want to spread any gossip,' Neil said with a shrug. 'But there were rumours at the rugby club.'

'Could you be more specific?' French asked.

'There is a little group of mums at the club. They seem to spend far too much time gossiping about Geoff.'

'Do you know if he was having an affair?' French asked.

'No,' Neil said, but he wasn't convincing. 'As I said, it was just gossip. But Geoff lapped it up.'

'He enjoyed all the female attention?' Georgie asked.

Neil snorted. 'Oh yeah. He was never happier than being in the company of women.'

'What about your wife?' Georgie asked, aware that it might be an inflammatory question. Neil bristled and sat up straighter.

'Zoe? What's she got to do with it?' Neil asked. He was getting angry.

'Your wife is one of the mums at the rugby club,' Georgie said with a shrug. 'I'm just asking if she spent time with Geoff?'

'Yes, I suppose so,' Neil said defensively. 'She liked Geoff more than I did.'

'And how did that make you feel?'

'I didn't care. If they wanted to flirt with each other, that was their business.'

'So, you would have described Geoff and Zoe's relationship as flirty then?' Georgie asked.

'I have explained already what he was like,' Neil said irritably. 'He didn't talk to women. He flirted with them.'

'And that didn't annoy you?'

'A bit,' Neil said. 'I didn't kill him because he flirted with my wife, if that's what you're asking me.'

French shook his head. 'I don't think we were suggesting you did. We're just trying to build up a picture of Geoff and what he was like.'

Neil shifted uncomfortably in his chair and uncrossed his legs.

Georgie asked, 'Just out of interest, do you know what size feet your wife has?'

'Can't you ask her?' Neil snapped.

'I can. But I just thought you would know.'

'Size 5. I think she takes a size 5.'

Georgie exchanged a furtive look with French.

CHAPTER 11

RUTH AND NICK CAME over the ridge of a hill as they headed down into the centre of Conwy. The sun was out and the huge medieval castle, with its eight circular turrets, loomed into view. It was an impressive sight as it rose high over the town and harbour with the dark skyline of the Snowdonia mountains in the background.

'Did I ever tell you that I used to play on that castle when I was a kid and we came to Conwy for our holidays?' Ruth asked.

Nick shook his head. 'I don't think so. I've seen it hundreds of times but it still takes my breath away. They built it in four years.'

'Bloody hell, it took my dad four years to build his two-room extension in Battersea,' Ruth joked.

'Of course, you know the castle is haunted by a hooded monk who roams the castle walls,' Nick said with a wry smile.

'Yeah, well I never saw him ... I do remember there were these huge spotlights that lit up the entire castle at night. It was stunning. I used to think I was a princess in a Disney film,' Ruth said, feeling lost in the innocent thoughts of childhood. 'We came from a concrete council estate in South London. We'd never seen anything like it.'

'And where were your parents when you and your brother were roaming around the battlements avoiding the ghost of the hooded monk?'

'Oh, you know. In the pub, getting pissed.' Ruth laughed. 'That was their idea of an educational experience. A bottle of coke with a straw, and a bag of crisps. Why don't you two go and play on the castle while we get drunk?'

'God bless the 80s, eh?' Nick gave a wry smile as he slowed at some traffic lights. As the lights changed and they pulled away, Nick gave her a meaningful look. 'Amanda asked me if you'd heard anything from the police in Paris.'

'I don't want to bore you with it,' Ruth said.

'If I don't go back with something to tell Amanda she'll hurt me. So ...?' Nick joked.

'The police in Paris found the premises where the escorts had been. Someone must have tipped them off about the raid,' Ruth explained.

'Have they got any idea where they went?'

Ruth shook her head. 'No, but they left all the passports behind so they're not going very far.'

'Okay. If they're stuck in one place, that sounds like progress.'

Ruth shrugged. 'I'm not convinced the police in Paris are treating it as a priority, but there's not a lot I can do.'

'Six months ago you would have jumped for joy to know that she was alive,' Nick pointed out.

'Yeah, I know all that. But that fact seems to have posed more questions than it's answered.'

Five minutes later, they pulled up outside the Williams' home. The SOCOs had just finished their second search of the property and were packing away their equipment. Ruth had organised for uniformed officers and the Dog Unit to conduct a thorough and protracted fingertip search of the woods that backed onto the houses. As a result the area was full of police vehicles, and the occasional bark of a German Shepherd could be heard.

Ruth and Nick ducked under the scene of crime tape, showed their warrant cards, and then pulled on their forensic gloves. The sun was trying to burn away the thick cloud cover, but it was still chilly. As they went inside, she could see that the house was now virtually clear of all forensic officers. Even the stepping plates had been removed.

'I want to do a walk-through of Geoff's final minutes,' Ruth said as she made her way through to the kitchen. There were still fingerprinting chemicals and dust on the work surfaces. She expected she would find photographs of the crime scene on her desk by the time she got back.

Ruth wanted to clear her head and do the walk-through without all the chaos of SOCOs being everywhere. It was in these moments that she sometimes gained an insight into a case. She imagined Geoff scrambling to get the door open before being stabbed in the back where he had been found.

They walked slowly and deliberately back out of the kitchen and down the hallway towards the stairs, studying the carpet, walls, and doors as they went.

'Whoever did this to him was full of rage,' Ruth said, thinking out loud. 'They wanted him dead.'

'In that case, I can't see this resulting from Geoff not putting a good word in for Louie. You might be disappointed with him, even angry. But you don't stab someone to death, do you?'

Ruth shook her head. 'No, it doesn't sound likely,' she agreed. 'My first instinct is to look at Claire Williams. We need CCTV from that hotel in Liverpool, and any witnesses.'

'Claire was away all weekend. If Geoff was having an affair, he knew he had the place to himself,' Nick said.

'And if she came back earlier than she said she would, Claire might have caught them together. Except, why hasn't that person been in touch with us?'

Nick shrugged. 'Maybe they're too scared? Or maybe something happened to them too?'

'How about Geoff was in the house alone. His mistress has left, but Geoff hasn't cleared up the house,' Ruth said, exploring another scenario as they climbed the stairs. 'He's not expecting Claire home. He has a shower. She arrives home early, sees signs of what he's been up to all weekend, loses the plot and kills him.'

'Sounds plausible,' Nick nodded. 'And unfortunately her DNA is going to be all over the house anyway so that doesn't help us.'

'We have a time of death for Sunday evening so we need CCTV and ANPR traffic cameras to see what time Claire actually came home.'

Walking into the en-suite bathroom, Ruth glanced around. It was neat and well-ordered, but impersonal. Even though she knew that the SOCOs would have done a thorough job, it was still important to check the house again.

Ruth moved over to the large wardrobe and opened it. Everything was as she expected – tidy, ordered, and expensive. There were sports bags neatly lined up along the bottom with a dozen or so pairs of trainers.

Ruth took a pair of pink Nikes and checked the size. 'I've got a pair of Claire's trainers here and they're a size four.'

Nick nodded. 'Forensics said it was only a partial match. I've seen them get a footprint wrong by a whole size before.'

Ruth knew he was right. 'But what it rules out is someone with, let's say, size nine or ten feet. Plus, we don't actually know how many people were in the house when Geoff was attacked.'

Moving slowly around the room, she saw a full-length mirror hanging on the left-hand wall. She peered at it for a moment. There was something slightly off with it. At first, she wasn't sure what it was. Then she realised it was something she had seen before on one of the first cases she had worked on after transferring to North Wales.

She approached, and inspected where the mirror joined the wall. It seemed to be part of the wall rather than fixed to it. Pressing her face against the cool glass, she cupped her hands to block out as much light as she could and peered ahead. Her breath made a neat circular pattern on its surface.

Standing back for a moment, Ruth could hear that Nick was in the en-suite bathroom.

'Nick, can you put the lights on in the bathroom?' she shouted.

'Erm ... Yes, Boss.' Nick sounded confused.

Going back to the mirror she cupped her hands again, and as the lights went on she could see the bathroom.

It was a two-way mirror.

Nick came in. 'Everything all right, Boss?'

Ruth gestured to the wall. 'It's a two-way mirror.'

Nick raised an eyebrow. 'We saw one of these at Owen Ankers' home in Harlech a couple of years ago.'

Ruth nodded as she remembered. 'Why do you want a two-way mirror between the bedroom and bathroom?'

Nick shrugged. 'Maybe they were a bit kinky, Boss.'

For Ruth it posed the question why did the Williams have a two-way mirror at all? She had seen all sorts of weird sexual practices and was shocked by little. However, it revealed a darker side to the couple.

'There's kinky, and there's plain weird,' Ruth said as she crouched down to look under the bed. Her lower back and knees struggled with the effort. *Bloody hell, I really am getting old.*

Having checked there was nothing on the floor under the bed, she went to get up. Out of the corner of her eye, she spotted something wedged between the wooden slats of the bed frame and the mattress.

'Something up?' Nick asked.

'I don't know.' Ruth lay down on the carpet, turned on her back, and shifted herself under the bed.

She reached up and took a small black object, about six inches long, from where it was positioned.

It was a pay-as-you-go mobile phone.

'Interesting place to keep a phone,' Ruth said dryly as she manoeuvred herself from under the bed and got slowly to her feet.

'It's almost as if it's been hidden there,' Nick said sarcastically.

Switching it on, the phone's screen lit up and asked for the four-digit security code. Ruth looked at Nick. 'One, two, three, four?'

Nick shrugged. 'Wouldn't be the first person to be that stupid.'

Ruth tapped in the four digits and the phone opened. With another click, she saw that there had been ten missed calls from another mobile phone. They were all from a two-hour period, 2pm to 4pm, on Sunday afternoon.

'Someone was desperate to speak to him,' Nick said.

'That's if this is Geoff's phone.' Ruth read the display which showed the calls made. The same number had been called on Sunday afternoon at 4.11pm.

'Trace it or call it?' Ruth asked Nick. Tracing it through the mobile provider would be difficult, unless it had been paid for with a credit card. That's what the criminals counted on by using them. Pay for them with cash, and they're virtually untraceable.

'Call it,' Nick replied.

Hitting the green call button, Ruth put the phone to her ear and heard the ringing tone.

She waited for about thirty seconds, but there was no answer.

'Sod it,' she said, feeling frustrated.

'I'd try it again, Boss,' Nick said.

'Why?'

'If you're calling another pay-as-you-go phone, it might be hidden. It needs to ring for longer for someone else to hear it and try to find it.'

Ruth raised an eyebrow. 'Very clever, Nicholas.'

'Not just a pretty face, Boss,' he quipped.

Hitting the button again, the ringing tone started.

Another thirty seconds went by and there was no answer.

And then another thirty seconds.

Taking the phone from her ear, Ruth went to hang up when she heard a woman's voice.

'Hello?' Hello?' the woman said, sounding very confused.

'Who is this?' Ruth asked, not wanting to give her identity away unless she had to.

'I'm sorry. Why are you calling this phone?' the woman asked.

'I'm wondering if you could tell me your name?'

'Erm ... actually, I'd rather not. I'm going to hang up now.'

'Wait. This is Detective Inspector Ruth Hunter from Llancastell CID. I need you to tell me who you are and why you have this phone in your possession?'

There were a few seconds of silence. Ruth prayed that the woman didn't hang up.

'This is Zoe Ellroy. We met yesterday?'

What?

'Hello, Mrs Ellroy. Is this your phone that I'm calling?'

'No, no. I don't understand ...'

'This isn't your phone?'

'No. I found it ringing in my house. I've never seen it before.'

'Could you tell me where you found it ringing, please?' Ruth asked.

There were another few seconds of silence before Zoe said, 'It was in my daughter Rhian's bedroom, hidden in a bag.'

CHAPTER 12

RUTH AND NICK WERE making the brief journey across Conwy from Geoff William's home to where the Ellroys lived. Across to the west of the town, Ruth could see Conwy Mountain which overlooked the harbour. Its dark ridges and uneven terrain were evidence of its origins as an ancient volcano millions of years ago. For a moment, she remembered hiking up it with Sian two summers ago and exploring the Neolithic hut circles and Iron Age hillfort at its summit. The views of Snowdonia from the hilltop at nearly 1,000 ft were incredible. It was one of those days that in hindsight she had taken for granted. She had assumed that there were going to be hundreds of days like that with Sian in their future.

Buzzing down the window, Ruth took a long drag on the cigarette she had just lit, blew out the smoke, and got her head back into detective mode. She tried to process what they had just discovered.

'Do we think that Rhian Ellroy was having an affair with Geoff?' Nick asked as he turned off the main road.

Ruth frowned. 'I don't know. She's only twenty-one but I guess that doesn't mean anything. Why would Geoff have a secret pay-as-you-go phone, and why would he and Rhian be calling each other? It's very suspicious,' she said, and then something suddenly occurred to her. 'Rhian Ellroy works as a chiropractor in Conwy, doesn't she?'

Nick nodded. 'That's what Zoe Ellroy told us.'

'Geoff is an ex-rugby player,' Ruth said as she finished the cigarette. 'Maybe they met that way?'

'She would have known him through her brother too.'

Ruth nodded. 'We need to pick her up and interview her straight after we've collected her phone.'

As they turned into the driveway of the Ellroy's home, there was a uniformed patrol car outside.

Ruth frowned. 'What are they doing here?'

'No, idea.'

Getting out of the car, Ruth pulled up the collar on her coat as it was getting chilly.

A tall uniformed officer came out of the house and approached them.

Ruth showed him her warrant card and frowned. 'Everything all right, Constable?'

'It's a Mrs Zoe Ellroy. She called us and claims that her daughter Rhian is missing, ma'am,' the constable explained.

Ruth and Nick exchanged a look – *what the hell is going on?*

'Her daughter's missing?' Ruth asked.

'Yes, ma'am. She seems to be very distraught.' He gestured for Ruth and Nick to follow him inside.

They made their way through the house and Ruth saw Zoe sitting at the kitchen table with a female PC.

'Thank you, Constable, we're from CID. We'll take it from here,' Ruth said with a kind smile.

'Yes, ma'am.' The officer got up from the table and left them to it.

'Okay if we sit down?' Ruth asked, approaching the table with Nick.

'Of course.' Zoe nodded and gestured to the chairs. She had clearly been crying, and she seemed anxious. 'I'm really sorry. I should have told you what was going on when we spoke, but I just panicked.'

'Do you want to tell us now what is going on?' Ruth said in a gentle tone.

'I don't know where Rhian is, and I'm really scared,' Zoe said, the stress showing in her eyes.

'When you say that you don't know where she is, what exactly do you mean?' Nick asked as he took out his notepad.

'Sorry ... I don't know where to start,' Zoe said as she blinked and tears appeared in her eyes.

Ruth gave her a sympathetic smile. 'It's okay. Let's start with the last time you saw Rhian.'

'I haven't seen her since Sunday afternoon. She was going over to Jason's house to stay the night with him.'

'And Jason is her boyfriend?' Nick asked to clarify.

'Yes. Jason Kelly. He lives with his brother Tom.'

Ruth nodded. 'And was it quite usual for Rhian to stay at Jason's?'

'Oh, yes,' Zoe said. 'She would go there two or three nights a week. She and Jason are saving up to buy a house together. Or at least that's what I thought was going on.'

Nick glanced up from his notepad. 'And she lives here with you the rest of the time?'

'Yes. I just don't understand where she is,' Zoe said, her voice now trembling.

Ruth leaned forward. 'When we spoke to you yesterday, you told us that Rhian was at work at the Conwy Therapy Clinic?'

'I thought she was. But then Neil got a call from the clinic to say that Rhian had sent a text to say she was ill and wasn't able to go to work. They were just ringing to see if she was okay. So, I texted Rhian and Jason to ask if she was all right or if she needed anything. But I didn't hear back from them.'

'Was that unusual?' Nick asked.

'Not really. Rhian can be a bit rubbish at texting me back straight away.'

'You weren't concerned at that point?' Ruth asked.

'Not really,' Zoe said as she shook her head. 'But then this morning we heard she had texted work again to say she wasn't well. By then I had left Jason a voicemail message to call me.'

Ruth felt uneasy about what Zoe was telling her. 'By this morning you hadn't heard from either Rhian or Jason since she left here on Sunday afternoon?'

Zoe shook her head. 'No, nothing. It wasn't like Rhian not to be in contact for that long. She loves her job, so I was surprised that she'd rung in sick two days running. And she wouldn't have just sent a text, she would have called them herself. I went over to Jason's house to see what was going on.'

'When was this?' Nick asked.

Zoe glanced up at the large clock on the wall. 'About two hours ago.'

'What happened when you got there?' Ruth asked.

Zoe blinked as she got upset again. 'Jason said he and Rhian had split up four months ago and he had no idea where she was.'

Ruth exchanged a furtive glance with Nick – there was definitely something troubling about what she was telling them.

'Did he say when he had last seen Rhian?' Nick asked.

'Not for months.' Zoe shrugged, and her eyes filled with tears. 'I came back here and went up to her room to see if I could find anything. That's when that phone rang. After that, I came down and called 999 to report her missing.'

Ruth nodded and looked directly at her. 'Okay. Don't worry. We will do everything we can to find Rhian, but you have to tell me everything you know. If you hide anything from us, that could jeopardise our attempts to find out where she is.'

Nick flicked over a page of his notebook. 'Can you think of anywhere else Rhian could have gone for the last two days? A relative? A friend?'

'No, I've thought of everyone,' Zoe said. 'My sister lives in France. I called Rhian's two best friends, but they haven't seen her for a few weeks. Neil's mum and dad live down in Devon and they would have called if she'd turned up there ... Please, I don't know where she is.'

Zoe was now visibly shaking as she rubbed her face nervously.

'Is it okay if DS Evans and I have a look around and go up to Rhian's bedroom? We're going to need to take the phone that you found too,' Ruth explained.

'And if you have details of Rhian's bank, credit cards, and mobile phone that would be useful,' Nick added.

'Of course. I'm guessing they'd be in her room.'

'I assume Rhian has a car?' Ruth asked.

'Yes. She's got a Mini.'

'If you could write down her registration, if you know it, that would be helpful too.'

Getting up from the table, Zoe nodded and gestured to the hallway and stairs. 'Do you want me to show you upstairs?'

'That's all right. We'll find our way around,' Ruth said with a benign smile. 'Tell you what you could do though. I'd love a cup of tea. DS Evans?'

Nick nodded. 'Great. If you don't mind. White, no sugar.'

'Same for me,' Ruth said.

It was a tactic she had used many times to keep someone both occupied and out of the way. There was nothing worse than searching a house with the owner hovering around, making comments and distracting them.

Nick glanced back for a second. 'Just a quick question. What size feet does Rhian have?'

Zoe frowned. 'Size 5. Same as me.'

'Thanks,' Nick said.

Taking her forensic gloves from her pocket, Ruth pulled them on with a snap. She walked slowly up the stairs that were covered in thick, fawn carpet. The walls were lined with framed family photos. She noticed an old sepia wedding photograph. The groom was in an old-fashioned soldier's uniform and she guessed it had been taken around the time of the Second World War.

'Have you got any evidence bags?' Ruth asked as they reached the landing.

Nick patted his coat pocket. 'Always prepared, Boss.'

'You must have been a cub scout as a boy?' Ruth quipped.

'I was a sixer, I'll have you know. Lots of badges all over my jumper. I was very conscientious,' Nick said with a grin.

Ruth snorted. 'Christ! What happened?'

'I moved up to the Scouts with Tim Blake and we spent most of our time smoking weed in the woods when we were meant to be building camps and whittling wood or something,' Nick explained.

Ruth laughed. 'Yeah, that sounds about right. I was a Brownie for about three weeks before I decided they were all too posh and boring.'

They got to the open door of a bedroom that was cluttered with clothes, sports gear, and had rugby posters on the wall.

'Three guesses as to whose room that is,' Nick said dryly.

Ruth pulled a face. 'I can tell from the smell that it's a teenage boy.'

They moved down towards another bedroom.

'Bet you're glad you had a daughter, aren't you?' Nick asked.

'Oh, teenage girls are a different species, Nick. You wait. There was many a time I wished for a monosyllabic, grunting boy as opposed to the acid tongue of an articulate, hormonal teenage girl.'

Nick rolled his eyes. 'Can't wait.'

Entering the next bedroom, Ruth could see that it belonged to Rhian. It was neat, tidy, and smelled clean. She inspected the bookshelves that seemed to have been arranged by the colour of the books' spines. *Nice idea*. Then she spotted a pro-life poster on the wall. It was in the same style as the recent *Black Lives Matter* poster. However, it read *Unborn Lives Matter – Pro-life*.

Ruth was surprised. In her experience, she would have guessed that a young, University educated woman like Rhian would be pro-choice. The people she had met who were pro-life were usually religious. She wondered where Rhian's strong views on the subject had come from?

As they searched the room, Nick pointed to a table where a laptop was sitting open. 'Right, here's her laptop.'

When he tapped a button, the screen lit up and asked for the security code.

'We need a code to get in,' Nick said.

Ruth shrugged. 'We'll have to take it to the tech boys.'

'I think it's her birthday,' said a voice behind them.

It was Zoe carrying two mugs of tea, which she handed them both. Ruth had meant for her to wait in the kitchen.

'Thanks,' Ruth said, taking the tea.

Zoe gestured to the laptop. 'Try seventeen, four, nineteen ninety nine. It's Rhian's date of birth. I'm pretty sure that's what she uses.'

Sitting down at the desk, Nick tapped in the suggested numbers. 'Bingo, we're in.'

Putting her tea down on the bedside table, Ruth continued to look through drawers and under the bed.

Zoe stood awkwardly by the door. 'I'll be down in the kitchen if you need me.'

As Ruth went over to the wardrobe, Nick turned to look at her with a serious expression. 'Boss, you need to see this.'

Going over to where Nick was sitting, Ruth glanced at the screen.

There was a selfie photograph of Geoff Williams and Rhian Ellroy lying in bed together, smiling at the camera. They were clearly naked.

'Oh my God!' said a voice from the doorway.

It was Zoe, and she was staring at the image on the screen.

CHAPTER 13

RUTH WENT OVER TO THE scene board in IR1. She had called together all the detectives that were available early evening. 'Okay guys, what have we got from today?'

Garrow gestured to his computer. 'CCTV from the Landor Hotel in Liverpool, Boss. Footage from the car park shows Claire Williams' car leaving the hotel car park at 5.48am yesterday morning.'

'Okay. So her alibi holds up,' Ruth said. They could now put Claire Williams' involvement in her husband's murder on the back burner and focus on what she and Nick had discovered about an hour ago. 'Right, just to update you on what I believe is our major line of enquiry. The Ellroys' home is now a crime scene and SOCOs are on their way to take away forensic evidence. The photo we found on Rhian's laptop indicates that she and our victim Geoff Williams were having a sexual relationship.'

Georgie looked surprised. 'Bloody hell, she's still a teenager isn't she?'

'She's twenty-one,' Ruth said. 'But it's quite an age gap.'

Georgie nodded. 'Maybe that explains why she ended her relationship with Jason Kelly four months ago.'

'And if Geoff and Rhian's relationship started back then too,' Nick said, '... then that's around April or early May.'

'Do we think that Rhian Ellroy is in danger, Boss?' French asked as he leant on the nearby table.

'She could well be,' Ruth said. 'Geoff was brutally murdered and Rhian is missing. She could have been in the house with him on Sunday.'

'Boss, we need to pull Jason Kelly in as soon as possible,' Nick suggested.

Ruth nodded. 'At the moment, we know that Jason Kelly was in a relationship with Rhian. They were supposed to be setting up home together. If Jason discovered she had left him for Geoff, then that gives him motive. Maybe he went to confront Geoff and things got out of hand.'

'And if Rhian was there, he might have attacked her?' Georgie suggested.

'We have the size 5 trainer print in our victim's blood. Rhian has size 5 feet and that might indicate that she was there too,' Nick said.

'Where is she now?' Ruth asked.

'Maybe Kelly took Rhian with him?' Garrow suggested. 'That would explain why she wasn't at work and why she only sent a text which we know was out of character.'

French nodded. 'It's the strongest lead we've got.'

'I need tech forensics to get everything they can from the two burner phones we've got,' Ruth said with a growing sense of urgency. 'And they need to see what they can pull off Rhian's laptop.'

'What about Jason Kelly?' French asked.

Ruth nodded. 'You and Georgie go over there now. Suss the place out. If he's keeping her there against her will, then there might be signs. Then ask him if he's willing to come to the station for a voluntary interview to help with our inquiries. But we want to stress that he's helping us to find Rhian. He's not a suspect. I don't want him spooked.'

'Yes, Boss,' French replied as he went to grab his jacket and then disappeared out of IR1 with Georgie.

Ruth looked out at the remaining detectives. 'I want us to pull all CCTV and ANPR footage. Did Jason Kelly leave his home on Sunday evening? If so, where did he go? Was he anywhere near the Williams' home? Where did he go after that? He's got a brother, hasn't he?'

Nick nodded. 'Yeah, Tom.'

'Someone should probably talk to him too. Get a statement from him.'

Garrow came into IR1 and approached, holding his notepad. 'Boss, switchboard just had a phone call from a Mrs Little. She's a neighbour of Geoff and Claire Williams. She claims to have seen someone running from the direction of the Williams' home at about 7pm on Sunday.'

Ruth frowned. 'But she's only just reported it?'

'She thought it was someone going for a run. Now she's seen the news, she's realised the significance of what she saw.'

'Did she get a look at the person?'

Garrow nodded. 'Yes. Girl, slim build, probably in her early 20s. She claims she got a good look at her.'

'Right, get her in. See if she can ID the woman as Rhian Ellroy,' Ruth said. 'And find out which way she was running.'

'Yes, Boss.'

ZOE WAS TRYING TO PREPARE spaghetti bolognaise, but she was finding it virtually impossible to concentrate. The pan on the hob boiled over and she blew on it to cool it down. Pouring herself another glass of wine, she knew she had probably drunk too much already but she didn't care. Where was Rhian? Why hadn't she called them to say she was okay? Was she really having an affair with Geoff Williams? The thought of that made her feel sick. Was she with him when he was murdered? Was Jason involved? What if the person who had killed Geoff harmed Rhian or taken her too? Her head was spinning.

'Mum?' said a voice behind her. She nearly jumped out of her skin.

'Bloody hell, Louie. You made me jump!'

'Sorry,' Louie said with a nonchalant shrug. 'Where's Rhian?'

For a few seconds, Zoe didn't know what to say to him. She had gone backwards and forwards about how much she should tell Louie about what she knew.

'Come and sit down, love,' she said, putting her hand gently on his shoulder and guiding him over to the table.

'How long's dinner?' he mumbled. 'I'm starving.'

Zoe sat down opposite her son. 'You know the police were here earlier?'

Louie nodded. 'Yeah.'

'Well, at the moment, we're not sure where Rhian is. I don't want you to worry. She's probably fine and this is just some big mix-up.'

'I thought she went to Jason's?'

'So did we. But apparently Jason hasn't seen her. They're not going out anymore,' Zoe said and then looked at him. 'Did you know they'd split up?'

'No,' Louie snorted. 'But it's not a big surprise. Jason's a retarded dickhead.'

Zoe frowned. 'I thought you liked him?'

'That's until I found out he was a drug dealer.'

'Jason's not a drug dealer!'

'He is! He sold some weed to Oliver Chase,' Louie said.

Zoe was pretty sure that Jason wasn't a drug dealer in any meaningful way. She wasn't about to tell Louie that she didn't really have a problem with Jason selling a bit of weed here and there. Especially as she and her old boyfriend Felix used to sell weed at Nottingham University in the 90s to make a bit of money.

'Okay. But we didn't know that Rhian wasn't going out with him any longer.' Zoe wasn't prepared to explain to him who his sister was in a relationship with now.

Louie bit his lip. 'You do know he's hit her?'

Zoe felt her stomach tighten. 'Jason hit Rhian?'

Louie nodded. 'Yeah. More than once.'

'Why didn't she tell me and your dad?'

'Why do you think?' Louie snorted. 'You know what Dad's like. He would have probably gone round there and killed him.'

Louie's revelation that Jason had sometimes been abusive to her daughter had only made her head spin more. Swigging more wine, Zoe peered down at her phone that was on the table. She was willing for it to burst into life. She just wanted Rhian to ring or text to say that she was all right.

'Where else could she be?' Zoe asked. 'You two talk. Did she say anything to you?'

'Not really,' Louie said with a frown.

Zoe nodded but her stomach was in knots.

The front door opened and Neil came in and walked down the hallway. He looked anxious. 'Have you heard from her?'

Zoe shook her head. 'No. The police were here again.'

'Maybe I should go out and look for her,' Neil said, sounding highly agitated.

Zoe looked at them both but she was lost in her own thoughts. 'We're not allowed to go into Rhian's room, and the police are coming at six in the morning to do a forensic search. We have to leave the house for a few hours.'

'Of course. Whatever they need to do,' Neil said as he went and poured himself a large tumbler of whiskey. 'What the hell happened between her and Jason then?'

Zoe shrugged. 'I've no idea. It happened months ago.'

She then noticed that Neil's hands and trousers were muddy. 'What have you been doing?'

'Helping dig a drainage trench,' he explained as he went over to wash his hands.

Zoe was confused. It had been ten years since Neil had done any manual labour on a building site. 'I thought you paid other people to do that?'

'Couple of the lads were off sick,' he replied with a shrug.

'Jesus, Neil! You're filthy!' Zoe said as she went over to the sink.

CHAPTER 14

JASON KELLY LOOKED tired and drawn as Ruth and Nick walked into Interview Room 3. Georgie and French had picked him up an hour earlier but had seen nothing suspicious that might suggest that Rhian was hiding in his house or being kept against her will.

At the moment, Ruth knew they didn't have enough to get a search warrant from a magistrate. However, she knew that the longer Rhian was missing, the more likely something untoward had happened to her.

Sitting down at the table, Ruth put her case folders down and glanced over at Jason. He had a flat nose, rounded chin, and piercing blue eyes. His hair was cropped, and he had tattoo sleeves on both arms.

'Afternoon, Jason. I'm Detective Inspector Ruth Hunter and this is my colleague, Detective Sergeant Nick Evans,' Ruth said. 'Thank you for agreeing to give us this voluntary interview. We're looking into the disappearance of Rhian Ellroy and the murder of Geoff Williams.'

Jason rubbed his nose nervously and sat back away from the table. 'Okay. I mean I don't know very much. But I'll do what I can to help. I didn't even know that Rhian was missing.'

Ruth gave him a reassuring smile. She didn't want him being defensive right from the start. 'That's great, Jason. Thank you.'

Nick moved forward in his chair. 'Could you tell us the last time you saw Rhian?'

Jason nodded. 'Yeah. It was about four months ago. We had split up, and she came to my house to get her stuff.'

'And that was definitely the last time you saw her?'

'Yeah. I haven't seen her since then,' Jason said.

'Have you had any contact with her at all?' Ruth asked.

Jason seemed very uncomfortable as he shifted in his chair. 'No, of course not.'

Nick looked at him. 'If we go into your or Rhian's phone records, we're not going to see any phone calls or texts between the two of you? And nothing on either of your social media accounts?'

Ruth saw Jason visibly swallow. 'I might have sent a text. I can't remember.'

'And what did that text say, Jason?' Ruth asked gently.

Jason took a few seconds and then mumbled, 'I honestly can't remember.'

Ruth nodded. 'Okay. You do know that we can get your phone records and we can print off every text you've made. You can tell us what the text said or we can go through your phone records. It's up to you.'

Jason bit his lip. 'I was drunk, and I called her a bitch.'

Ruth nodded. 'Okay. Anything else?'

'No, I don't think so,' Jason said, staring hard at the floor. *He's definitely lying.*

Nick stared at him. 'If you lie to us today, Jason, it could be brought up in court.'

'Court? But I haven't done anything.'

'What did your text say?' Ruth asked in a very authoritative tone.

'I ... I told her to watch her back,' Jason mumbled, and then bit the nails on his right hand.

'You threatened her?' Ruth asked.

'Yeah, but I didn't mean it. I was drunk. And I was annoyed that she'd dumped me. I wasn't gonna do anything to her. I'm not like that,' he babbled nervously.

'Where were you on Sunday evening, Jason?' Nick asked.

'At home.'

'Can anyone vouch for that?'

Jason shrugged. 'My brother, Tom.'

'You were home all evening?' Ruth asked.

'I might have popped out for a packet of fags, I can't remember,' Jason said. 'Look, if something's happened to Rhian it's got nothing to do with me.'

Nick frowned. 'You were in all evening, but you might have gone out to get some cigarettes?'

'Yeah.'

'When might you have gone out to get cigarettes?'

'Early. About six maybe.'

'And you didn't go anywhere else?' Ruth asked.

'No. You've got cameras so you can check, can't you?'

'And you didn't see or have any contact with Rhian on Sunday evening?' Ruth asked.

Jason snorted. 'No. I've told you that. I haven't done anything.'

Ruth waited for a few seconds as she turned the pages of her folder – she wanted the tension in the room to build, placing Jason under more pressure.

Closing the file, Ruth looked directly at him and asked, 'Did you know a man named Geoff Williams?'

'Not really. I knew who he was,' Jason said with a growing look of panic on his face. 'I know he was murdered ... What the hell is this all about?'

'How did you know Geoff Williams?' Nick asked.

'Me and Rhian were together for a long time. He was her brother Louie's rugby coach. I met him at barbeques at their house once or twice,' Jason explained as the colour drained from his face.

'Were you aware that Rhian and Geoff were in a relationship with each other?' Ruth asked.

'Eh?' Jason was utterly gobsmacked. 'What? No way! He's got to be nearly fifty! That's bullshit.'

Jason's reaction seemed to be genuine – or he was a very good actor.

'You had no idea that Rhian and Geoff had any type of relationship?' Nick asked.

'No! No way,' Jason said with his eyes widening in fear. 'Oh my God, you think I killed him because he was with Rhian?'

'Did you kill him, Jason?' Ruth asked.

'No, no. Of course not! Jesus!' Jason was shaking. 'Anyway, there's no way that Rhian would have been with that Geoff. That would have been sick!'

Ruth frowned. She had no idea what Jason was getting at. 'Why do you say that?'

'Because Rhian was convinced that her mum was having an affair with Geoff. She said that she had once caught them snogging in the garden.'

CHAPTER 15

NICK LOGGED OFF HIS computer, then gathered up his things. It had been a long day in CID and it was time to go home. He was thinking about the interview with Jason Kelly. From his reaction, Nick thought that Kelly really didn't know about Rhian and Geoff's affair. But he had seen some very convincing actors in interviews throughout his career.

Looking over towards Georgie, he saw that French was standing by her desk. They were chatting and laughing about something. Nick felt a pang of jealousy, even though he knew he had no right to. He was going home to his pregnant partner and beautiful daughter. He was sober and his career was going well. So why was he looking over at French and feeling annoyed that he was making Georgie laugh? Ever since Georgie had walked through the doors, Nick had been attracted to her. They had flirted once in a while in recent months with the odd secret text message that he couldn't help but find exciting.

But why was she flirting with *French*? He clearly wasn't her type. He was too straight-laced, over-educated and, frankly, a bit boring. He knew that himself and Georgie sparked off each other which is what made it sometimes exhilarating. And being a narcissistic fantasist, Nick's mind would get carried away with secret sexual liaisons with Georgie, or even just a romantic walk down the river. Yet the other side of his mind would point out to him how utterly selfish and ridiculous he was being. He had a beautiful wife and daughter at home, and another child on the way. Wasn't that everything he had ever dreamed of? When he had woken in his urine-soaked trousers, shaking and sweating, then frantically searching his home for more booze, what would he have given in that moment to have all that he has now?

Nick knew what was really going on. His fantasies and flirtations with Georgie were just another external *fix*. Nick was an addict. He could basically become addicted to anything that boosted the serotonin and dopamine levels in his brain. He didn't know if it was his dysfunctional or traumatic upbringing that had led him to a dark mixture of anxiety, agitation and depression. What he knew was that he was drawn to anything that would relieve those feelings. In the past he had been addicted to sex, exercise, gambling, work, and alcohol of course. Anything that would change the chemicals in his brain and make him feel better. Eventually it was alcohol that he had seized and finally backed as the most effective solution to change the way he felt.

Since being in the rooms of Alcoholics Anonymous, Nick had learnt that the external fixes for emotional and mental well-being were dangerously transient and decreasingly effective – hence the addiction. Now he needed to combat his demons with the peace and serenity that could be found in meditation, a walk in the countryside, friendship, and ultimately love and compassion.

With an exasperated huff at his own idiocy, Nick pushed his chair away from his desk, ready to leave for the evening.

French approached and came over to his desk.

'What were you two giggling about?' Nick asked with a smile.

French grinned. 'You know what Georgie's like, Sarge. She's hilarious.'

'Yeah, she is,' Nick said. 'And Dan, you don't need to call me Sarge now you're an acting DS.'

'Oh yes. Sorry,' French snorted. 'Force of habit ... Can I ask your advice about something?'

Nick nodded but realised from French's expression that this wasn't going to be advice about what his next car should be. If he was to guess, French was about to ask him about Georgie. He had watched their growing friendship in recent weeks with envy.

'Pull up a pew,' Nick said, gesturing to a chair.

French sat down, leant forward and scratched his face awkwardly. 'It's a bit embarrassing if I'm honest.'

Nick raised an eyebrow and joked, 'If you've got a strange rash or growth on your body somewhere, I'm not going to have a look, mate.'

French laughed. 'No, it's not that. I wanted to ask you about Georgie. We're really getting on and I, you know ... like her.'

'Okay,' Nick said, pulling a face. 'My advice, for what it's worth, is not to go there.'

French seemed disappointed. 'Why's that?'

'You like spending every day with Georgie as your partner, yes?'

French nodded. 'Well, yeah.'

'As soon as DCI Drake or DI Hunter get a sniff that there's anything romantic going on between you, you'll never work with her again,' Nick said. 'It's police policy. It's dangerous territory.'

'I didn't know that,' French said. 'What about DI Hunter and Sian? I thought they ...?'

'They weren't partners, and they rarely worked side by side,' Nick explained. 'Plus, there's something else you should know.'

'What's that?'

'I heard a couple of rumours from when Georgie was in uniform. She did a right number on a couple of PCs down there. They didn't know if they were coming or going. One of them put in for a transfer,' Nick said under his breath. 'You do not want someone like that playing mind games with you and sending you round the bend. Not with the job that we do.'

'Oh God. Okay,' French nodded and got up from the chair. 'Thanks, Nick.'

With a growing feeling of guilt that he had embellished the truth, Nick watched French go back to his desk.

Georgie took a detour from the photocopier and came over to Nick's desk.

Nick pointed to his watch. 'Shouldn't you be getting home?'

Georgie leant in close and said, 'You and Dan have a little heart to heart, did you?'

Nick glanced up and saw that French was leaving IR1 for the day.

'None of your business,' Nick said with a grin. 'Boys' talk.'

Georgie plonked herself down on a nearby chair. 'Oh yeah? Comparing porn sites, were you?'

Nick laughed. 'You know he's got a thing for you, don't you?'

Georgie frowned. 'Has he? Really?'

'Fuck off, Georgie, you know he has,' Nick said.

Georgie shrugged. 'Asking your advice was he? Man to man?'

'I told him to stay well clear of you.'

Georgie's eyes widened in mock indignation. 'That's not very nice.'

'He's not your type and you know it.'

'Warning him off?'

His phone buzzed on his desk. It was Amanda. He cancelled the call and saw that Georgie had spotted him doing it.

'Oh right. And you know what my type is then do you?'

'I think I've got a fair idea,' Nick said, giving her his best sexy grin and rubbing his chin. 'You told me you like men with beards for starters.'

'Well, Dan's got a beard.'

'Fuck off. You could remove that thing with a hairdryer,' Nick joked.

Georgie laughed. 'That's true. Go on then. What's my type?'

'Tell you what,' Nick said, getting up from his desk and turning off his phone. 'Buy me a drink and I'll tell you.'

Georgie looked at her watch and then laughed. 'Go on then. I'll see you in The Crown in ten minutes.'

RUTH POURED HERSELF a glass of wine and walked from the kitchen to the living room. For a second, she thought about Sian sitting on the sofa and making some inappropriate comment. Even though it was still painful, she had reached the stage where she could smile and focus on some of the lovely moments that she and Sian had shared.

Going over to the Bluetooth speaker, Ruth clicked it on and scrolled through her phone to find some music to play. She had recently discovered Jorja Smith and put on the track *Slow Down*.

As she slumped down on the sofa, her mind turned to the current investigation. Jason Kelly was their prime suspect. He had the three key elements – means, motive and opportunity. Rhian had finished with him to be with Geoff Williams. If he had gone to Geoff's home to confront him and found them together, then things could have got out of hand very quickly. It posed the question of what had happened to Rhian? Had Kelly injured or killed her and taken her somewhere else? There was also the matter of Rhian's car, which was still missing. Once they had Kelly's DNA, they could check for traces at Geoff Williams' home. It would have been virtually impossible for him not to have left some.

Ruth reached for her laptop and opened it. She had spotted an email from Stephen Flaherty. She felt frustrated at the lack of progress from the police in Paris or Interpol. She had spent the previous evening trawling the Internet trying to piece together what she knew about Sarah and what she had been doing since her disappearance. As far as she could see, finding Sergei Saratov would be the key.

Stephen's email subject line was *Patrice Le Bon*. The email explained that the Paris police believed the premises they had raided in Montmartre had been owned by Patrice Le Bon. They were trying to track down Le Bon, who had been linked to Saratov in the past.

Ruth Googled the name Patrice Le Bon and found an article in *The Times* from 2019. He was in his sixties, and was the owner of a Paris-based model agency. He had been arrested in connection with supplying underage models to both Sergei Saratov and Jeffrey Epstein. Paris prosecutors had told *The Times* that Le Bon was being questioned for alleged rape, sexual assault of minors, sexual harassment, and human trafficking of underage girls for sexual exploitation. However, the French press agency, Agence France-Presse, reported that all charges had been dropped in November 2019 due to lack of evidence.

Ruth read that Le Bon, who had founded the ZE7 Model Agency in Paris in the 1990s, had previously been investigated by the BBC for a documentary about abuse in the fashion world. Le Bon had bragged that he had slept with over 1,500 models by the time he was forty.

At the bottom of *The Times* article there was a photograph of two men having dinner, with the caption – *Patrice Le Bon and disgraced Russian billionaire Sergei Saratov dining at The Dorchester Hotel, London 2018.*

Ruth had a strong feeling that finding Patrice Le Bon in Paris was the key to finding Sarah.

CHAPTER 16

WEDNESDAY 16th September

'Call from Control, Boss,' Nick said as he went into Ruth's office. 'Uniformed patrol have found Rhian Ellroy's car.'

'Right,' Ruth said. 'Where is it?'

'In the woods at Parc Mawr, which is about two miles south of Conwy. Dog walker found it and called it in. First reports are that it looks like the car has been driven there and hidden.'

Ruth felt uneasy and said, 'Oh God. That doesn't sound good to me.'

'No, Boss.'

'We'll get straight over there after briefing,' Ruth said, getting up from her chair.

Nick left and Ruth watched him as he walked past Georgie and cracked a joke. Georgie dissolved into giggles.

What is he up to? she thought.

Grabbing her files and coffee, Ruth marched out of her office and saw DCI Drake, her direct boss, coming her way. She hadn't updated him on the case since yesterday, so it was useful to see him.

'Thought I'd sit in on the briefing, Ruth,' he said as he reached her. 'How are we doing?'

Ruth nodded. 'Not sure. I know we're running a murder investigation, but my major concern is a missing person, Rhian Ellroy.'

'This is the girl who you now think was in some kind of relationship with the victim?' Drake asked.

'Yes, sir. I spoke to Nick briefly last night. We've got explicit photos on her laptop, and a burner phone with calls and texts between her and Geoff Williams.'

'Do you think she's in danger?'

'Yes. She has no reason to go missing. It's completely out of character and no one knows where she is,' Ruth explained. 'Her car has just been found up at the woods in Parc Mawr. Sounds like someone was trying to hide it.'

'You think she was caught up in the murder?'

'I think it's a strong possibility,' Ruth replied. 'I'm wondering at what point we escalate this to a missing persons case too and put those wheels in motion?'

'Do we have any physical evidence that she's come to harm?'

'No, just that she's missing.'

'How old is she?'

'Twenty-one,' Ruth said. 'If she was under 18, then I would say put out a press release now.'

'Okay. Leave it with me. You know how tight budgets are. I don't want to mobilise the whole of North Wales Police to look for her if we think she might be off on a jolly for a couple of days,' Drake explained.

'Yes, Boss. Thanks,' Ruth said as she then walked to the middle of IR1. 'Morning everyone. DCI Drake will join us this morning so that he can keep up to speed with the case ... Right, Nick and I interviewed Jason Kelly last night. He claims that he was at home with his brother Tom at the time of the murder. However, he might have gone out for cigarettes. Georgie and

Dan, can you track down Tom Kelly and see if he'll corroborate his brother's alibi?'

'Yes, Boss,' French said, scribbling in his notebook.

'Do we think that Jason Kelly is our prime suspect at the moment?' Drake asked.

Ruth nodded. 'He has a decent motive. We suspect that Rhian, his long-term girlfriend, ended their relationship because of Geoff Williams.'

Nick looked over. 'Kelly also admitted to sending an angry text to Rhian threatening her and telling her to watch her back.'

'However, Kelly told us that Rhian suspected her mother, Zoe Ellroy, of having an affair with Geoff Williams and that she had seen them kissing,' Ruth explained.

'Any physical evidence to link Kelly to the crime scene?' Drake asked.

Ruth shook her head. 'His DNA isn't on the system and we don't have enough for a search warrant for his home.'

Drake nodded. 'Do you think he would give us a voluntary DNA sample?'

'No, Boss,' Nick said. 'He seemed terrified when we asked him about Geoff Williams. There's no way he'd agree to that.'

'Then I think we arrest Kelly, which means we can get his DNA and fingerprints,' Drake said.

'Any news on when we can look at Rhian's bank and phone records?' Ruth asked.

'Hopefully any minute now, Boss,' Garrow said, pointing to his computer.

'What about the neighbour who has a spare set of keys? Myra something?' Ruth asked.

'She's been with family in Cardiff all last week, Boss,' French explained.

'Any way of us checking that those spare keys haven't been stolen?' Ruth asked.

'I can check that,' French said.

'We also have a neighbour who saw a young woman running away from the direction of the Williams' home on the night of the murder,' Ruth said.

Drake seemed concerned as he rubbed his hand over his beard and thought for a second. 'Ruth, I think we should escalate this to a missing persons right now. I trust your instincts that Rhian Ellroy is caught up in Geoff Williams' murder somewhere along the line. The fact that no one can find her makes me very uneasy.'

'Yes, Boss,' Ruth nodded. She was relieved that they could now mobilise more resources to look for Rhian.

'I'll talk to the media office at St Asaph about a press release,' Drake said as he headed for the door. 'Come and update me on any progress through the day, Ruth.'

Garrow looked over at her. 'Boss, something I need you to see.'

'What is it?' Ruth asked as she went over to the monitor.

She saw CCTV footage from some kind of toll booth with several cars slowing to go through.

'This is the Mersey Tunnel Toll. We got an ANPR hit for Claire Williams' car reg,' Garrow said as he pointed to an Audi A4. 'This is her car here. It slows down and the driver throws money into the basket, and then the barrier goes up and they drive on.'

Ruth frowned. 'Okay? It's 6.05am, so it's the right time frame.'

Garrow clicked to an overhead camera at the Mersey Tunnel Toll, played the footage of the Audi coming to the barrier and then pointed. 'Thing is, Boss, that's not Claire Williams driving the car.'

As Ruth peered closely, she could see that the driver was a middle-aged man with a beard. 'Bloody hell. Is there anyone in the passenger seat?'

Garrow shrugged. 'I've checked every angle, but it's impossible to see.'

Ruth looked at him. 'If she wasn't driving the car back, that means she could have been at the house murdering her husband.'

RUTH AND NICK REACHED the edges of Parc Mawr, a large wooded area on the western side of the Lower Conwy Valley, close to the villages of Henryd and Rowen.

As they took the turning to Parc Mawr, Ruth could see the steep slopes of the Carneddau Mountains which stretched away and touched the early morning clouds at their peaks. Below that, a patchwork of green fields divided by dark hedgerows and trees, and occupied on the higher terrain by sheep. Across to the west, a distant canopy of grey cloud was heading their way and bringing a storm with it.

They got out of the car where two marked patrol cars were now parked. The woods to the south were a blaze of golds, browns and yellows.

A uniformed officer approached. Ruth took out her warrant card and identified herself and Nick.

'What have we got Sergeant?' she asked.

'Dog walker found the car down that path there, ma'am,' he said, pointing. 'I ran a PNC check on the plate. The car is registered to a Rhian Ellroy. Address in Conwy.'

'How come you called us in, Sergeant?' Nick asked with a frown.

It was a good point, Ruth thought. The discovery of an abandoned car in some woods wouldn't normally warrant a call to CID.

'When I opened the passenger door, I saw what appeared to be blood stains on the seat,' he explained.

Ruth and Nick looked at each other. It wasn't good news, and made Ruth feel very uneasy.

Following the sergeant down the stony track, the daylight was blocked out by the array of pines, cedar and fir trees, along with beech and oak. The wide pathway had become a stunning carpet of leaves that crunched as they made their way downhill.

'Just down here,' he said, pointing to a gap in the undergrowth.

A few yards further on, Ruth saw the black Mini Countryman. She noticed that branches had been placed over the car to deliberately hide it from view.

As she and Nick approached, two uniformed officers stepped out of the way and retreated to let them get on with their job. Taking blue forensic gloves from her pocket, Ruth put them on. Her mind was now racing. Why was Rhian's car hidden in the woods?

She went over and carefully opened the passenger door. Immediately she saw the smears of blood on the fabric of the passenger seat.

A grim expression crossed Ruth's face. 'Substantial amount of blood on the seat here.'

Nick was inspecting the other side. 'Nothing obvious on the driver's side.'

'Whoever sat on the passenger seat was covered in blood,' Ruth said, trying to piece together the various scenarios.

Nick opened the back door, then crouched down and pulled a face. 'Blood-stained trainers under the seat, Boss.'

Ruth's heart sank. 'At a guess, what size?'

'Four or five. Could be a match for the footprint we found at Geoff Williams' home.'

As she peered carefully at the inside of the passenger door, Ruth could see there were more dark smudges of blood on the handle.

The picture was getting increasingly macabre. Had someone brought Rhian out to the woods in her own car and buried her here?

'Let's get SOCOs down here and seal this whole area off,' Ruth said. 'We're going to need a fingertip search and maybe get the Dog Unit out here too.'

They walked back through the undergrowth as the wind picked up and swirled the leaves above them noisily. A crow cawed above them. It echoed around the trees.

'Why is Rhian's car hidden out here?' Nick asked.

'If we still think Jason Kelly is our prime suspect, then maybe he murdered Geoff and Rhian. He placed Rhian in her car and drove her out here where he buried her in the woods,' Ruth said, thinking aloud.

The constable beside the car nodded, 'Ma'am.'

Ruth gave him a smile. 'Thank you, Constable. We'll take it from here. You and your colleagues can seal off this whole area now. I don't want anyone coming down that pathway. Close the car park off too.'

'Yes, ma'am,' the constable said as he left them.

Ruth's phone rang. 'DI Hunter?'

'Boss, it's Jim,' Garrow said. 'We've been sent some footage by traffic.'

'Okay. What's on it?' Ruth asked.

'We got an ANPR hit for Rhian Ellroy's car at around 6.30pm on Sunday evening. CCTV from the traffic lights on Morton Lane.'

'Have you had a look?'

'Yes, Boss,' Garrow said. 'It's not her driving the car. It's a young man who looks very much like Jason Kelly.'

CHAPTER 17

GEORGIE AND FRENCH sat opposite Claire Williams in a corner of the bar at the hotel where she was staying until the forensic search of her home had been completely signed off. Claire looked tired and drawn as she nervously bit the cuticles on her nails.

'Do you want us to get you a coffee or tea?' French asked in a concerned tone.

Claire shook her head and said in a virtual whisper, 'I just want you to find out who ... killed my husband.'

Georgie nodded. She could see that Claire was on the verge of tears. However, she had lied about driving the car home from Liverpool and they had to confront her with that. Georgie reached for a case file and took out the screenshots that Garrow had discovered from the Mersey Tunnel Toll.

'Claire, I'm going to show you some still images that we've taken from the CCTV at the Mersey Tunnel Toll,' Georgie explained as she laid four printouts on the table that they were sitting at.

'Okay,' Claire said, looking defensive.

That's thrown her. She wasn't expecting that, Georgie thought.

French leaned forward and pointed to one of the images. 'So, this is your vehicle approaching the toll here. Is that right?'

Claire leaned forward and peered. 'Yes. That's my car.'

Georgie nodded. 'In this one, we have your car stationary at the toll.'

Claire shrugged as she grumbled, 'Why are you asking me about this?'

'If you look carefully at this one which is taken from the overhead camera at the toll,' French said, turning the image so that she could see it clearly, 'you can see that it's not you driving your car.'

Claire closed her eyes for a second and let out a sigh. 'No, it's not me driving.'

Georgie looked over at French – *she's not putting up much of an argument.*

'Could you tell us who is driving your car?' Georgie asked.

'Paul Marlow.'

French gave her a quizzical glance. 'And who's Paul Marlow?'

'He's someone I work with. He's the Regional Manager for the North West,' Claire explained.

'And where were you when this CCTV was recorded?' Georgie asked.

Claire frowned as if this was a stupid question. 'I'm sitting in the passenger seat, of course. You can see that.'

Claire reached for the image, picked it up and peered closely at it. Her face reacted when she realised that it wasn't possible to see who was in the passenger seat.

'Unfortunately, we're not able to see if there is anyone sitting in the passenger seat or who it might be,' French said calmly.

'For Christ's sake!' Claire growled. 'Where the hell do you think I was?'

Georgie shrugged. 'We don't know. But you told us that you drove back from Liverpool to your home on Monday morning. Clearly, you didn't.'

'I'd drunk too much the night before, so Paul drove us back.'

'Where was Paul's car?' Georgie questioned.

'He didn't have one. I gave him a lift up to Liverpool,' Claire explained.

'But you didn't mention that on Monday morning when we asked you about your movements?' French said.

Claire shrugged. 'I didn't think it was important.'

'If it wasn't important, why did you lie to us?' Georgie asked.

'I didn't want to complicate things by bringing Paul into it.'

'And when we go and talk to Paul, he's going to confirm that he drove you and your car back to North Wales early on Monday morning?' French asked.

Claire took a few seconds to answer. Something was bothering her. 'I think that depends.'

Georgie shot French a look – *why is she stalling?*

'Is there a reason why you don't want anyone to know that you and Paul were in the car together?'

Claire nodded her head. 'Yes ...'

'Are you and Paul having an affair?' Georgie suggested.

'Yes.'

RUTH AND NICK PULLED up outside Jason Kelly's house. A uniformed patrol car pulled in behind them. She didn't want

Kelly to do a runner, and she needed his home to be sealed off as a crime scene as quickly as possible.

Ruth banged on the door and waited. Kelly opened the door and peered at them with bleary eyes. The smell of weed was coming from inside the house.

Ruth flashed her warrant card. 'Jason Kelly, I'm arresting you on suspicion of the murder of Geoff Williams, and the abduction and murder of Rhian Ellroy. You do not have to say anything but it may harm your defence if you do not mention, when questioned, something that you later rely on in court. Anything you do say may be given in evidence. Do you understand?'

The colour drained from Jason's face. 'Yeah.'

'I'm going to need you to accompany us to the station now,' Ruth said.

'I didn't have anything to do with it.'

'You own a car, Jason?' asked Nick.

Jason nodded, 'Yeah.'

Nick gestured to the garage. 'Is it in there?'

Jason nodded again as Ruth put him in handcuffs.

'Is it locked?' Nick asked.

Jason shook his head and said in a virtual whisper, 'No ...'

Nick took out his forensic gloves and headed over to the garage.

A man in his early 20s appeared walking down the stairs. 'What the bloody hell is going on, Jase?' The man had a shaved head and arms covered in tattoos. He was wearing a vest and boxer shorts.

'Who are you?' Ruth asked.

'I'm his brother, Tom,' he said aggressively.

'Right, Tom. I'm going to need you to put some clothes on and accompany us to the station too,' Ruth said calmly.

'What you arresting Jason for? He hasn't done anything,' he said with a sneer.

'We can talk about that at the station.'

'I ain't going nowhere,' Tom growled.

'Okay, Tom,' Ruth said as she gestured to the burly constable who was now on the path nearby. 'You either go and put some clothes on and come with us quietly, or my officer is going to come in, pin you to the floor, and handcuff you. Then you're going to have to walk around the custody suite in your boxer shorts.'

'You can't do that!' Tom snapped.

'Watch me,' Ruth said.

Tom glared at her but stomped off back up the stairs.

Ruth turned to the constable. 'Make sure that these two are kept separate in the custody suite, please. I don't want them getting their stories straight before we talk to them.'

The constable nodded. 'Of course, ma'am.'

As she led Jason down to the car, Ruth saw Nick coming back from the garage with a grim expression. She opened the rear door to the car and pushed Jason down and inside.

'What did you find?' she asked Nick as he reached her.

'The car stinks of bleach, Boss. Someone's tried to clean every surface,' he said. 'But I found what looks like a droplet of blood in the footwell on the passenger side. I'm sure that the SOCOs will find more.'

Ruth thought it increasingly likely that Jason Kelly had killed both Geoff and Rhian and had disposed of her body up in the woods at Parc Mawr, possibly with the help of his brother.

RUTH HAD ASSEMBLED the CID team in IR1 for a briefing to update them on developments. If Kelly was responsible for Geoff's murder, and possibly Rhian's disappearance, they needed to move quickly to gather the evidence to charge him.

'For those of you who haven't been brought up to speed, Jason and Tom Kelly are in custody downstairs,' Ruth said. 'We've arrested Jason Kelly on suspicion of Geoff's murder and the abduction and possible murder of Rhian Ellroy. We suspect that his car has been bleached and cleaned in the last few days. In addition, he was seen driving Rhian's car at 6.30pm on Sunday, around the presumed time of Geoff's murder. We've found her car abandoned and hidden in woods at Parc Mawr. There are significant blood stains inside, and a pair of blood-stained trainers, size 5. I have ordered a fingertip search of the area around the car and we've got the Dog Unit going up there. Has anyone been onto forensics?'

Garrow looked over. 'If we can swab Kelly for DNA, they can fast-track it and see if it matches samples they took at Geoff Williams' home. The tests for the blood found in Rhian's car and on the trainers won't be back until tomorrow.'

Georgie signalled she wanted to say something. 'We spoke to Claire Williams this morning, Boss. She claims that the man driving the car, Paul Marlow, was someone she was having an affair with. They'd gone to Liverpool together and she was in the passenger seat when that image from the toll was taken.'

'Did you believe her?' Ruth asked.

Georgie nodded. 'Yeah, I thought she was telling us the truth.'

Ruth nodded. 'Thanks Georgie. We'll put Claire Williams on the back burner. I want us to focus all our efforts into getting enough evidence to charge Jason Kelly. I want his phone records, bank statements, anything where he might have slipped up.'

Nick came into IR1 and approached Ruth. 'Boss, good news.'

'What is it?'

Nick looked at the assembled team. 'SOCOs started up Jason Kelly's car. When they turned on his GPS tracker and sat-nav, they found details of his last journey.'

'Which was?'

'Parc Mawr.'

Ruth's eyes widened. 'In that case, we've got him.'

CHAPTER 18

BY THE TIME RUTH AND Nick went to interview Jason Kelly, the duty solicitor had arrived and had been briefed on Kelly's arrest. Interview Room 1 was sparse and cold. Kelly was now dressed in a regulation grey tracksuit as his clothes had been taken for forensics. He had also been swabbed for his DNA. Ruth leant across the table to start the recording machine. The long electronic beep sounded as Ruth opened her files and gave Nick a quick look of acknowledgement.

'Interview conducted with Jason Kelly, Wednesday 16th September, 3.20pm, Llancastell Police Station. Present are Detective Sergeant Nick Evans, Duty Solicitor Pat Clough and myself, Detective Inspector Ruth Hunter.' Ruth then glanced over at Kelly. 'Jason, you understand that you are still under caution?'

'Yeah,' he mumbled, staring down at the table.

Ruth brought out a document from the folder. 'Jason, I have here your previous statement here where you claim that last Sunday night you were at home all night with your brother Tom. However, you might have popped out for cigarettes? Is that correct?'

Jason nodded.

'For the purpose of the recording, the suspect nodded,' Nick said.

Ruth slid a photograph across the table. 'I'd like you to take a look at this image for me, Jason. For the purpose of the recording I am showing the suspect Item Reference 374.'

Jason sat forward and peered at the photo of him driving Rhian Williams' car. Then he sat back and looked at her.

'Could you tell us why you were driving Rhian's car at 6.30pm on Sunday 13th September in Morton Lane, Conwy?' Ruth asked.

Kelly stared at the floor. 'No comment.'

Nick delved into the folder he was holding and pulled out three more photos. 'For the purpose of the recording, I am now showing the suspect Item References 386, 387 and 388. The images show Rhian's car hidden in the woods at Parc Mawr, as well as significant blood stains on the passenger seat and interior of the car. Is there anything you would like to tell us about these, Jason?'

'No comment.'

Even though she was irritated that Kelly was now going for a 'no comment' interview, Ruth continued. 'Have you ever driven Rhian's car before Jason?'

'No comment.'

Nick sat forward. 'Could you tell us whose blood is in her car?'

'No comment.'

'Have you ever visited the home of Geoff and Claire Williams at Bay Road, Conwy?'

'No comment.'

Nick glanced back at Ruth, who waited for a few seconds. Clearly it was frustrating that Kelly wasn't going to answer their questions, but she was used to career criminals opting for the 'no comment' route. It put the onus on the police to find enough evidence to persuade the CPS to charge a suspect and take them to trial. However, she was determined to let Kelly know what they knew.

'Jason, I'm going to tell you what I think happened,' she said. 'I think that when Rhian ended your relationship, you were upset and very angry. You suspected that there was someone else and eventually you found out that person was Geoff Williams. In a rage, you went to confront Geoff at his home. You found him and Rhian there together and they had just had sex. You attacked Rhian and then you stabbed and killed Geoff. Rhian was bleeding, so you put her into her own car and drove her out to the woods at Parc Mawr. You killed her there, buried her in the woods, and tried to hide her car. Your brother Tom came to pick you up and drive you home and then you attempted to clean the car in case there was any forensic evidence. How am I doing?'

'No comment.'

Ruth rolled her eyes at Nick and then looked over at the duty solicitor. 'Okay, interview terminated at 3.30pm. Jason, you will be held here overnight and we'll talk to you again in the morning.'

'YOUR BROTHER JASON was at home with you all evening on Sunday?' Georgie asked.

'Yeah. That's what I just said,' Tom snapped. He was sitting with his legs wide open and a surly look on his face.

Georgie and French had been interviewing Tom for fifteen minutes but weren't getting anywhere. It was a voluntary interview as there was nothing to arrest him with yet. However, he was telling lies and it was time to call him out on them.

French took the photo of Jason Kelly driving Rhian's car and turned it around to show him.

'Could you tell us what you can see in this photograph, Tom?' French asked.

Tom leant forward, looked at it and shrugged. 'I can't really see. It's someone driving a car isn't it?'

'Can you tell us who's driving that car?' Georgie asked.

Tom began to smirk at Georgie as he sat back. 'Not really. It's not a very good photo. It could be anyone.'

He's such a prick, Georgie thought to herself.

'Looks a lot like your brother Jason, doesn't it?' French commented.

Tom smiled as if someone had just told him a joke. 'Does it? I don't think so.'

Georgie continued. 'Unfortunately for Jason, that photograph was taken at 6.30pm on Sunday, and it's Rhian Ellroy's car that he's driving. The car was found today in the woods at Parc Mawr. Would you like to say anything about that?'

Tom shook his head with a smug smile. 'No. Jason was with me all evening so it can't be him. Not a clue what you're talking about.'

French frowned. 'You see the thing is, what I can't work out is how Jason got home once he had disposed of Rhian and hidden her car. The only thing I can think of is that someone picked him up from Parc Mawr.'

Tom laughed. 'Still don't know what you're talking about.'

Georgie rolled her eyes and looked at French. 'I think a night in the cells might refresh Tom's memory. What do you think?'

French nodded as he got up from the table. 'Yeah, it sometimes has that effect.'

Tom shot up from his chair and glared at them. 'I'm not going in a fucking cell, I can tell you that much.'

French reached for the handcuffs attached to his belt. 'I'm afraid you are.'

Suddenly, Tom sprinted for the door, barging French out of the way and sending him flying. He took a swing at Georgie as she stood in his way, but she ducked and kneed him hard in the crotch. Tom went down onto the floor in a groaning heap.

French leant over him, pulled his hands roughly behind his back and cuffed him. 'Tom Kelly, I'm arresting you for the assault of a police officer and attempting to pervert the course of justice.'

CHAPTER 19

BY THE TIME RUTH HAD sat down to conduct the North Wales Police press conference, she was already aware that someone had leaked to the press the discovery of the car at the local woods. Her phone buzzed and she took it out of her jacket pocket. There was a tweet in Twitter:

BBC Wales@BBC Wales Breaking News

Sources claim that an abandoned car has been discovered at Parc Mawr, close to Conwy, by officers today. The area has been sealed off and local woodland is being searched. Sources also suggest that the discovery and search are linked to the North Wales Police investigation into the murder of Geoff Williams in Conwy last Sunday.

Ruth was always in two minds about how useful the extensive use of social media coverage was in a case like this. Once she had informed journalists that Rhian was missing, and that her disappearance was linked to Geoff Williams' murder, there would be an explosion on sites like Twitter. On the plus side, she hoped that it might jog the memory of witnesses from Sunday evening who might have seen something they previously assumed was irrelevant. However, the coverage would also encourage a lot of timewasters, and trolls looking to lash out or hurt the vulnerable.

Looking out at the assembled reporters, Ruth took a moment. She had never liked holding press conferences. Even though she had held about half a dozen since arriving in North Wales, it was her least favourite part of the job. She wondered if she would ever get used to it.

Sitting next to her was Kerry Mahoney, the Chief Corporate Communications Officer for North Wales Police, who had come up from the main press office in Colwyn Bay. Ruth had met her before and there was little love lost between them.

On the table in front of Ruth was a row of microphones. She cleared her throat and said, 'Good afternoon, I'm Detective Inspector Ruth Hunter of North Wales Police, and I am the Senior Investigating Officer in the murder of Geoff Williams and the disappearance of Rhian Ellroy. Beside me is Kerry Mahoney, our Chief Corporate Communications Officer. This press conference is to update you on the case and to appeal to the public for any information regarding Mr Williams' murder and Miss Ellroy's disappearance on Sunday evening between approximately 6pm and 10pm. Rhian's family are understandably very concerned. We are looking for any information that can help us bring Rhian back home safely, and we are doing everything we can to bring Mr Williams' murderer to justice.'

'At this stage in the investigation, we believe that Rhian's disappearance is directly linked to Mr Williams' murder. If you were in or around the Bay Road area of Conwy, or the car park or woods at Parc Mawr, on Sunday evening, we would like you to get in touch with us. If you saw anything out of the ordinary, however insignificant you think it might be, please contact us so we can come and talk to you. I have a few minutes to take some questions.'

'Can you confirm that the search taking place in the woods at Parc Mawr is for Rhian Ellroy's body?' asked a reporter from the front row.

Bloody great! Ruth thought. She wanted the focus of the press conference to stay firmly on the idea that Rhian was missing, not dead.

'As far as I and my officers are concerned, we are looking for Rhian to bring her back to her family safely. There is a thorough examination taking place of the local woods, and if there is anything significant we will let you know,' Ruth explained.

'Can you confirm that Rhian Williams' car was found at Parc Mawr, and that you are now treating her disappearance as a possible murder?' asked another reporter.

Let's wrap this up, Ruth thought.

'I can only reiterate what I've already told you. As far as we are concerned, Rhian is missing and we are doing everything in our power to find her and bring her home safely,' Ruth said, but she knew she sounded a little irritated. 'Right, thank you, everyone. No more questions.'

As Ruth stood and gathered up her files, she noticed Mahoney giving her a slightly conceited look. She had spotted that Ruth was a bit rattled and she was judging her.

Right, I need a ciggie and a coffee, Ruth thought.

Zoe sat at the kitchen table and finished her glass of white wine. The preliminary forensic search of their house had been completed and she had spent the last hour putting things straight again. The BBC news was burbling away in the background. It had been an hour since Ruth Hunter had arrived to update her on developments in their search for Rhian. Even though Ruth had told her they still believed Rhian was alive, she knew that there was growing evidence to suggest something awful had happened to her. She couldn't believe that Jason had been arrested in connection with her disappearance. The fact that Rhian's car had been discovered hidden in some nearby woods made her feel sick.

As she got up to pour herself more wine, Zoe felt unsteady on her feet. It was all too much for her and she burst into tears. She leant over the kitchen counter sobbing and trying to get her breath. How could this be happening? It didn't feel real. She just wanted Rhian to come walking in through the front door with some silly tale about why she hadn't been in touch. But Zoe knew that just wasn't going to happen. Something terrible had happened to her daughter, and it was unbearable to think about. What if she never saw her again?

Finishing the wine, she put the glass down and took a deep breath. It was no use – the tears just kept coming. What if Rhian was being kept against her will somewhere? What if she was chained up in some terrible, dark place by a maniac? She tried to ignore the hideous thoughts and images that spun around her head. She would do anything to have her back. She would never tell her off and criticize her again. *Just please God, let her come home safely.*

Drawing in a breath, she dabbed her eyes, poured more wine and gulped it down. She didn't want to feel anything. The press conference from earlier came on the TV and for a moment she watched Ruth talking to reporters.

Neil appeared at the doorway. 'I don't know why you have that thing on?'

'In case there's a development, why do you think?' Zoe snapped.

There was part of her that was so angry with him. His inability to ever show real love, affection or warmth to their daughter. She had seen Rhian's face when she watched Neil and Louie when they used to play wrestle and laugh. She knew what she was thinking. Why was my father never like that with me? Did I do something wrong?

Neil walked over to the cabinet, poured himself a whiskey and came and sat down.

'I just can't get my head around what Rhian was doing with a man like Geoff? Christ, the man was older than me,' he mumbled.

'Really?' Zoe said through gritted teeth.

Neil frowned. 'What?'

'That's what's worrying you, is it?'

'I'm just saying ...'

Zoe gave him a withering look. 'At the moment, I just want her back safe. I don't care about any of that.'

'I always said Jason wasn't to be trusted,' Neil growled. 'She was far too good for him. If he's done anything to her ...'

'What? What are you going to do, Neil?' Zoe growled.

'I'll fucking kill him,' Neil said coldly.

'Great,' Zoe said caustically. 'That's a great idea.'

'Hey, we need to be sticking together through this, don't we?'

Zoe ignored him. None of it interested her. The tension in her stomach and her whole body was making her feel physically sick.

Louie appeared at the door and came in to join them.

'Do you want something to eat, love?' Zoe asked.

'No, thanks,' Louie said as he shook his head. 'I'm not hungry.'

Zoe watched as he paced the kitchen. She didn't blame him. How was he meant to deal with having his sister missing and all over the news?

'Why don't you go for a run, Louie?' she suggested. 'Might make you feel better.'

Louie shrugged. 'I can't find my trainers anywhere.'

Zoe frowned. 'What do you mean?'

'I went out for a run on Sunday, remember? I took my trainers off by the front door like always. Now they've gone.'

'Have you searched for them?' Neil asked.

Louie nodded. 'Yeah, everywhere.'

MOVING HIS CHAIR BACK, Nick looked at the paperwork he needed to fill out and then at his watch. It was time to get home or he would miss Megan's bedtime again. It had been over a week since he had read her a bedtime story, and going to the pub last night with Georgie had made him feel very guilty. He had also received a text from his AA sponsor Bill wondering why he hadn't seen Nick at any of the Llancastell AA meetings in recent weeks. Nick felt bad that he hadn't been, because he knew that this could be the start of a slippery slope.

'Sarge?' called a voice from behind him.

He turned to see Georgie approaching with a folder.

'What's up?' he asked, feeling a little flicker of excitement.

Plonking herself on the next chair, Georgie showed him a document she had taken from the folder. For a moment, he admired the shape of her legs in the dark grey trousers she was wearing.

'This is the statement from the eye witness, Mrs Little,' Georgie said.

'The one that claimed to have seen a young woman running from the direction of the Williams' home on Sunday evening?' Nick asked to clarify.

Georgie nodded. 'Yeah, she came in about an hour ago.'

'What's the problem?'

'She identified a photograph of Rhian Ellroy as the woman she had seen,' Georgie explained.

'Right. And that's an issue because ...?'

'Our theory is that Jason Kelly attacked both Geoff and Rhian in the house, and that he took Rhian away from the property, either injured or dead, in her own car. So, how was she running down the road?'

Nick took a few seconds to process what she'd said. 'How reliable is this Mrs Little?'

Georgie pulled a face. 'She's got to be eighty if she's a day. And she's a bit doddery.'

'Not great as a witness at trial then?' Nick said raising an eyebrow. 'Run it past the boss in the morning and see what she says.'

'Thanks, Sarge,' Georgie said with a smile. 'I need to pick your brains for a second.'

'Pick away,' Nick said with a grin.

'There's a PIP Investigative Interviewing Course coming up. Level 2. I wondered if you'd found it useful?' she asked.

Nick shrugged. 'I've only ever done the Level 1 training to be honest.'

'Really?' Georgie said in an excited voice. She reached over and touched his arm. 'Come and do it with me then. It's residential. Five days out of this place. We'd have a right laugh.'

Nick wasn't sure what Georgie's agenda was but he was flattered. His phone started ringing. It was Amanda. He thought about answering and then pressed the call cancel button.

Georgie raised a mocking eyebrow. 'Being summoned, are you?'

'I keep missing Megan's bedtime.'

'Well, stop asking me to the pub then,' she laughed. 'Or are you actually trying to miss the whole bath and bedtime thing? I know I would.'

'No, it's not like that,' Nick protested, feeling uncomfortable.

His phone rang once more – it was Amanda again.

Georgie mimed cracking a whip. 'Naughty, naughty.'

Nick let out an audible sigh of frustration and rolled his eyes. 'Yeah, I'd better answer this or I will be in real trouble.'

Georgie got up, touched his arm and looked directly at him. 'Yeah, you do that. Like a good boy, eh?'

Nick gave her a sarcastic smile and answered the phone as she left.

'Nick?' Amanda said. He could instantly tell from her voice that something was wrong. She sounded distraught.

'Amanda? What's wrong?' Nick asked as his stomach clenched.

'I'm really sorry, it's the baby,' she said as she burst into tears. 'I had cramps, then bleeding ... and then ...'

Nick knew what she was telling him – she had lost the baby.

'It's okay,' he said gently. 'Where are you?'

'I've just got back from the hospital,' Amanda said, her voice breaking with emotion. 'I'm so sorry, Nick.'

'Don't worry. I'll be home in twenty minutes ... I love you.'

CHAPTER 20

IT WAS 11PM WHEN ZOE went into the darkness of the kitchen. She had drunk too much and was thirsty. Now she was awake, her mind was racing again and it was torture. She clicked on the light switch. Nothing. Maybe it was a power cut? Power cuts were a regular occurrence in the area and didn't normally last much longer than a few minutes. She saw that the digital clock on the cooker was off too which confirmed her suspicion.

She poured herself a glass of water, and walked carefully across the dark room to the doors that led from the kitchen out to the patio and garden. It was raining outside and the droplets pattered rhythmically onto the glass panes. There was a buzz from inside the kitchen as the electricity came back on. The clock on the cooker now flashed 00:00, and the freezer started to buzz with a loud hum as it readjusted its temperature.

Gazing out into the garden, Zoe thought of Rhian. Where the hell was she? The wind picked up and rattled the doors. She sipped her water and noticed that her hand was shaking a little. Her nerves were frayed and her whole body felt heavy with exhaustion.

A sudden explosion of light in the garden startled her. She squinted outside through the doors. Obviously a motion sensor had triggered the security lights. The wind, or those damned foxes again. It had made Zoe almost jump out of her skin.

She started to feel paranoid. Moving closer to the glass she peered cautiously outside.

Could it have been a cat or another animal?

Everything outside went dark again as the motion sensor switched off.

Not a moment later, the garden was flooded with light once more.

Where previously there was just an empty lawn, a shadowy figure stood.

OH MY GOD!

Zoe shrieked and jumped away from the window.

The figure was backlit. Zoe couldn't see anything but the outline of a person standing there.

Although she couldn't see their eyes, she could feel their stare boring into her. She took another step back from the door.

She was about to turn and run when the figure stepped forward.

It was Rhian.

Oh God, Rhian!

CHAPTER 21

SITTING IN THE ARMCHAIR, Nick looked over at Amanda who was lying on the sofa. She sensed his gaze, turned, and gave him a sad smile. Her eyes were puffy and red from crying.

'You look tired, Babe,' Nick said.

'I thought we'd agreed ages ago that you weren't going to call me Babe,' Amanda said, trying to make a joke.

Nick smiled back at her. 'Why don't you go to bed, eh?'

Amanda shook her head. 'I want to stay down here with you.'

'I can come up with you, if that helps?'

'It's okay,' Amanda said and gestured to a comedy programme they were watching. 'I'm all right lying here with you and watching the telly.'

'Of course.'

There were a few seconds of silence between them as they went back to watching the television, before Amanda turned back to look at him. 'You know what? There was this bloody nurse at the hospital who told me not to worry, that miscarriages were very common and it wouldn't affect me getting pregnant again. And I thought, but I don't want to brush over it and make light of it. I lost a baby and it's okay for us to be really sad about it. And it's all right to feel grief. I don't want someone telling me how to feel and to start thinking about getting pregnant again.'

Nick nodded as he thought about the child they had lost and the thoughts he'd had about Megan having a little brother or sister. 'It's really sad. I had a picture in my head of Megan and how she'd react when she met our new baby.'

Amanda smiled. 'Don't, or I'll start crying again. Megan's lucky to have you as a dad, you know that?'

Nick nodded. 'Thanks.'

Amanda went back to watching the television as Nick took stock of how he really felt about himself. It wasn't good. In fact, he had felt this kind of self-loathing for a long time.

As he gazed back over at Amanda, he saw that she had fallen asleep. He got up and took the blue knitted blanket from behind the sofa and lay it gently over her. She looked so peaceful, so beautiful. Why was he acting like such a prick? Why was he risking everything that he loved?

Sitting back down in the chair, he heard his mobile phone buzz. It was a text from Georgie. He had vaguely explained to her what had happened as he left CID earlier.

Everything okay at home? G xx

As Nick replayed their earlier conversation in IR1, he felt ashamed. He had lied to Amanda yesterday about working late while he went to the pub with Georgie. What kind of a husband or father does that?

He read the text again and thought about replying. And then he made a resolution. No more secret texts, no more flirty conversations. It was time for him to grow up and be responsible.

ZOE BROUGHT A MUG OF tea over to Rhian, who sat at the kitchen table with a towel around her shoulders. She was shivering.

'Oh my God,' Zoe said as she hugged her daughter tightly. 'I'm so glad you're here.'

For a second, Zoe prayed that this wasn't some cruel dream.

Putting her hands either side of her face, Zoe looked at Rhian's terrified eyes. 'Where have you been?'

'I didn't kill him, Mum,' Rhian said as she began to cry.

'What?'

'I didn't kill Geoff. I promise,' Rhian sobbed. 'I was there but I didn't kill him.'

Zoe held her again. 'Of course you didn't. No one thinks you did.'

'Don't they?'

'No, of course not.'

They looked at each other for a few seconds.

'Drink your tea,' Zoe said. Tears came into her eyes. 'Oh my God. I can't believe that you're sitting here. I thought we'd lost you. I didn't think you were coming back.'

'I'm so sorry, Mum. Really,' Rhian said as she reached out to hold her mother's hand.

For a few seconds they just sat and stared at each other.

'Where have you been?' Zoe asked as she wiped the tears from her face.

'A friend of Jason's in town,' Rhian said.

'Why? What happened on Sunday?' Zoe asked.

Rhian bit her lip and began to cry. 'It was so awful. I can't believe this has happened. I've been sitting in a flat too scared to go anywhere.'

'Rhian, you need to tell me what happened. Whatever it is.'

'You know about me and Geoff?' Rhian asked in a virtual whisper.

Zoe nodded. 'Yes. The police found your secret phone and looked through your laptop.' As Rhian tried to take a sip of tea, Zoe could see that her hands were shaking. 'It's all right, love, take your time.'

Rhian nodded and sniffed. 'I ... I was at Geoff's house on Sunday. We'd had a bit of a row. So, I said I was going for a walk to get some fresh air ... and he said he was going to have a shower.' Taking a deep breath, Rhian started to sob. 'And ... when I came back, I saw him there ... and he was dead ...'

'I'm so sorry. That must have been horrendous,' Zoe said as she leaned over and hugged her. 'Why didn't you call the police, or us?'

Rhian sat back and wiped her face. 'I just panicked. I stepped in the blood. I tried to give Geoff CPR so I was covered ... I just thought the police would think I'd done it.'

'Why?' Zoe asked. 'You tried to save him.'

Rhian stared into space and shook her head as tears rolled down her face. 'I rang Jason.'

'Jason? Why?'

'I just thought he would know what to do,' Rhian mumbled.

'And he told you to hide?'

Rhian nodded. 'He said the police would think it was me. He said it's always the partner or someone like that. He came over and we went up to Parc Mawr and hid my car. Then Tom came and picked us up and I went and got cleaned up. Then Jason dropped me at this Kevin's flat. He told me to lie low until he worked out what to do next.'

Zoe couldn't believe that Rhian had been so naïve. But the fact that she was home safe was all that really mattered.

'You'll have to talk to the police, darling,' Zoe said gently.

Rhian nodded. 'I know. I saw the press conference on the news. That's why I came back tonight. But I'm so scared. Everyone's going to hate me for what I've put them through.'

'No, they won't,' Zoe said as she hugged her. "It's going to be fine. You haven't done anything wrong, okay? We'll sort it out.'

CHAPTER 22

THURSDAY 17th September

It was early morning as Ruth and Nick approached the dark blue double doors that led to the Llancastell University Hospital mortuary. Ruth looked over at Nick to check that he was okay. As they'd set off from Llancastell CID he had told her that Amanda had had a miscarriage the previous night. Despite her insistence that he take a day of compassionate leave, Nick had refused. His Auntie Pat had gone to look after Amanda and pick Megan up from nursery. Amanda had told him to go to work as she would probably sleep for most of the day.

'Nick,' Ruth said gently.

'Yeah?'

'It's okay to grieve when you have a miscarriage,' Ruth said.

Nick nodded. 'Yeah, I know. I'm not sure what I'm supposed to feel.'

'I had a miscarriage about a year after Ella was born,' Ruth admitted. 'And it was horrible. Me and Dan were excited about Ella having a new baby brother or sister. And then all that was taken away. It was so sad.'

'I didn't know that.'

'Some people will tell you that one in four pregnancies ends in miscarriage. They make you feel that because it's quite common you shouldn't be upset or feel loss. But you and Amanda were excited about bringing a new life into your family and this world. You need to know it's okay to feel grief for the loss of that.'

For a few seconds, Nick didn't say anything and then he turned to her. 'Thank you.'

Ruth nodded and gave him a kind smile. 'Just don't feel that you've got to forget and move on. Not until you're both ready to.'

Nick nodded. 'Yeah.'

Ruth gestured to the doors. 'You okay to do this? I can do it on my own?'

Nick shook his head. 'I just need to keep occupied, Boss. It's fine.'

As they entered the mortuary, Amis gave them a cheery wave and got up. Ruth could see Geoff Williams' body laid out on the metal gurney at the far side of the room.

'Here they are again,' Amis quipped in his usual jovial manner.

'Who are we this week, Tony?' Ruth said rolling her eyes.

'Ooh, you've got me there,' he replied, deep in thought. 'Hart To Hart?'

Ruth frowned. 'They were a married couple and millionaires.'

Tony shrugged. 'Best I could come up with this early, I'm afraid.'

'Something you wanted to show us?' she asked, trying not to sound too impatient. She had a murder and a missing persons investigation to get on with.

'Come over here,' Amis said, putting down his mug of tea that had '*Yes, I am a doctor. No, I don't want to look at it.*' emblazoned across it.

Ruth and Nick turned and followed Amis to look at Geoff's colourless body that glared under the harsh post-mortem lights.

'Your victim was in very good shape for his age. However, I found some severe degeneration at the base of the spine,' Amis said. 'Possibly a sporting injury.'

Nick nodded. 'He played rugby.'

'Yes, that would explain it,' Amis confirmed. 'Bloody stupid game.'

Ruth caught Nick's eye. She knew his passion for the game but he let it go.

'It would have been very painful, and with the enlargement of the liver I would guess that your victim was taking a lot of opiate painkillers,' Amis explained. 'I won't know more until the toxicology report comes back. There are a couple of things that don't really sit right with me at the moment though.'

'You mean the cause of death?' Ruth asked, wondering what Amis meant.

'No, no. He definitely died from the two stab wounds. Internal bleeding and damage to a lung and kidney, plus some nasty defensive wounds to one hand.'

'What's the problem?' Nick asked.

'Not necessarily a problem,' Amis said as he pointed to the chest. 'Your victim had a broken rib and bruising to the sternum.'

Ruth shrugged. 'Probably from fighting with his attacker?'

Amis shook his head. 'No, not from what I can see. The bruising and broken rib are from severe compression.'

Ruth still didn't know what Amis was getting at. She was used to having to go around the houses for him to get to the point but it was starting to frustrate her now.

'Compression?' Ruth frowned. 'I don't know what you're getting at Tony.'

She saw Nick smirk. He knew Amis was getting to her and was finding it amusing – so she gave him a playful kick.

'My guess would be that someone tried to revive your victim with excessive CPR,' Amis explained. 'They compressed his chest so hard that it cracked a rib. I've seen it before.'

'Any clues?' Ruth asked, wondering if the pattern of the bruising could tell them anything.

'Small bruises from the fingers, so the hands were pretty small too,' he suggested.

Ruth and Nick exchanged a look – not quite what they had expected if Jason Kelly was their prime suspect. But then again why revive him? Or did Rhian try to perform CPR on Geoff before Jason attacked her?

'Looks like there were three people at the house when Geoff Williams was murdered,' Nick said thinking aloud. 'Someone stabbed him and left. And then someone else found him and tried to save him.'

'Not necessarily actually,' Amis said, peering over his mask at them.' I worked a case a few years ago. The husband flew into a rage with his wife and strangled her. Five minutes later, when he had calmed down and come to his senses, he tried to revive her. He broke every rib in her body trying to restart her heart – but of course, it was too late.'

RUTH SIPPED HER COFFEE and ran through her plans for the day. The post-mortem hadn't given them any more evidence against Jason Kelly or his brother Tom. She hoped that a night in the holding cells might have softened them up enough for another interview. She had seen it many times before. A suspect, tired, scared and bewildered, after an uncomfortable night in the cells, would start to crack on the second interview. And it was often the kind, gentle and friendly approach that worked best in these situations. She knew that television, films and books were full of cliches. Good cop, bad cop. The maverick cop who loses his temper and puts the suspect against the wall by his throat. She had only ever seen that a few times when she was a PC in South London. The perceived wisdom was that the softly, softly approach produced far better results than intimidation.

Grabbing her coffee, she walked out into the CID office and went over to the scene board.

Garrow approached and said, 'Boss, I've checked with Companies House. There are some irregularities with GW Gym and Sportswear Ltd, the company that Geoff Williams owned with Lynn Jones.'

'How do you mean?' Ruth asked.

'Lynn Jones told us that there were no problems and that she made a decent amount of money from the business every year. According to the tax and VAT records, they're operating at a huge loss,' Garrow explained.

'Maybe Lynn Jones didn't know that?' Ruth said. 'Can we get detailed records sent over, Jim?'

'Of course, Boss,' Garrow said.

Was that a source of conflict between Geoff Williams and Lynn Jones? Had they fallen out about the way the company was being run? Lynn had seemed very upbeat about her business dealings with Geoff. Either she didn't know the true financial picture, or she was hiding it from them.

Garrow looked over at her from his desk. 'Boss, I've just had the first batch of forensics through.'

'Anything interesting?'

'They've got a decent soil sample from the hallway carpet and the kitchen,' Garrow explained.

'How long is that going to take to analyse?'

'A day or two. They've also fast tracked Jason Kelly's DNA through, but there's no match for any of the DNA found at Geoff Williams' home,' Garrow explained.

Ruth shrugged. 'I guess if Kelly was wearing a hat or balaclava and gloves, he might not have left any DNA.'

'True, Boss,' Garrow replied. 'Rhian Ellroy's DNA is everywhere, including the body, but I don't suppose that's particularly surprising?'

'No, not really,' Ruth said. 'What about her phone records?'

Garrow shook his head. 'Some time this morning, Boss.'

The doors to CID flew open and Nick approached – he seemed perplexed.

'You okay?' Ruth asked as he marched towards her.

'Rhian Ellroy is downstairs with her parents,' he said.

CHAPTER 23

'SO, YOU THEN PERFORMED CPR on Geoff in the kitchen?' Ruth asked.

A very tearful Rhian nodded and sniffed. 'Yes.'

They had been interviewing Rhian for ten minutes in Interview Room 2, and had established the key facts of what she said had happened and where she had been. Even though it was a voluntary interview, Rhian was under caution and the interview was being recorded in case it needed to be used at trial.

Ruth was hugely relieved that Rhian was alive and well. However, if they believed what she was telling them, it put Jason Kelly out of the frame for Geoff's murder, which meant they were back to square one. It also meant that Geoff's killer was still out there and the longer they remained undetected, the more likely it was that they would never be caught. With both the media and Senior Management breathing down their necks to solve the crime, Ruth was starting to feel the pressure.

'Did you have to move Geoff's body so that you could give him CPR?' Ruth asked.

'Yes,' Rhian nodded. 'I had to turn him over.'

Nick glanced up from taking notes. 'What did you and Geoff argue about before you left?'

'His wife,' Rhian replied.

'What about his wife?'

'Geoff had said he would leave her and we'd be together,' Rhian said. 'But it never happened, so I said he was stringing me along.'

'So, you had a row and you left the house to get some fresh air?' Ruth asked.

'Yeah,' Rhian said.

'Were you very angry?' Ruth asked.

'No, I was more upset than angry,' Rhian explained. 'I ... loved Geoff and I wanted us to have a life together.'

'You weren't worried about the age gap?'

'No, of course not. We'd even talked about having children. Geoff's wife couldn't get pregnant, but he was desperate for kids.'

'And when you rowed, it didn't escalate to become physical?' Nick asked.

'Oh God no,' Rhian said. 'Geoff wasn't like that.'

'What about you?' Ruth asked.

'Me?'

'It can work both ways. You were never physical when you lost your temper?'

Rhian looked confused by the question. 'No, of course not.'

'How long did you walk for?' Nick asked.

Rhian thought for a few seconds. 'Twenty minutes, I guess.'

'Did you see anyone?'

'I don't think so. I wasn't really paying attention.'

'Which way did you go?'

'I went left down Bay Road. There's a little park at the end with swings and I sat on a bench there.'

'Do you think anyone saw you there?'

'I don't think so. It was dark and it had started to rain.'

Nick stopped writing and asked, 'And then you walked back and that's when you found Geoff?'

Rhian nodded, closed her eyes and began to cry. 'Yes.'

'Was the front door closed when you got back?'

'No, I don't think so ...'

Ruth raised an eyebrow. 'Are you sure?'

'I don't remember using my key to get back in.'

'Didn't it strike you as strange that the front door was open?' Nick said with a frown.

'I'm sorry,' Rhian said. 'I just can't remember. But yes, it would have been weird for the door to be open so I must have used my key. I don't know.'

Ruth took a few seconds and then asked, 'Did you see anyone on that road as you walked back?'

'No, no one,' Rhian said.

'You went in and what was the first thing you did?'

'I saw blood on the carpet in the hall and so I called out for Geoff,' Rhian explained.

'Did you hear anything at all?'

'No, I just followed the stains down to the kitchen and that's when I found Geoff lying there,' Rhian said. She took a deep breath as tears rolled down her face. 'Sorry ...'

Ruth gave her a kind smile. 'It's fine. Just take your time, Rhian. There's no rush.'

'Thank you,' Rhian said. 'I'm first-aid trained, so I felt for a pulse but there wasn't one. Then I pushed him onto his back. He wasn't breathing so I tried CPR.'

Rhian wiped her face with a tissue.

'Was there anything that made you suspect there might have been someone else in the house?' Nick asked.

'No,' Rhian said, but then she thought of something. 'The boiler came on.'

Ruth frowned. 'What do you mean?'

'When I was trying to give CPR to Geoff, the boiler clicked on and fired up,' Rhian explained.

Ruth frowned – she still didn't know what she was getting at. 'I don't know what that means?'

Rhian's face was completely perplexed. 'I didn't think of it before. I remember thinking it was weird for a second but ...'

Ruth looked directly at her and said gently, 'Rhian, you're not really making any sense.'

'Sorry,' Rhian said, staring into space. 'The boiler only fires up when you put the central heating on, or if you run hot water. And the central heating wasn't on.'

Nick nodded at Ruth. 'Which means that someone was in the house running hot water.'

Rhian put her hand to her face. 'Oh my God. They were there, weren't they? The person that killed Geoff. They were there in the house when I got back?'

IT WAS 2PM BY THE TIME Ruth had assembled her CID team in IR1. The fact that Rhian Ellroy had walked into Llancastell nick that morning was big news and the room was buzzing with chatter.

'Right guys, if we can settle down,' Ruth said, striding into the middle of the room. She watched as Drake came in through the door, gave her a nod, and positioned himself at the back. Although she had managed to inform Drake that Rhian was alive, she hadn't debriefed him since she and Nick had interviewed her. 'Right, as you all know Rhian Ellroy came into this police station this morning, which is fantastic news. She seems very upset and scared, but she's safe and well. Nick and I interviewed her under caution and she has given us her account of the events last Sunday evening. Nick?'

Getting up from where he was perched on the table, Nick came to the front of the room. 'Rhian told us that last Sunday, she and Geoff Williams had argued about the fact that he had not yet left his wife as promised.' Nick went over and pointed to the enlarged map of Conwy where the Williams' home was marked with a red pin. 'Rhian claims she went for a walk down Bay Road to this park where she sat for a while. She thinks she was out for around twenty minutes in total. It was dark and raining and she didn't see anyone while she was out. When she returned, she spotted blood on the hall carpet. She followed the blood down to the kitchen where she found Geoff lying face down on the floor. She checked his pulse, rolled him over and carried out CPR but it was too late. Rhian was now covered in Geoff's blood, very scared and upset.' Nick pointed to a photograph on the scene board. 'She rang her ex-boyfriend Jason Kelly. He told her not to call the police. He managed to convince her that no one would believe her story and said she could be convicted of Geoff's murder. Kelly came over and drove Rhian in her car up to Parc Mawr where they hid the car. His brother, Tom Kelly, then drove them back to their house where Rhian cleaned herself up and burned her clothes. Kelly then dropped her at a friend's flat and told her to stay there until he worked out what to do next.'

'Thanks Nick,' Ruth said and then looked out across the room. 'Of course, this is only Rhian's version of events.'

'What did you think when you interviewed her?' Drake asked.

'I was convinced that she was telling us the truth, Boss,' Ruth admitted. 'She has no record of violence. And having a row with Geoff Williams about when he was going to leave his wife doesn't feel like motive to stab him to death.'

Drake raised an eyebrow. 'If that's what they were rowing about.'

Nick glanced over at Drake. 'Rhian's very young. And she's terrified. I don't believe the girl we spoke to this morning stabbed a man and then chased him downstairs to make sure he was dead. And then decided to try and give him CPR. That doesn't make any sense, Boss.'

Drake nodded. 'I tend to agree with you there. She's also had two days to think of a decent alibi. Going for a walk and sitting in a park doesn't do her any favours, does it?'

'No, Boss,' Ruth said. 'There is something else. Rhian claimed that when she was giving Geoff CPR, the boiler in the kitchen came on. That suggests that there was someone else in the house running hot water when she got back.'

'That would make sense if you were covered in blood,' Georgie said. 'You'd try and wash it off before you left.'

'Did forensics find any sign of that?' Drake asked.

Ruth shook her head. 'No, Boss. But if someone made a decent job of clearing up after themselves, it might not have been spotted. SOCOs were concentrating on the areas where Geoff had been stabbed and made his way downstairs.'

'Okay. Then we need forensics to go back in and have another look,' Drake said.

'Talking of forensics, anyone hear anything back on that soil sample they found at the premises?' Ruth asked.

'They said it would be tomorrow,' French explained.

Ruth nodded and then went over to the board and pointed to a photograph of Claire Williams. 'We know that Geoff and Rhian were having an affair. Claire Williams, Geoff's wife, claims that she was in Liverpool on Sunday evening and drove home early on Monday morning, which is when she discovered her husband's body. However, we know that she wasn't telling the entire truth because a work colleague, Paul Marlow, was driving her home. Has anyone managed to speak to him to confirm her story?'

French looked over. 'Georgie and I are going to talk to him later today.'

Ruth nodded. 'Okay. Let's see what he has to say. And see if you can get a feeling whether he's covering for her or if she really was in the car.'

'Who else do we have in the frame for Geoff's murder?' Drake asked.

'We haven't looked at Zoe Ellroy properly yet, Boss,' Nick said.

Drake frowned. 'Does she have motive?'

'Jason Kelly told us that Rhian had seen Geoff and Zoe kissing and that she suspected them of having an affair,' Nick explained. 'What if they were having an affair and Geoff finished with her to be with Rhian? It's a double whammy. She's furious because he's chosen her twenty-one-year-old daughter over her.'

'She doesn't have an alibi for the time of the murder either,' Ruth said. 'She was out dog walking.'

'Weren't you looking at the father and son after some dispute at the rugby club?' Drake asked.

Ruth shook her head. 'We were but I can't see there's anything in it.'

'If what you've said is true, then Neil Ellroy has motive too, Boss,' Georgie said. 'If he knew that Geoff was shagging his wife and then his daughter?'

Nick snorted. 'Nicely put, Georgie.'

'Yes. That's a good point,' Ruth said.

'He hasn't got an alibi either,' French said. 'Didn't he claim he was out at a building site fixing a fence and no one saw him?'

Nick nodded. 'Yeah.'

'Nick and I will go and talk to Neil and Zoe Ellroy. Right, thank you everyone. Let's get cracking on this,' Ruth said loudly, trying to instill a sense of urgency into everyone.

CHAPTER 24

IT WAS LATE AFTERNOON by the time Ruth and Nick knocked on the front door of the Ellroys' home. The door opened and Zoe peered out at them and smiled. Even though she looked tired, Ruth could also see the relief on her face.

'Hi there,' Zoe said as she gestured for them to come inside. 'Actually, Rhian's asleep at the moment. She's exhausted after the past few days.'

'She's been through a lot,' Ruth said as she and Nick came through to the kitchen. 'You must be so pleased to have her home?'

'God, yes,' Zoe said. 'I can't believe everything that's happened. The past few days feel like some horrible nightmare, but it's hard to describe how happy I am to have Rhian back safely. Do you have children?'

'Yes,' Ruth nodded as they sat down at the kitchen table. 'I have a daughter Ella. She's only a couple of years older than Rhian.'

'Then you'll know what I mean.'

Ruth thought back to the Andrew Gates case from a few years ago when she feared she would lose Ella. It made her shudder. 'Yes, I know exactly what you mean.'

'Do you want tea or coffee while I go and wake Rhian up?' Zoe asked.

Nick leant forward and said in a friendly tone, 'Actually Zoe, we wanted to talk to you first.'

'Oh, okay,' she said and pulled a face. 'I just assumed you'd want to go through more stuff with Rhian. But I'll do anything I can to help.'

Ruth moved her chair nearer the table and smiled at Zoe. She didn't want her to become instantly defensive. 'We just wanted to talk to you about your relationship with Geoff.'

Zoe frowned but didn't reply for a few seconds. 'Okay ... I thought we'd talked about that?'

Zoe shifted awkwardly in her seat and sat up straight.

'Just a few things we'd like to clarify,' Nick said as he clicked his pen to take notes. 'Would you say that you and Geoff were close friends?'

Zoe hesitated and then said, 'Erm, yes, I suppose so.'

She didn't like that question, Ruth thought. There was something about this line of questioning that was unnerving Zoe.

'You don't sound sure?'

'I saw him at the rugby club, and I also saw him socially. He was good company,' Zoe explained cautiously.

'Your husband described your relationship with Geoff as flirtatious,' Ruth said.

Zoe huffed and seemed instantly annoyed. 'Well, he would.'

'So it wasn't then?'

Zoe rolled her eyes. 'Geoff's relationship with every woman he came into contact with was flirtatious. I wasn't singled out for special attention.'

'But it was never more than that?' Ruth asked.

'Me and Geoff?' Zoe said and then gave a little laugh. 'God, no.'

Ruth looked at her. However hard she was trying to laugh at the insinuation, Zoe was clearly finding answering the questions excruciating.

'Are you sure?' Nick said and read from his notepad. 'We heard you were seen kissing Geoff at a party in your garden?'

Zoe shook her head but took a few seconds to respond. 'I don't think so, although when Geoff has a drink, his definition of personal space changes. And sometimes he tried to lean in for a kiss. But I never responded ... Who told you that?'

Ruth ignored her question and asked, 'Was your husband jealous of your relationship with Geoff?'

'Not really. It was a bit of joke between us all,' Zoe said and then looked at them. 'Neil didn't have anything to do with what happened to Geoff, if that's what you're thinking.'

Ruth waited for a moment and then asked, 'Did you know that Rhian and Geoff were having a relationship before he was killed?'

'What?' Zoe snapped. 'You know I didn't! I was there when you found that photograph.'

That touched a nerve.

'It's just that Rhian lives here, and I assume that you two are close,' Ruth said. 'When she finished with Jason, I thought she might have confided in you what was going on?'

Zoe shrugged but was clearly annoyed. 'Well, she didn't.'

A bleary-eyed Rhian appeared at the doorway and was surprised to see them.

'How are you feeling, darling?' Zoe asked as she gestured to the table. 'Come and sit down and I'll make you a coffee.'

Rhian frowned. 'It's okay, if you're in the middle of something.'

'It's fine,' Zoe said as she got up and went to make the coffee. 'We were just talking about you.'

Ruth could see that Zoe was desperate to take the spotlight away from herself, and Rhian's appearance at the kitchen door was a welcome distraction.

With a slightly hesitant expression, Rhian came over and sat with them.

'Are you up to talking to us for a few minutes now?' Ruth asked. It didn't appear that Zoe was going to tell them any more about her relationship with Geoff.

Rhian nodded as Zoe returned with a mug of coffee which she placed down in front of her daughter. 'There you go, love. DI Hunter was asking if you had told me that you'd split up with Jason and were seeing Geoff?'

Rhian's eyes widened as if that was a hideous question. 'No.'

Ruth raised an eyebrow. 'Can you tell us why not?'

Rhian pulled a face. 'Erm, I just thought my mum would think it was very weird.'

'Because of the age gap and the fact that Geoff was married?' Nick asked.

'Yeah. For all sorts of reasons. It's not the sort of thing you tell your mum is it?' Rhian said.

Ruth thought that it was exactly the sort of thing her daughter Ella *would* tell her, but they were incredibly close and told each other everything.

Rhian sipped her coffee and looked at Zoe. 'I didn't want you telling dad either.'

Ruth picked up on the comment. 'Why not?'

Rhian shrugged and said, 'He hated Geoff as it was. He would have gone mental. I've been trying to avoid him since I got home.'

'You don't get on?' Ruth asked.

Rhian shook her head. 'Not really. Louie was a medical miracle whereas I was from the lost and found.'

'Rhian!' Zoe protested.

'Oh come on, Mum,' Rhian said. 'My Dad is a miserable git with a nasty temper. And he likes to pretend that I don't exist.'

Ruth exchanged a look with Nick – should they be taking a closer look at Neil Ellroy?

GEORGIE AND FRENCH made their way down the water-front beside Conwy Harbour. To her left, Georgie could see the rounded stone turrets of Conwy Castle looming over them. To the right, the tide was low and twenty or so small boats sat motionless on the shallow water, the reflections of their white masts in a neat diagonal line on the water's still surface. Less than a mile across the water were more boats, and behind them the town of Llandudno.

'I love sitting outside a pub next to the water,' Georgie said.

'There's a couple on the river in Llancastell if you fancy a quick drink after work one night?' French said.

Oh my God, is he actually asking me out?

'Yeah, that would be nice. Not sure it's the weather at the moment, though,' Georgie said with a smile. French was her partner, but she just didn't fancy him. However, if he had a crush on her, she was more than happy to use it to her advantage.

As they continued down the harbour, Georgie gazed at the sporadic pools of water and rippled dunes of sand that lay side by side as gulls pecked holes in their search for food. The air smelled of the salty sea mixed with the greasy food from a nearby fish and chip shop.

'That's it,' French said, pointing to The Liverpool Arms pub which was traditional looking, with a white and black painted exterior, and seemed to have been built within the grey walls of Conwy. There were various customers sitting at the dark wooden tables outside. It was where they had been told they would find Paul Marlow when they rang his home earlier.

Georgie saw a middle-aged man sitting at the far table nursing a pint. She thought she recognised him from the photo they had seen from the Mersey Tunnel Toll CCTV.

'I think he's over there,' she said to French.

Approaching the table, Georgie got out her warrant card and asked politely, 'Paul Marlow?'

Marlow looked up at them and frowned. 'Yeah?'

'DC Wild and DS French, Lancastell CID. Mind if we ask you a few questions?' Georgie asked in a low voice so as not to draw attention to themselves.

'Llancastell, eh?' Marlow said, and gestured to the table that he was sitting at. 'Be my guest.'

'Thanks,' Georgie said as she and French sat down. The wind came off the sea, and the dark red umbrella that was folded away above them fluttered noisily.

'This is about Geoff Williams' murder isn't it?' Marlow said calmly as he sipped his beer.

He seems to be taking this in his stride, she thought.

'That's right,' Georgie said, taking out her notepad and pen. 'We understand that you know Claire Williams?'

'Yeah, we work together.'

'And you were at a work conference with her in Liverpool last weekend?' French asked.

Marlow nodded. 'Yeah. Sales conference. Very boring.'

'Claire claims that you drove both of you back in her car to Conwy early on Monday morning? Is that right?' Georgie asked.

'Yeah.'

'What time would that have been?'

'Must have left Liverpool at about six,' Marlow explained.

'Can you tell us why Claire didn't drive her own car?'

'She'd had a few too many the night before. I told her it was safer for me to drive.'

Georgie frowned. 'You didn't drink on Sunday night?'

'Couple of pints. I had an early night. But a few of them were up 'til the early hours. Claire was the worse for wear, so I drove and she had a kip in the car on the way back,' Marlow said.

'Claire told us that you two are having an affair,' Georgie said bluntly.

Marlow seemed unruffled by the question and shrugged. 'Yeah, she texted me to say that she'd told you that. I've been divorced for a few years now and we get on like a house on fire.'

'Except that Claire's married,' Georgie said raising an eyebrow.

'Yeah, I suppose so. But only in name.'

'Did Geoff know that you two were having an affair?' French asked.

'I don't think so, but you'd have to ask Claire that.'

'What time did you drop Claire off at her home?'

'About seven.'

'How did you get home then?'

'I drove home in her car. I only live a couple of miles away so I said we'd sort it out later. I think she just wanted to crawl into bed for the day,' Marlow said quietly. 'I couldn't believe it when she told me what had happened when she went in.'

'You didn't go into the house with her?' French asked.

'No. I just watched her go in and then I drove home,' Marlow said. 'I wouldn't have gone in anyway. Not if Geoff was home.'

'You'd met Geoff before?'

'At a few work dos. And Christmas parties,' Marlow explained.

'You didn't like him?' Georgie asked.

'No,' Marlow said with a withering look. 'Not to speak ill of the dead, but Geoff Williams was a prick. I had no time for him. And I didn't like the way he treated Claire.'

'What makes you say that?' French asked.

'He'd spent years shagging everything that moved. And he rubbed her face in it. He was bloody full of himself,' Marlow said. 'That's what made what happened to him so ironic.'

Georgie looked up from her notepad. 'What do you mean?'

'Claire was going to leave him this week. She was panicking about how to tell him. Worrying about how he would react. And then ...' Marlow shrugged. 'You know.'

CHAPTER 25

AS RUTH AND NICK CAME down the North Wales Expressway, they took the turning for Conwy. Putting her phone away, Ruth looked at Nick. 'That was the CPS. They're going to charge Jason and Tom Kelly, and Rhian Ellroy with perverting the course of justice.'

'You think they'll go to prison?' Nick asked.

'I'm guessing suspended sentences,' Ruth said. 'Although Jason Kelly might get a short sentence as he persuaded Rhian not to call the police, picked her up, hid the car, and took her to his friend's.'

Nick shrugged. 'Oh well. I didn't like him.'

Ruth frowned. 'I'm not sure our justice system should be based on who you do or don't like.'

'No,' Nick grinned. 'That would be a bad idea.'

Nick turned left and slowed as the street narrowed.

'How are you and Amanda doing?' Ruth asked.

'You know,' Nick said. 'It's still a bit raw.'

'Yeah,' Ruth said with a supportive smile. 'If you guys want some time together to go out or something, I'm more than happy to babysit.'

'Actually that sounds like a good idea,' Nick said cheerfully. 'I think it would do Amanda the world of good.'

They pulled up outside GW Gym, got out of the car, and walked inside.

Flashing his warrant card at the attractive young woman on reception, Nick asked, 'Is Lynn Jones around?'

The woman nodded and pointed to the office where they had spoken to her previously.

'I might come back and enquire if she does personal training sessions,' Nick said under his breath.

'Pack it in,' Ruth said as she shook her head. 'You do know that I'm your daughter's godmother.'

'Traditionally evil, cold and manipulative,' Nick quipped. 'Sounds about right.'

Ruth said, 'That's the wicked stepmother you twerp!'

Knocking on the door, Ruth didn't wait for an answer before opening it. Lynn Jones was sitting at a desk behind a computer. She was the only person in the office and was clearly startled to see them.

'Hi Lynn,' Ruth said approaching the desk. 'There's a couple more things that we'd like your help with, if you've got five minutes?'

Lynn nodded and pointed to two chairs, 'Erm, yes, of course. Sit down. Do you want me to get you a drink?'

'We're fine thanks,' Ruth said with a smile and then gestured to the case file she was carrying. 'We've had a look at the accounts for GW Gym and Sportswear Ltd.'

'Oh, okay,' Lynn said. 'As I told you, Geoff dealt with that side of things.'

Nick took out his notepad and pen. 'Were you aware that the company was running at a huge loss, Lynn?'

Lynn's eyes widened. 'What? No, that can't be right.'

Ruth flicked open the file. 'According to Companies House, the company made a £70,000 loss in the last tax year.'

'But Geoff always said we were doing well. He paid me a dividend at Christmas,' Lynn said looking bewildered. 'I don't understand what's going on?'

'According to HMRC, the company owes back taxes of £90,000,' Nick explained.

'Are you sure that Geoff never mentioned this to you?' Ruth asked.

'No, never. I feel really stupid,' Lynn said shaking her head.

Ruth looked at her. 'Do you have a company safe here?'

Lynn nodded, got up from her seat and pointed to the corner of the room where there was a small black commercial safe about four foot by two foot. 'It's over there, although I can't remember the last time anyone opened it. I think it's just got company papers inside and stuff like that.'

'Could we have a look?' Nick asked.

'Of course,' Lynn said as she frowned and then picked up her mobile phone. 'I think I saved the combination on my phone somewhere.'

Ruth and Nick exchanged a look – Lynn clearly didn't have a clue about the company that she had invested heavily in.

'Here it is,' she said with a nod as she walked across the office and reached the safe.

Ruth and Nick followed her over and watched as she punched the combination into the keypad on the front of the safe. There was a clunk as the electronic locks moved.

Lynn opened the door and her jaw dropped.

Ruth went over and peered inside. The safe was full of plastic-covered packs of £50 notes.

'What the hell is going on?' Lynn gasped.

Ruth glanced at Nick. 'That's a lot of cash for someone who is meant to be on the verge of bankruptcy.'

Nick nodded and did a quick tally of the packs – each one had an authorised bank strap around it that read *£50 notes x 100 - £5000.*

'There's fifteen packs,' Nick said. '£75,000.'

Ruth looked at him – it was a very suspicious amount of cash to be carrying in a company safe.

CHAPTER 26

FRIDAY 18th September

Sitting up in her chair, Ruth arched her back and stretched. She was craving a cigarette, but the thought of getting the lift to the ground floor and standing outside didn't appeal. She would wait another half an hour and get a decent coffee from the cafeteria on the way out.

She got up from the desk and took a quick look out of her window over the skyline of Llancastell. For a second, she remembered the first time she had looked out at the view from the sixth floor. The scene she had observed that day had seemed so alien to her, and it was strange to think that this was now home. She felt so comfortable now in Llancastell CID, it was rare for her to think of her time in the Met in London.

Wandering out into IR1, she spotted a few detectives at their desks making phone calls or working on their computers. She glanced at the scene board and then at the photo of Geoff Williams. Somewhere on that board, amongst all the photos, details, and maps, there was a clue as to why he had been killed so brutally. At the moment, the investigation seemed like a vague mesh of suspects with motives, and none of them had become a clear prime suspect. It would be methodical detective work that would solve the case and she needed to trust that her team would deliver – as they had done on so many occasions before. For a moment, she experienced a twinge of great pride that they were her team.

Garrow turned around on his chair. 'Boss, I've just got the call log data from Geoff Williams' mobile phone provider.'

'Anything interesting, Jim?' Ruth asked.

'Yes, Boss. The last call, or calls, that Geoff received were from a mobile phone registered to Neil Ellroy,' Garrow explained.

'Okay. That's strange, as the picture we're getting is that Neil really didn't like Geoff one bit,' Ruth said thinking out loud. 'Did Geoff answer the call?'

Garrow gestured to what was on the screen. 'No, Boss. But there wasn't just one call. There were seven calls in the space of five minutes just before 5pm. Looks like Neil was desperate to get hold of Geoff for some reason.'

Ruth raised an eyebrow. 'Or Neil had lost his temper for some reason and rang Geoff to confront him?'

'And if he couldn't get hold of him on the phone, maybe Neil went down to the Williams' house?'

'Maybe,' Ruth said, still deep in thought. 'Have we established if there are any CCTV cameras at the Shore Lane building development that Neil owns?'

'Yes. Company called Site Security. They're based in Chester but they're proving to be a nightmare to get hold of.'

'Can you chase them up, Jim? Tell them if we don't get the CCTV footage we need from them soon, we'll turn up at their premises with a search warrant and take everything we find.'

Garrow gave her a wry smile. 'Yes, Boss. I'm sure that will do the trick.'

Ruth was beginning to think that the key to Geoff's death lay somewhere within the Ellroy family. Had Neil discovered Geoff's relationship with Rhian, called to confront him, and then gone to his home. Did he then confront Geoff in his own home and stab him? That posed the question of why Geoff was initially stabbed in his bedroom. It implied that the killer had gained access to the house while Geoff was in the shower. Maybe Rhian had left the door open in her haste to leave and clear her head?

Ruth's train of thought was broken as Georgie and French came through the doors of IR1.

'Did you find Paul Marlow?' she asked them.

'Yes, Boss,' Georgie replied. 'He confirmed Claire Williams' story that he drove her home in her car.'

Ruth frowned. 'Why didn't she drive?'

French looked at her. 'He reckoned that she had drunk too much the evening before to drive back that early.'

Ruth shrugged. 'Makes sense.'

Georgie raised her eyebrow. 'It would do if they weren't both bloody lying.'

French came over with a printout of an image. 'This is an image of Claire Williams' car on the north side of the Mersey Tunnel Toll in Liverpool. It's taken this long for them to send anything back to us.'

'That's Scousers for you,' Nick quipped as he came over to see what was going on.

Ruth rolled her eyes. 'Glad to see you're clinging on to your old prejudices, Nicholas.'

French pointed to the image. 'There's no one in the passenger seat. Paul Marlow was driving the car on his own.'

'So where was Claire Williams?' Ruth asked.

Nick nodded. 'And why is she lying to us?'

'It gets better, Boss,' Georgie said, showing Ruth a computer printout. 'This is the PNC check we did on Claire.'

'Something interesting?' Ruth asked.

Georgie nodded. 'She received a two-year suspended sentence when she was twenty for stabbing her boyfriend after a row.'

'Right. That's a worrying coincidence,' Nick said.

'And Paul Marlow told us that Claire was about to leave Geoff. She was just worried about when to tell him,' French said.

'Claire went back on Sunday evening to tell Geoff that she was leaving him,' Ruth said thinking aloud. 'She can see that Rhian has been there all weekend. Geoff comes out of the shower and she confronts him. They argue, she stabs him, and leaves. Rhian comes back to find Geoff dead in the kitchen.'

French frowned. 'It doesn't explain why she didn't drive her own car back and why Paul Marlow is lying for her.'

'Which would suggest this is premeditated. She goes home with the express purpose of murdering her husband, leaving her car at a hotel in Liverpool to provide an alibi. Marlow is in on it,' Ruth said. 'Right Georgie and Dan, get Claire Williams in and find out why she's lying to us.' Ruth tossed Nick the car keys. 'Come on.'

'I take it we're going somewhere?'

'We need to go and have a chat with Neil Ellroy,' Ruth said heading for the doors. 'You drive and I'll smoke.'

Nick laughed. 'You haven't said that for ages, Boss.'

'I know. I thought I'd bring it back.'

CHAPTER 27

WHEN RUTH AND NICK arrived at the Shore Lane building site, there was a hive of activity on the far side with a yellow digger carving out a trench in the soil. Guide ropes marked off each plot of land where the houses were to be developed. Ruth calculated there were fifteen new houses being built on the plot.

A man with a shaggy blonde beard, high vis jacket, and hard hat approached. She and Nick clearly didn't look like they belonged on a building site.

'Can I help?' the man asked in a confrontational tone.

Ruth reached for her warrant card and thought *This will shut him up.*

'We're trying to find Neil Ellroy,' she said as she held her warrant car in front of his face.

'Oh, right. Yeah, he's over there in that Portakabin,' the man said, now adopting a helpful tone.

'Thanks,' Nick said with a wry smile.

Making their way over to the Portakabin, Ruth looked at Nick. 'Is it Neil Ellroy funding this development or does he run the site for someone else?'

'No idea, Boss,' Nick said. 'The Ellroys have a nice house but you would need millions to fund the building of fifteen houses.'

Ruth knocked on the door and opened it without waiting for an answer.

Neil was sitting with his feet up, nursing a mug of tea. He took his feet off the desk and sat up as they came in.

'Hi Mr Ellroy,' Ruth said as she approached. 'We just wondered if you've got a few minutes? There are a few things we'd like to clarify with you.'

Neil nodded but didn't look overjoyed at the prospect. 'Not sure what else I can tell you ...'

Ruth and Nick sat down on two hard plastic chairs close to his desk. Ruth spotted a calendar on the wall behind him showing a scantily-clad woman– *Jesus, what a bloody cliché.*

She paused for a few seconds to let the tension in the room mount a little before saying, 'We're just trying to get a picture of everyone's whereabouts last Sunday afternoon.'

Neil nodded but seemed anxious. 'Okay, but I've been through that a couple of times now.'

Nick peered down at his notepad. 'You left your home at around 5 – 5.30pm as someone had reported that part of the fence here had been broken down. Is that right?'

'Yes.'

'Could you tell us who told you that?' Ruth asked.

'Jack Meyers. He's one of the foremen here. He happened to be passing in his car and he spotted it and gave me a ring.'

'And he'd confirm that would he?' Nick asked.

Neil shrugged. 'Yeah, of course. Why wouldn't he?'

'Is he here today?' Ruth asked.

'No, he worked Saturday so he gets time off in lieu,' Neil explained.

Nick looked over at him. 'You came here, repaired the fence, and then went straight home?'

'Yes, that's right ... No, actually I stopped at the garage for petrol.'

'And that would be on their CCTV, wouldn't it?' Ruth asked.

'I guess.'

'What time do you think you stopped for petrol?'

He shrugged. 'Twenty past seven, I guess.'

'And you went straight home from here via the garage, and nowhere else?'

Neil nodded. 'Yeah. That's it.'

Ruth frowned. 'It's not far from here to Bay Road where the Williams' home is, is it?'

Neil's eyes darted around the room as he thought. 'No. About a mile, I suppose.'

'And if you cut across the playground?' Ruth asked.

'I don't know.'

'A five or ten minute walk?' Ruth suggested.

'Yeah. I don't really know. I've never walked to Bay Road from here.'

'And you've never visited Geoff Williams at his home?'

'No.'

Ruth nodded and let a few uncomfortable seconds pass as Neil shifted awkwardly in his chair.

'Neil, if I can take you back. You said that you received a phone call from the foreman to tell you that the fence was broken. Can you remember if you made or received any phone calls while you were out?' Ruth asked quietly.

'No.'

'For example, you didn't ring Zoe to tell her how long you'd be here at the building site?' Nick asked.

'No.'

Got you! Why are you lying to us?

Ruth frowned and removed a printout from the case folder she was carrying. 'You see, I'm confused. We've got the records for your mobile phone here. And you made seven phone calls in a five-minute period just before 5pm. Could you explain that to me?'

Neil frowned but he was clearly rattled. 'I don't know. I can't remember making those phone calls.'

'Do you want to know whose number you called seven times in five minutes at that time?'

Neil looked at her but didn't say anything.

'I'll help you out. You rang Geoff Williams' mobile phone seven times but he didn't answer. You must have been desperate to talk to him about something?'

'I can't remember. Maybe I rang him to talk about Louie and the trials?'

'But you don't know if you did ring him?'

'No.'

Ruth exchanged a look with Nick – *he's tying himself in knots here.*

'Did you leave Geoff a voicemail message?' Nick asked.

Neil shook his head but his eyes were darting nervously around the room. He was hiding something from them.

'It strikes me that if you ring someone seven times in five minutes but don't leave a voicemail message, you are feeling very emotional about something. Maybe you were feeling angry?' Ruth suggested calmly. 'What were you angry about Neil?'

Neil sat forward, staring into space. 'I don't know ... I wasn't.'

Letting a few more tense seconds tick past, Ruth stared at him. 'Neil, can you tell me when you found out that Rhian was having an affair with Geoff.'

Neil rubbed his face and then met her gaze. 'When Zoe told me you'd found stuff on her laptop.'

'Are you sure about that?'

'Yeah.'

'Because if you'd found out last Sunday, then you might have called Geoff to confront him because you were angry,' Ruth said quietly. 'And if you couldn't get hold of him, you might have jumped in the car to go down there and have it out with him?'

Neil shook his head. 'No. That's not what happened.'

'You must have been furious that Rhian, your twenty-one-year-old daughter, was sleeping with a man who was nearly fifty,' Ruth said with a growing intensity. 'A man that had flirted with your wife and every other woman at the rugby club. A man you probably knew had had countless affairs. And now he's having sex with your daughter who is only two years beyond her teenage years. What kind of a man does that?'

Neil looked down at the floor and closed his eyes. 'I didn't know about their affair.'

'I wouldn't blame you for being angry. No one would. Who the hell did he think he was? And you went to confront him. And maybe you saw Rhian coming out of his house. And that just did it. She had left the door open so you went in. You grabbed a knife from the kitchen. Geoff was in the shower, washing after he had just had sex with your daughter. And when he came out, you confronted him. Geoff said something that really got to you and you just lost it and stabbed him.'

'No, you've got that all wrong. I didn't kill him,' Neil said and then he looked at both of them. 'And I'm not going to say anything else to you unless my solicitor's present.'

CHAPTER 28

GEORGIE AND FRENCH walked along the ground floor of Llancastell Police Station towards the interview rooms. After his remark about them going for a drink, Georgie was getting the distinct impression that French was attracted to her. He had made a couple of clumsy remarks in the last week but it was more an instinctive feeling. She had no intention of doing anything about it. For one thing, dating someone in CID would be a disaster for her career. She was twenty-six and the next step for her was to get the Sergeants' Exam passed and find an acting DS post somewhere in North Wales. In her head, she had it all mapped out. DS by thirty. DI by thirty five, if not earlier. She didn't want anything to get in the way of that. She also wasn't attracted to French in any way, shape, or form. He was nice looking, in a conventional way, but he seemed immature for his age and there just wasn't any spark.

The same couldn't be said for the lovely DS Nick Evans. He had an edge and a darkness that made him incredibly sexy and attractive. She had fantasised about what he would be like in bed. There would be a variety of benefits to having a fling with Nick. He was a DS, which would be useful for her within the department. Plus he was married with a child. He was never going to leave his wife and child, which meant that a clandestine relationship could never develop into anything more than that.

They could flirt and have great sex – and that suited Georgie down to the ground.

She would string French along a little bit, feeding him the odd tit bit. Knowing that your partner had a crush on you could be very useful when push came to shove.

'Here we go,' French said as they arrived at Interview Room 2.

They went in and found Claire Williams sitting at a table and looking very nervous.

Georgie took the lead, sitting down opposite Claire and putting her case files on the table. 'Okay, as you know Claire, this is a voluntary interview today. However, we are going to record it in case anything you say needs to be used at a potential trial. Do you understand that?'

Claire nodded but her eyes revealed her anxiety. 'Yes.'

Georgie reached over to the recording device, pushed the red button, and waited for the long electronic beep to end.

'Interview with Claire Williams. Friday 18th September, 1.25pm. Interview Room 2, Llancastell Police Station. Present are Claire Williams, Detective Sergeant Daniel French and Detective Constable Georgina Wild,' Georgie said as she sat back and arranged her case files on the table. 'Okay, Claire. We are trying to establish your whereabouts last Sunday evening and Monday morning. We have now spoken to Paul Marlow. He did confirm to us that he drove you and your car back from Liverpool last Monday morning between 5.45am and 7.00am,' Georgie explained.

Claire nodded slowly and seemed relieved. 'Good.'

French opened the file in front of him. 'However, we'd like you to look at this image for us. For the purpose of the recording, I am showing Claire Williams Item Reference 438, which is an image taken on the north side of the Mersey Tunnel Toll in Liverpool.'

Georgie watched as French turned the image around so Claire could see it clearly. It was a photograph of her car with only Paul Marlow sitting at the wheel. The passenger seat was conspicuously empty.

'Oh shit,' Claire muttered under her breath.

Oh shit, indeed Georgie thought to herself.

French looked at her and asked calmly, 'Could you explain why Paul Marlow appears to be driving your car on his own and why you are not in the passenger seat?'

Claire squirmed and shifted uncomfortably in her chair. 'Not really.'

Georgie looked directly at her. 'You told us that you were in the car and that Paul Marlow drove you home on Monday morning. He confirmed that. Why are you lying to us, Claire?'

Claire pulled a face and said in a virtual whisper, 'I can't tell you, but I'm not lying.'

Georgie frowned – *what the hell does that mean?*

French pointed to the image. 'Claire, you are clearly not in your car.'

Claire didn't say anything for a few seconds as she bit her lip. 'You're wrong, I *am* in the car.'

Georgie exchanged a look with French. *What are we missing here?*

'What do you mean, Claire?' Georgie asked, unable to hide her frustration. 'How can you be in the car?'

Claire stared down at the floor. 'I was giving Paul ... oral sex.'

What?

There were a few awkward seconds in the room as they took in what she had said.

'You're not in the photo because your head was in Paul's lap while you were performing oral sex on him?' French asked.

Claire nodded and fidgeted uncomfortably. 'Sorry, this is really embarrassing.'

Georgie looked at French – *this is a new one on me!*

'And this is going to be your alibi? Come on, Claire, no one's going to believe that for one second,' Georgie said.

'It's the truth. It was Paul's idea. He thought it would be really kinky for me to ... you know ... while he was driving through the Mersey Tunnel,' Claire explained. 'I can prove it.'

Georgie raised an eyebrow and asked hesitantly, 'You can prove it?'

Claire took the phone out of her bag and put it down on the table. 'We filmed it on my phone.'

Georgie shrugged. 'Right, well we'd better see it then.'

Claire logged into her phone, found the video, and pressed play. She turned it around for them to see.

The video showed the sign to the tunnel, the car coming to a halt – and then the graphic footage of what Claire had described.

Georgie blinked and glanced over at French, whose eyes had widened – *Well, that's one hell of an alibi!*

CHAPTER 29

SATURDAY 19ᵗʰ September

Ruth came out of her office clutching her files and coffee and strode over to the scene board.

'Morning everyone,' she said brightly as she began the briefing. 'Lovely to see you all so bright and bushy-tailed on a Saturday morning.' She sipped her coffee and looked out at her assembled team.

'Okay, I want today to be the day that we find a prime suspect in this investigation. I know you're all frustrated that we seem to be struggling to do that, but I think Rhian Ellroy's disappearance and our arrest of Jason Kelly didn't help us to get off on the right foot ...' Ruth walked over to a photograph of Rhian. 'I've spoken to the CPS again. Clearly, Rhian was with Geoff just before he was murdered. She claims to have gone out, only to come back and find him dead when she tried to revive him. In terms of forensic evidence, her DNA is all over our suspect and his home. However, I can't see a decent motive.'

Nick nodded. 'And why would she try to give CPR to someone she had just stabbed?'

'Maybe she came to her senses and tried to save him?' Georgie suggested.

'That doesn't feel right,' Ruth said and then frowned. 'We also don't have any kind of motive yet.'

'And if you've stabbed your boyfriend dead, do you ring your ex and fabricate a story that you've found your current boyfriend murdered?' French asked.

'Unless Jason Kelly is in on it,' Georgie chimed in.

'My instinct is that Rhian is telling us the truth,' Ruth said. 'So, unless she's a well-practised actress and sociopath, I think she should go on the back burner. So, what else have we got?'

Garrow looked over. 'Some more forensic stuff came back. SOCOs searched through the bins at the property.'

'Anything interesting?' Ruth asked.

'Anti-depressant blister packs, but I think they've been flagged up,' Garrow said. 'And a pregnancy test.'

'Positive or negative?'

Garrow shrugged, 'I'm not sure. I'll find out.'

Ruth addressed the team again. 'Anything else?'

French looked over with a slight smirk. 'Bit of a weird one, Boss. Georgie and I interviewed Claire Williams late last night. We confronted her with the image of her car at the Mersey Tunnel Toll where she's not visible.'

'And how did she explain that?' Ruth asked.

'Erm, she said that she was giving Paul Marlow oral sex, which is why she wasn't visible in the picture,' French said as he rolled his eyes.

There was laughter and chatter from the assembled detectives.

Ruth shrugged. 'First time I've ever heard that one as an alibi.'

'Yeah,' French said. 'Thing is, Claire has video proof of what she was doing.'

Ruth's eyes widened. 'What?'

There was more low level laughter and chatter in the room.

'Yeah, Boss,' Georgie said. 'She videoed herself giving Marlow oral sex as they entered the Mersey Tunnel.'

'You've seen this video?'

Georgie nodded. 'We had to make sure she wasn't lying, Boss.'

Garrow glanced over at her. 'Get any tips, Georgie?'

There was more laughter as Georgie gave Garrow the finger and a sarcastic smile. 'Never had any complaints, Jim, so no.'

Ruth held her hand up before the laughter and comments got out of hand. 'All right, children. Let's settle down.' She went over to the photograph of Claire Williams that was on the scene board. 'So, we can rule out Claire being at home at the time of her husband's murder.' She then pointed to a photo of Neil Ellroy. 'Nick and I spoke to Neil Ellroy last night, and if we have a front runner at the moment, it's going to be him. Phone records show that he phoned Geoff Williams seven times in the space of five minutes at around 5pm on Sunday afternoon. He didn't get a response. That kind of pattern of calling would suggest that Neil was very agitated about something and wanted to talk to Geoff as he didn't leave a voicemail message. He claims that he wanted to talk to him about his refusal to put Louie forward for the Welsh rugby trials.'

'We don't think that's a decent motive though, do we Boss?' Garrow asked.

A phone rang on one side of the room and Nick went over to answer it.

Ruth looked at Garrow and shook her head. 'No. Both Zoe and Rhian have made it clear that Neil disliked Geoff. In fact, Neil admitted it himself. Not only do we know that Geoff and

Zoe had a very flirty relationship, we suspect that they might have had some kind of affair.'

French frowned. 'Do we know if Neil ever found out about that?'

'No,' Ruth replied. 'However, if Neil did know, and then became aware over the weekend that Rhian was having an affair with Geoff too, that is definitely a motive to go and confront him. Or worse. The erratic phone calls might suggest that too.'

'And if he went and saw that Rhian was there, he might have waited for her to leave and then gone into the house,' Georgie said.

Ruth nodded. 'That definitely sounds plausible.'

'Do we have any DNA matches for Neil Ellroy?' Garrow asked.

'No,' Ruth said, 'But it doesn't mean he wasn't there.' She went to the map and pointed to the Shore Lane building site. 'This is where Neil claims he was early on Sunday evening. And that's less than a mile from the Williams' home on Bay Road here.'

Garrow nodded. 'CCTV from the building site should be with us today.'

Nick approached. 'Boss, that was Pearce Accountants. They handle the accounts for GW Gym and Sportswear Ltd.'

'Okay. What did they say?' Ruth asked.

'Last week, Lynn Jones requested all the accounts for GW Gym and Sportswear Ltd for the last two tax years. They emailed them over to her on Friday.'

'What?' Ruth frowned as she processed what he had said. 'She's told us all along that she had no idea that the company was verging on bankruptcy.'

French raised his eyebrows. 'Boss, didn't you say that you'd seen a load of money in the safe at GW Gym?'

Ruth nodded. 'About £75,000. But Lynn Jones said she didn't know it was there.'

'If she had the weekend to look over the accounts, she might well have wanted to talk to Geoff straight away,' Nick suggested.

'She seems to be lying to us about something. Let's pull her in for a chat.' Ruth looked at her team. 'Right, everyone. I still believe the focus of this investigation should be Neil Ellroy. Let's get out there and do some good work today.'

CHAPTER 30

TAKING THE LAUNDRY out of the dryer, Zoe felt something solid and pulled out one of Louie's trainers. *What the hell is that doing in there?* As she pulled the rest of the laundry into the basket, she saw the other trainer too. *Why did he put his trainers in the washing machine?*

She took the basket to the kitchen table and started to fold and sort the clothes into piles. She was worried about Neil. He had hardly said a word since speaking to the police the previous day. As she folded Louie's jogging pants, she noticed that the bottoms were stained with something. She inspected them closely. *That looks like oil,* she thought.

Her train of thought was broken as Rhian came into the kitchen. She seemed tired and preoccupied. After what she had been through in recent days it wasn't surprising. Trying to resuscitate your lover who had been stabbed to death must have been horrendous.

Zoe smiled warmly. 'Hello, love. How are you doing?'

'Yeah, you know,' Rhian said with a tiny shrug. 'I can't seem to get it out of my head. Every time I drift off to sleep, I can see Geoff lying there on the kitchen floor. Then my heart starts to race.'

Zoe could see tears forming in her daughter's eyes. She went over to her. 'Hey, it's all right. What you've been through is horrible. Do you want me to talk to Dr Doyle and get something to help you sleep?'

Rhian sniffed, wiped her face, and nodded. 'Yeah, if you don't mind?'

'Of course. He gave me something when your nan died. What you've been through is a lot worse than that.'

'I'm really sorry, Mum,' Rhian said. 'Really I am. What I put you all through.'

Zoe went over to the table, sat down next to her and took her hand in hers. 'You need to forget all about that. You were in shock and you weren't thinking straight. What Jason told you to do was bloody stupid but all that matters is that you're here and you're safe.'

'Thanks Mum,' Rhian said in a virtual whisper.

'I keep thinking about what might have happened if you hadn't gone out of his house when you did,' Zoe said feeling choked. 'With some bloody maniac in there, anything could have happened to you.' Zoe felt her eyes water. 'Bloody hell, you've got me going now.'

They glanced up as they heard approaching footsteps. It was Louie.

'Have we got any cereal?' he mumbled.

'Yeah. In the cupboard with the crisps,' Zoe said, gesturing to where it was always kept. Today wasn't the day to nag him. 'I found your trainers.'

Louie pulled a face. 'Where were they?'

'You must have put them in the washing machine.'

'No,' Louie said angrily. 'If you put decent trainers in a washing machine or a dryer you'll ruin them.'

'Hey, I didn't put them in there, sunshine,' Zoe said. She was worried that Louie hadn't said anything about what had happened to Geoff or his sister even when she had tentatively tried to broach the subject.

'Everything all right?' Neil asked grumpily as he came into the kitchen looking for something.

'Yeah, fine love,' Zoe said. 'You going somewhere?'

Neil looked at her. 'I've got to work. I can't sit here all day. Where are the keys for my van?'

'By the phone,' Louie said.

Zoe frowned. She couldn't believe that Neil was going to work as if nothing had happened. 'You're going to work? I'd have thought you'd want to be here with us after everything that's happened?'

Neil snorted. 'That place won't run itself.'

'It's not a big surprise, Mum,' Rhian mumbled under her breath.

Neil glared at her. 'What did you say?'

Zoe put up her hand to pacify him. She could see Neil was about to explode. 'Neil, just leave it. Go to work.'

'After all you put me and your mum through?' Neil growled. 'Anyone with half a brain would have picked up the phone and called the police. I don't know what the hell is the matter with you!'

'Neil, that's enough!' Zoe snapped.

'Well I do actually,' Neil said under his breath as he went and snatched the keys to the van and headed out towards the front door.

Zoe knew exactly what he was implying. It wasn't the first time. Neil was convinced that Rhian's birth parents were what he termed *junkie scum*. It was a horrible thing to say, and she had spoken to him about it.

'He's such a prick!' Rhian hissed.

'I know, love,' Zoe said. 'But you mustn't take any notice of him.'

Rhian started to cry and Zoe went and hugged her. 'I hate him, Mum. I really hate him.'

'CAN YOU TELL US WHY you failed to inform us that you had requested and received the company accounts last week?' Nick asked Lynn Jones.

Although Lynn was attending a voluntary interview at Llancastell Police Station, Ruth had made it very clear from the outset that they took a very dim view of the lies she had told them in the previous two interviews.

'I don't know,' Lynn said. She seemed very shaky as she looked over at them. 'I didn't want Geoff to get a bad name.'

Ruth frowned. 'I'm sorry, Lynn. I don't really understand what you mean by that.'

'I was so upset when I heard what had happened to Geoff. I didn't want to tell anyone that he had bankrupted the company.'

Ruth shrugged. 'Didn't you think that would come out as soon as we looked into the business?'

'No,' Lynn said. 'I feel so stupid but I didn't even realise you would be looking into the company accounts. I just thought ... I don't know what I thought. Sorry.'

Ruth sensed that Lynn did seem genuine but they had to pursue it as a line of enquiry, especially as she had misled them.

Nick glanced up from taking notes. 'Could you tell us when you actually opened the accounts to look at them?'

Lynn thought for a few seconds. 'It would have been Saturday afternoon.'

'And what did you think?'

'I was shocked I suppose,' Lynn replied.

Ruth nodded. 'But you must have been angry too?'

Lynn shook her head. 'No. I was just very confused. Geoff had always been very straight with me. I got my regular dividends. He told me not to worry about the accounts.'

'Can you tell us why you chose to ask for the accounts then?' Nick asked.

'I was in the process of buying a new house. The mortgage company asked me about the business and its turnover. I needed to see the accounts to tell them what profits the company was making,' Lynn explained.

Ruth raised her eyebrow. 'And then you saw that the company was running at a huge loss?'

Lynn nodded. 'Yes. Even I could see it was a mess and it wasn't what Geoff had been telling me over the past two years.'

'But you didn't think to contact him?' Nick asked.

'Not at first. I wanted to talk to my brother who is a solicitor, but he was away with his family for the weekend,' Lynn explained. 'I wasn't going to say anything to Geoff until I'd spoken to him.'

'And he'll verify that you tried to contact him?' Ruth asked.

'Yes. Since it happened I've spoken to him every day. We're very close.'

Ruth waited for a few seconds before presenting her hypothesis. 'You see, Lynn, there is a different way this might have played out. When you saw the accounts on Saturday, you could have become very angry with Geoff. You'd invested your inheritance in his company. He'd lied about how the company was doing financially and as far as you could see, he'd effectively lost your money. That would make most people incredibly angry.'

Lynn shook her head. 'But it didn't. I thought there might have been some kind of explanation for it. I'm not a businesswoman so I didn't know what to think.'

'And you didn't go to Geoff's house last Sunday evening to confront him with what you had found?'

'No,' Lynn said, sounding upset. 'No. I didn't do anything of the sort.'

Nick looked across at her. 'You don't have an alibi for Sunday evening, do you?'

'I didn't do anything to Geoff, you have to believe me,' Lynn said as she shook her head and began to cry. 'I wouldn't do that. I was in love with him.'

Ruth and Nick exchanged a look as Lynn began to sob.

'You were in love with him?' Ruth asked quietly.

Lynn nodded. 'Yeah. I never said anything to him of course. And he would never have looked twice at someone like me. I'm far too old. But I could never have hurt him.'

Ruth looked at her. There was nothing about Lynn and what she had told them that would suggest she could stab Geoff to death.

CHAPTER 31

RUTH AND NICK HAD BEEN sitting in her office playing through the different scenarios with Drake for about twenty minutes. Ruth was always happy to have Drake's input on any investigation. His instincts as a copper were second to none, and she respected anyone who had spent years working in the roughest areas of Manchester.

'The footage of Claire Williams and Paul Marlow in her car in the Mersey Tunnel seems to have given Claire an alibi. Do you think it rules her out completely?' Drake asked.

Ruth nodded. 'I guess so, but it has crossed my mind that she might have paid or persuaded someone to kill her husband while she was away.'

'Being in Liverpool that night is the perfect alibi,' Nick said, continuing Ruth's train of thought.

'Plus, we now know that she was having an affair with Paul Marlow, which gives her motive,' Ruth said.

'Anything in the evidence that suggests Geoff didn't know his killer?' Drake asked.

Ruth shook her head. 'We're still struggling to see how the killer got into the property, Boss. Claire told us that Geoff kept the front door locked. However, if we believe Rhian's account then, when she left the house, the front door would have still needed a latch key to get in.'

'What about the business partner?' Drake asked.

'Lynn Jones lied to us about seeing the accounts. But Nick and I interviewed her an hour ago and she went to pieces. I can't see the woman we just interviewed arriving at Geoff Williams' home to stab him to death because he had almost bankrupted their company.'

Drake looked at Nick. 'What did you think?'

Nick nodded. 'Yeah. She admitted that she was in love with Geoff and wouldn't have done anything to harm him. I don't think she's our killer.'

'What does that leave us with?' Drake asked.

'My instinct is that the key to this investigation still lies within the Ellroy family,' Ruth said.

'Neil Ellroy?' Drake asked.

'If I had to make a call on who killed Geoff Williams right this minute, then yes, my money would be on Neil Ellroy. But we're a long way from getting any kind of evidence to prove that.'

'You know we're taking a hammering on social media?' Drake asked.

Ruth nodded.

Garrow appeared at the doorway and knocked on the open door. 'Sorry, Boss.'

'Jim?'

'Couple of things I thought you should know about right away,' he said, and then looked at Drake. 'Unless you want me to come back later?'

Drake shook his head and beckoned to him. 'Come in, Jim. What have you got?'

'We've received the phone records from the GW Gym landline. If you remember, Lynn Jones reported hearing Geoff

Williams having a heated argument on the phone on the afternoon of Friday 11th September,' Garrow said. 'She thought she heard the name Zoe mentioned.'

'That's right,' Ruth confirmed.

'The phone records shows that Zoe Ellroy rang the gym at 2.58pm on Friday afternoon from her mobile phone.'

Ruth raised her eyebrow. 'So, she was lying to us.'

'Looks that way,' Garrow said. He then held up a memory stick and gestured to Ruth's computer. 'There's something else I need to show you, Boss.'

'Help yourself,' Ruth said.

Garrow put in the memory stick, clicked the mouse, and then turned the monitor so that Drake, Ruth, and Nick could see. 'Okay, I've been trawling through some of the videos from Conwy Rugby Club that are on YouTube, and I came across this.'

The footage was a shaky hand-held clip that had been filmed on a mobile phone. It showed teenage boys playing rugby. Ruth couldn't see anything interesting, but she trusted that Garrow wasn't wasting her time.

Garrow pointed to the far right of the screen. 'So, this video was taken about five months ago. And this, here, is the car park at the rugby club. These two people caught my eye so I had the image cleaned up and zoomed in.' He clicked on the next MPEG file and a video came up that focused solely on the car park.

Ruth frowned at the man who was standing to one side of a black 4x4. 'That's Geoff Williams isn't it?'

Garrow nodded. 'Watch this.'

As the video played, the figure of a woman walked over to Geoff, put her hands on his waist, and leaned in towards him. They kissed.

Ruth's eyes widened.

'Have we got her face?' Drake asked.

Garrow gave a wry smile, 'Oh yes.'

The woman turned to leave the car park and Garrow paused the image.

'Zoe Ellroy,' Ruth said looking over at Drake.

CHAPTER 32

'JUST TO REMIND YOU, Zoe, you are under caution and we are recording this interview in case we need to use anything as evidence at trial. Do you understand that?' Ruth asked.

Zoe nodded as she peered over from the other side of the table. Next to her was her solicitor, a small woman in her 50s with greying hair and glasses.

Nick reached over, pressed the red recording button, and waited for the long beep to end.

'Interview with Zoe Ellroy. Saturday 19th September, 11.30 am. Interview Room 1, Llancastell Police Station,' Nick said. 'Present are Zoe Ellroy, solicitor Marianne Hughes, Detective Inspector Ruth Hunter and myself, Detective Sergeant Nick Evans.'

Ruth removed a printout from the case file in front of her. 'I'm showing the suspect Item Reference 212, a phone log from GW Gym, Conwy. Zoe, we have a record here of you phoning GW Gym just before 3pm on Friday 11th September. We also have witness testimony from Lynn Jones, Geoff Williams' business partner, that he received a phone call at that time and that he called the person Zoe.'

Zoe shrugged but she seemed jittery. 'I rang Geoff. I've rung Geoff lots of times. I don't see your point?'

'Could you tell us what you talked about in that conversation?'

'I'm organising a fund-raising night for the rugby club. Geoff said he would be able to get some signed rugby shirts for the auction. I was ringing him to see if he'd managed to get hold of them yet.'

'Lynn Jones claims that the conversation was heated. In fact, she described it as an argument,' Nick said.

'An argument?' Zoe said pulling a face. 'No. I think I teased Geoff that he always promised stuff and sometimes didn't deliver, but I wouldn't have described it as an argument.'

Ruth looked directly at Zoe and waited for several seconds before moving on to the actual reason why she had been arrested.

'Could you describe the nature of your relationship with Geoff Williams?' Ruth asked.

'Oh my God! We've been through this before,' Zoe said, sounding very frustrated. 'I've known Geoff for years because he's been Louie's rugby coach. We get on and I sometimes see him socially.'

'And that's it?' Nick asked.

Zoe glared at him. 'What does that mean?'

Ruth continued. 'It means, did your relationship with Geoff ever go beyond just friendship?'

'No, of course not,' Zoe said shaking her head. 'I'm married and so is Geoff.'

'That doesn't always stop people being together,' Ruth said.

Zoe shifted awkwardly in her chair. 'Nothing has ever happened between me and Geoff, if that's what you're asking.'

'And you're sure about that?' Ruth asked.

'Yes. Look, whatever anyone's told you about me and Geoff is just gossip. And it's just not true,' Zoe said, getting angry.

Nick opened his laptop and turned it on. 'For the purpose of the recording, I'm showing the suspect Item Reference 453. A video taken at Conwy Rugby Club on April 3rd.'

Zoe peered anxiously at the screen on the laptop. 'What the hell is this?'

Now she's rattled, Ruth thought.

Nick pressed play and the enhanced image of Geoff standing in the car park came onto the screen. Nick paused the footage. 'This man standing here is Geoff Williams.'

Zoe frowned and looked at her solicitor.

Nick let the footage continue, and it showed Zoe walking over and kissing Geoff. As Zoe turned to walk away, Nick paused the footage again with her face clearly visible. 'And that is you, Zoe.'

Ruth looked directly at Zoe, who seemed shocked. 'So, I'm going to ask you again, what was your relationship with Geoff Williams?'

Zoe's eyes flicked wildly around the room as she tried to think of what to say next.

'Did you have an affair with Geoff, Zoe?' Ruth asked her.

Zoe still wasn't answering, and Ruth could see that her breathing was shallow.

'Zoe?' Ruth said in a louder, sterner tone. 'Did you have an affair with Geoff Williams?'

Zoe stared at the floor and nodded.

'For the purpose of the recording, the suspect has nodded her head,' Nick said.

After a few seconds, Ruth asked quietly, 'Zoe, could you tell us about your affair with Geoff?'

Zoe peered over at her and took a deep breath. 'It only lasted a few months. It didn't mean anything.'

'When was this?' Ruth asked.

'It started about a year ago.'

'Could you tell me when it finished?'

'Last April some time.'

Ruth frowned as something occurred to her. 'Wasn't that about the time Rhian started to see Geoff?'

Zoe's eyes were watering. It was all getting too much for her. 'I don't know. I think so.'

Zoe started to sob loudly.

'Did Geoff stop seeing you so he could be with Rhian?' Ruth asked.

'I don't know, do I?' Zoe said as she sniffed and wiped her face.

'When did you realise that Geoff might have stopped seeing you because he wanted to be with your daughter?' Nick asked.

'The other day. When I saw that stuff on her laptop,' Zoe explained.

'Are you sure you didn't find out before then?' Ruth asked.

Zoe looked at her across the table. Her eyes were filled with tears. 'No, of course not.'

Ruth looked at her. 'Because if you had found out before then, I'm assuming you would have been incredibly angry?'

Zoe didn't say anything.

'It's one thing for someone to end an affair with you. But to find out it was because the man was now seeing your 21-year-old daughter ... that must have really got to you? Nick suggested.

Zoe shook her head and murmured, 'Geoff ... didn't finish with me. It was ... the other way around.'

Ruth frowned. It wasn't what she expected. 'Sorry? I don't understand.'

'I stopped seeing Geoff.'

'Can you tell me why you ended your relationship with Geoff?'

Zoe shrugged and avoided eye contact. 'I don't know. It was all getting too much.'

Ruth sensed Zoe was lying or hiding something.

'Zoe,' Ruth said very gently. 'Why did you break off your relationship with Geoff?'

'I don't know.'

'Zoe, you need to tell us the truth here,' Ruth said.

Zoe peered over the table at her and said very quietly, 'Neil found out.'

Ruth and Nick exchanged a look – that's motive right there.

'Neil discovered that you were having an affair with Geoff?' Ruth asked.

Zoe nodded as tears came again. 'Yes. He went mad.'

'What did he say about it?'

'He said ...' Zoe said, taking a breath. 'He said that if I didn't stop seeing Geoff, he would kill the pair of us.'

For a few seconds, Zoe's statement hung in the air.

'Can I just confirm that Neil threatened to kill you and Geoff if you didn't stop the affair?' Ruth asked.

Zoe nodded uncomfortably. 'Yes.'

Ruth leant forward over the table and looked directly at her. 'On Sunday evening, was Neil at the building site?'

Zoe shrugged. 'I don't know. That's what he told me.'

'What do you think?' Ruth asked.

'I don't know.'

'How did Neil act when he came back on Sunday evening?'

'He was fine.'

'Was he?' Ruth snapped. She didn't believe her.

'He was a bit flustered, you know. He was soaking wet.'

'What was he flustered about?'

'He'd cut his hand ...' Zoe said but then stopped mid sentence.

For a moment Zoe's eyes widened as if she had suddenly realised something.

Ruth wanted to keep the pressure on her. 'What do you mean he'd cut his hand, Zoe? Like a graze?'

Zoe was lost in thought and then said, 'No. It was a deep cut on his left hand by his thumb.'

'How did he say it had happened?'

'When he was mending the fence.'

'Is Neil right handed?'

'Yes.'

'Can you describe the cut to us? Was it jagged or straight?'

Zoe frowned. 'It was straight like it had been sliced open by a knife.'

Ruth looked over to Nick – they both knew that in a frenzied attack like the one on Geoff, where there had been defence wounds and a struggle, the attacker often injured themselves with their own weapon.

CHAPTER 33

AS SHE MARCHED INTO IR1, Ruth was feeling energised. For the first time they had a prime suspect that ticked all the boxes – motive, means and opportunity.

Nick was on his mobile phone as he strode towards her. 'Uniformed patrol just arrived outside the Shore Lane building site, Boss. They confirm that Neil Ellroy is there. What do you want them to do?'

'Keep a visual on him but stay put,' Ruth said. 'If he tries to leave, arrest him, but I want us to be first on the scene.'

Nick went back to his phone call as Ruth approached Garrow at his desk. 'Jim, I need that CCTV of the Shore Lane building site like yesterday.'

Garrow pointed to his computer screen. 'Just arrived, Boss.'

'Great, is Neil Ellroy there that night?'

Garrow nodded. 'Yes, Boss. He arrived at six on the dot.'

'Okay,' Ruth said. 'I need the exact time he left. Does he go anywhere during the time he's there? What is he doing - does he look like he's actually mending a fence, or is he up to something else?'

'I'm on it, Boss.'

Nick approached. 'Okay, uniformed patrol will stay at the location and maintain visual on Neil Ellroy.'

'Right, we need an arrest warrant and a Section 18 Search Warrant,' Ruth said, feeling her adrenaline pumping. 'I'd better go and see Drake.'

French looked over from his desk where he was working. 'Boss, message from the forensic lab. There's something they need you to see.'

'Can it wait?' Ruth asked. She didn't want anything to get in the way of nicking Neil Ellroy.

French shook his head. 'They said it was urgent, Boss.'

Ruth thought for a second. She needed every bit of evidence to hand to secure the search warrant.

'Nick, go and get Drake up to speed with what's going on. Ask him to rush those warrants through. I'm going to forensics and I'll see you back here.'

'WHAT HAVE YOU GOT FOR me?' Ruth said as she stood at the entrance to the forensic lab in the new building opposite Llancastell nick. The chief lab technician handed her gloves and a mask which she put on before entering.

'First thing is a series of fingerprints that the SOCOs lifted from the windows at the victim's address. We cross-matched them with elimination samples and got a couple of hits.'

'Go on,' Ruth said.

'We've got fingerprints inside matching both Rhian and Zoe Ellroy,' he explained. This wasn't news to Ruth – they had both been sleeping with Geoff.

'What about Neil Ellroy?' Ruth asked hopefully.

The technician shook his head. 'Not inside. But we did match prints found on the back door and the windows to the rear of the property to Neil Ellroy.'

Ruth nodded – it was good news. Neil Ellroy denied ever being at the property. 'Anything else?'

He nodded and showed her a coloured graph. 'This a breakdown of the soil that we found on the hall carpet. Essentially it's local soil. Stoneless, with a mixture of silt and clay. However, we also found substantial traces of calcium aluminate and lime.'

Ruth shrugged. 'Does that help us?'

'Yes. Calcium aluminate and lime are found in both concrete and house bricks. My guess is that whoever came into the hallway of the victim's house probably worked in construction, maybe on a building site.'

Bingo!

Ruth nodded as her face brightened. 'That's brilliant work. Thank you.'

'I take it that's helpful?'

Finally, they had their prime suspect.

She nodded slowly. 'Yes, that is *very* helpful.'

AN HOUR LATER, NICK and Ruth drove into the Shore Lane building site at speed with their lights flashing.

'Garrow says that the CCTV shows Neil Ellroy arriving here at six on the dot,' Ruth said. 'That gives him time to have gone to Geoff Williams' home, killed him, and come back here.'

'And a building site is a pretty good place to get rid of a murder weapon.'

'Yeah, I just hope it's not buried under ten feet of concrete, or we'll never find it,' Ruth said.

As they pulled up, Ruth glanced in the rear view mirror. Behind them was the local patrol car that had been keeping tabs on Neil Ellroy, plus two more patrol cars. The speed of their arrival had thrown dust and dirt up into the air.

The workmen were startled by their sudden arrival.

Getting out of the car, Ruth could feel the adrenaline pumping around her body.

She marched over to a nearby builder in a yellow hard hat and flashed her warrant card. 'I'm looking for Neil Ellroy?'

The builder, who looked a little scared, pointed over to the Portakabin where Ruth and Nick had interviewed Neil before. 'Last I saw him, he was in there.'

Just as Ruth turned, the Portakabin door opened. Neil came outside with a perplexed look on his face. 'What's going on?'

Ruth stared at him. 'Neil Ellroy, I'm arresting you on suspicion of the murder of Geoff Williams. You do not have to say anything, but it may harm your defence if you do not mention, when questioned, something that you later rely on in court. Anything you do say may be given in evidence. Do you understand?'

Neil pulled a face. 'What the hell are you talking about?'

Ruth signalled to the two uniformed officers who went over to Neil and cuffed him. She then pulled a folded document from her coat pocket. 'I am also executing this Section 18 Search Warrant for the whole of the site. Where's the foreman?'

'That's me,' said a burly man with tattoos. He was looking as bewildered as everyone else.

Ruth approached him and said, 'I need you to tell all the workers that this building site is now an active crime scene. I also need everyone to give a statement to one of my officers before they leave.'

'This is crazy,' Neil growled. 'I didn't go anywhere near Geoff's house.'

'We can talk about that at the station,' Nick said.

As the officers took Neil towards one of the marked patrol cars, Ruth approached them. 'Wait a minute, Constable.'

They stopped. Ruth went over to Neil and said in a very quiet voice, 'Neil, I have a very strong suspicion that you've hidden the murder weapon somewhere on this building site. It would make both of our lives much easier if you just tell me where you put it.'

'I have no idea what you're talking about,' came the reply.

Ruth let out an audible sigh. 'Neil, you do know that my officers are going to rip this place apart looking for that weapon. Come on, why don't you do everyone a favour and tell us where to look?'

Neil glared at her and sneered, 'Why don't you go and fuck yourself, you sanctimonious bitch!'

Ruth nodded but didn't react. 'Okay. I'll see you back at the station, Neil.'

The officer pushed Neil's head down as they shoved him into the back of the car and shut the door.

CHAPTER 34

AS ZOE TIDIED UP THE kitchen, she had half an eye on the BBC news. Taking a couple of dirty plates over to the dishwasher, she wondered where Neil had got to. He had promised to come home early so they could go to the supermarket together.

As she closed the dishwasher door, Zoe glanced up at the television screen as a BBC Wales presenter was speaking.

'There has been a major development in the investigation into the murder of Geoff Williams, the rugby coach who was brutally murdered in his home in Conwy last Sunday. A police spokesperson has confirmed in the last hour that a local man has been arrested in connection with the murder and is helping them with their enquiries.'

Just as the news moved on to the next item, the phone rang making Zoe jump.

'Hello?' she said, still lost in the news item she had just seen.

'Mrs Ellroy?' asked a serious voice that she didn't recognise.

Zoe got a very uneasy feeling. 'Yes?'

'It's Kenneth Davies from SPR Solicitors in Llancastell.'

'Okay.'

'I'm afraid I have some bad news, Mrs Ellroy,' Kenneth Davies said. 'I've had a phone call from Llancastell Police Station to inform us that your husband, Neil, has been arrested this afternoon in connection with the murder of Geoff Williams. We have been instructed to act on your husband's behalf.'

'Oh my God!' said Zoe desperately. She couldn't believe what she had just been told.

'I'm sorry. This must be very difficult for you. Neil will be interviewed under caution later this afternoon and I will be representing him. I think it is likely that he will be held overnight at Llancastell Police Station.'

'I don't understand. That's ridiculous!'

'I know this is a shock for you.'

Zoe's head was spinning. It felt like she was in some terrible anxiety nightmare.

'They've got it all wrong,' she said as her voice trembled.

'Let's find out what the police have to say, Mrs Ellroy.'

'*Why* has he been arrested?'

'We won't know that until we get to the interview.'

'Can I see him?' Zoe asked as her heart raced.

'I'm afraid that's not possible at the moment. I will have some time with Neil before the interview and after, so I will call you later to tell you how he is, what happened in the interview, and what to expect next. Is this the best number for me to contact you on?' Kenneth asked.

'Erm, yes. Do you know when that might be?' Zoe said, fighting the growing tremor in her voice as her body began to shake.

'Not at the moment. My guess would be late afternoon or early evening, Mrs Ellroy. So, I'll speak to you then, okay?'

'Yes, thank you. Goodbye.' Zoe's head was a jumbled mess with the news of Neil's arrest.

She went and sat at the table to calm down and collect her thoughts. *There must be some terrible mistake.* She didn't think for one moment that her husband was capable of murder. It was ridiculous.

'Mum?' Rhian said in a concerned voice as she came into the kitchen. 'What's wrong?'

'I've just had a phone call,' Zoe gasped, wondering how she was going to break the news to her children. 'Your ... father's been arrested.'

Rhian stared blankly at her. 'What are you talking about? What's he been arrested for?'

Zoe looked at her and before she could tell her, Rhian's eyes widened in horror. 'What? Are you joking? Dad?'

Zoe got up from the table and they hugged.

'It must be some horrible mistake,' Zoe said wiping a tear from her face.

'Mum, you're shaking,' Rhian said. 'They've got the wrong person. It's going to be fine.'

CHAPTER 35

RUTH AND NICK CAME out of the lift and walked purposefully down the corridor towards Interview Room 1 where they were due to question Neil Ellroy. Nick was on his phone as Ruth ran through the questions in her head. Even though she was certain that Neil was their man, she was worried that the evidence against him was circumstantial. She feared it wouldn't reach the CPS threshold for them to charge him with Geoff's murder and they would have to release him tomorrow.

Nick ended his call and looked at her. 'Nothing from the Shore Lane building site yet.'

'Sod it,' Ruth said. 'I was banking on something turning up.'

'They've searched his van and there's nothing in there either,' Nick explained. 'But the SOCOs have arrived with the GPR so they might turn up something. '

GPR stood for Ground Penetrating Radar and was used by UK police forces to examine earth, foundations, or concrete for evidence without the need to excavate.

They arrived at Interview Room 1 and entered to see Neil sitting beside his solicitor, Kenneth Davies.

Ruth and Nick sat down and pulled their chairs up to the table. She was feeling a little apprehensive as to how the interview was going to go. Neil Ellroy didn't strike her as the kind of man to lose his bottle and openly confess to a crime.

'Neil, I just need to remind you that you are still under caution and that you have been arrested on suspicion of the murder of Geoff Williams,' Ruth said. 'Do you understand that?'

Neil nodded, his face devoid of emotion. 'Yes.'

Ruth leant forward, pressed the red button on the recording equipment and waited for the long eletronic beep to finish.

'Interview with Neil Ellroy. Saturday 19th September, 7.15pm. Interview Room 1, Llancastell Police Station. Present are his solicitor Kenneth Davies, Detective Sergeant Nick Evans, and myself, Detective Inspector Ruth Hunter,' Ruth said as she moved the case files so they were directly in front of her.

Nick leaned forward with his forearms on the table and looked at Neil. 'Neil, since we last spoke we've had several developments in the case, which is why you're sitting here today.' Nick opened a file and pulled out a photograph. 'For the purpose of the recording, I'm showing the suspect Item Reference 393.' He moved the photo so that Neil could see it. 'As you can see, this image shows the back door to Geoff Williams' property. There are several fingerprints on the glass that have been circled in red, and another set of fingerprints on the door handle circled in blue. Would it surprise you to know that we have matched those fingerprints to the sample fingerprints that you gave us?'

Neil locked eyes with Nick. 'Not really.'

Nick raised an eyebrow. 'Neil, you told us that you had never been to the property before. How can you account for your fingerprints on the glass and handle of the back door?'

Neil shrugged. 'I had to drop off some consent forms to Geoff for Louie to play for North Wales Rugby. I knocked on his front door but there was no reply, so I went around the back. I cupped my hands to look through the back door and tried the handle.'

'When was this?'

'About two weeks ago.'

Ruth gave Neil a withering look. 'Come on, Neil. That doesn't make any sense. Why didn't you post the forms through the front door letterbox for starters?'

'They were in an A4 envelope. It wouldn't fit.'

'So you decided to go and see if the back door was open?'

'I wasn't going to go in. But if it was open, I was going to shout hello,' Neil replied defensively.

'Where are those forms now?'

'I had to wait until last Saturday and I gave them to Geoff at the rugby club.'

Ruth shook her head. 'And you expect us to believe that?'

'That's what happened.'

Nick took out another photo from the file and showed it to Neil. 'I'm now showing the suspect Item Reference 295. This image shows a partial footprint from the hallway at the victim's home. A soil analysis from that footprint showed significant traces of concrete and brick. Forensics believe the soil was likely to have orginated from a building site. Is there anything you would like to say about that?'

Neil shook his head but didn't look remotely fazed. 'I'm probably not the only person to have walked close to some building work in this area. It doesn't prove that I was there, does it?'

He's a very cool customer, Ruth thought. Even someone who was innocent would have been slightly rattled by these two new pieces of evidence.

Ruth looked directly at him and said, 'How did you feel about Geoff having an affair with your wife, Neil?'

This time Neil shifted uncomfortably in his seat and took a deep breath.

Now that's thrown him, Ruth thought.

Neil didn't answer for several seconds and then leant in to talk to Davies.

'No comment,' Neil said.

Ruth let out a loud sigh. 'Really, Neil? We're going to go down this route now are we?'

Nick glared at Davies. 'You're advising your client to continue giving us a 'no comment' interview are you?'

'That's my client's legal right,' he answered stiffly.

'Okay. I'm guessing that you were very angry when you found out Zoe had been sleeping with Geoff. How could you not be? In fact, your wife remembers you making a comment,' Ruth said as she checked through her notes and then read out, *'He said that if I didn't stop seeing Geoff, he would kill the pair of us.'* Is there anything you'd like to tell us about that, Neil?'

Neil stared down at the floor. 'No comment.'

'Can you see how suspicious that looks to us? And how suspicious that might look to a jury? You made a threat to kill Geoff Williams because he'd had an affair with your wife,' Ruth said.

'My guess is that when you found out he was now having sex with your twenty-one-year-old daughter, it was all too much for you. You decided that you actually were going to kill him. Is that right?' Nick asked.

'No comment.'

Nick waited for a few seconds before looking directly at Neil. 'That must have made you pretty angry. Your son thought the world of Geoff. He was like a father to him. In fact, Louie respected and liked Geoff far more than you, his own father. And on top of this, Geoff began to sleep with your wife. Already you're probably thinking of killing him.'

Ruth spotted Neil leaning forward and clenching his fists. It was all getting too much for him.

'And then last weekend, to rub salt into the wound, you find out that Geoff is now having sex with your daughter, who only left school a couple of years ago and ...'

Suddenly Neil sprang out of his seat and launched himself across the table. 'How fucking dare you!'

Jumping to her feet, Ruth dragged Neil back and away across the room. 'Oy, calm down, Neil, or we're going to add assaulting a police officer to the charges.'

Davies looked at Ruth. 'I think my client needs a break. And your sergeant there needs to think about the tone of his questioning.'

CHAPTER 36

ARRIVING AT DRAKE'S office, Ruth peered in and saw that Fiona Gatward, the Senior Lawyer for the North Wales Crown Prosecution Service, was sitting by his desk.

'Come in and sit down Ruth,' Drake said. 'You've met Fiona Gatward before, haven't you?'

Ruth nodded, smiled, and shook her hand. 'A couple of times, yes.'

If she was honest, Ruth had a bit of a crush on Fiona. She was full figured, with wavy brunette hair, and wore 40s-style makeup. Ruth thought she looked like a femme fatale from one of those film noir detective films she used to watch as a kid.

'Did you get anything from the interview with Neil Ellroy?' Drake asked.

Ruth raised an eyebrow. 'Not really. He tried to throttle Nick and I had to restrain him. He's cooling off for a bit in the holding cell. His brief has instructed him to go 'no comment' which is very frustrating.'

Drake held up the paperwork relating to the investigation. 'I've run through this with Fiona.'

Ruth's heart sank. She knew what was coming next.

'At the moment, I'm not satisfied that we've met the threshold to charge him with murder,' Fiona said. 'How sure are you that your suspect murdered Geoff Williams?'

'About ninety percent before I saw him go for DS Evans in the interview,' Ruth said. 'I'm not going to pretend that DS Evans wasn't trying to goad him, but his reaction to the questions about his wife and daughter's affairs with Geoff Williams sealed it for me.'

Fiona nodded. 'My big problem is the evidence linking your suspect to the scene of crime.'

'We have fingerprints on the back door and the soil sample from the hallway,' Ruth pressed.

'The defence will dismiss both of those as circumstantial. Neither of them conclusively put him at the scene of the crime at the time your victim was murdered.'

'We have motive and we have a threat to kill Geoff Williams,' Ruth continued. 'Plus, the suspect doesn't have a decent alibi.'

'Which is great for the prosecution, but it doesn't get us over the line at the moment,' Fiona said with an apologetic shrug.

Drake looked over at Ruth. 'What about the search of the Shore Lane building site?'

Ruth shook her head. 'Nothing yet, Boss.'

Fiona gave her a sympathetic smile. 'Sorry, Ruth.'

As she got up from her seat, Ruth looked at them both. 'We still have some more forensics to come back from the house. Something might turn up there.'

Drake nodded. 'Keep me posted, Ruth.'

With a sense of frustration, Ruth left Drake's office and headed back towards IR1. She didn't want Neil Ellroy to be released from custody. It might give him a chance to cover any tracks that he was still worried about. So that effectively gave them a full day tomorrow to find something to convince the CPS that they could take it to trial. They were running out of time.

She turned into the main CID corridor as Nick came out of IR1. He looked at her with a sense of urgency. 'Boss, I've been waiting for ...'

'... a girl like you, to come into my life,' Ruth said, interrupting him with song lyrics. She needed something to lighten her mood.

Nick laughed. 'I'm gonna say the band Chicago.'

'Nah, I'm pretty sure it's Foreigner,' Ruth said. 'And I need some good news as I've just had a very depressing conversation with Fiona Gatward from the CPS.'

Nick grinned. 'Oh yeah, she's quite fit for an older woman.'

'Older woman? She's in her 40s!' Ruth protested.

'Yeah. Sorry to break it to you, Boss, but 40s is older-woman territory.'

Ruth sighed. 'Anyway, what have you got?'

Nick gave her a meaningful look. 'They've found something at the building site and want us to go down there now.'

Ruth frowned. 'Why didn't you just say that when you first saw me!'

'Erm, because you were quoting soft rock lyrics to me?'

'Come on,' Ruth said as they turned around and made their way to the car park.

BY THE TIME NICK AND Ruth arrived at the Shore Lane site, not only was it dark, it had also started to rain. Ruth pulled up her collar as she got out of the car. The air was thick with the pungent smell of wet concrete and bricks. She could see that the SOCO team had erected several halogen lights to illuminate their search. A jackhammer was being used to break up the concrete base of one of the units. As they approached, the noise grew louder.

The man with the jackhammer stopped, and two SOCOs in their full white forensic suits stepped in to carefully remove the pieces of concrete that had been smashed.

As the rain turned from heavy drizzle to a downpour, another SOCO approached them.

'What do you think we've got?' Ruth said blinking the raindrops from her eyelashes.

'The GPR picked up a metallic object buried in that concrete base,' he explained. The rain was splashing noisily on his forensic suit.

'How far down?' Nick asked as he hunched his shoulders up against the downpour.

The SOCO glanced back to where the search was taking place. 'I'm guessing it's only two or three feet. But we've got to go slowly so we don't damage it.'

'Do you think it's a knife?' Ruth asked.

He shrugged. 'Hard to say. It's metal and it's about eight to ten inches long by the looks of it. But the GPR isn't good at defining specific shapes.'

'Okay, thanks,' Ruth said as the SOCO went back to his colleagues.

Ruth pushed a wet strand of hair from her face and looked at Nick. 'What do you think?'

'If I ran a building site and I had to get rid of a murder weapon, I would bring it here and hide it somewhere, especially if I knew it was going to be covered in concrete the following day.'

Ruth gave a wry smile. 'Yeah, so would I.'

Looking up to the black sky, she allowed the raindrops to fall on her face.

The jackhammer started again and Ruth could hardly hear herself think, let alone have a conversation.

There was a sudden shout from one of the SOCOs who signalled for the man to cut the jackhammer.

Two SOCOs crouched down and began to carefully remove more broken fragments of concrete. Ruth could see that they had found something and exchanged a look with Nick.

'Looks like we timed our arrival just right, Boss,' he said.

'Yeah, well fingers crossed that's a Sabatier kitchen knife and not a misplaced spanner or wrench.'

'I think they're the same thing. Isn't wrench just American for spanner?'

Ruth shrugged. 'You're asking the wrong person.'

One of the SOCOs stood up, turned around, and approached them. He was holding something that was wrapped in a cloth of some sort.

'I think you're in luck, ma'am,' he said as he reached them. The object he was holding appeared to be wrapped in a muddy tea towel that bore the Welsh Red Dragon.

'What have we got?' Ruth asked.

The SOCO opened up the tea towel to reveal a blood-stained kitchen knife that was about eight inches long.

Ruth scanned the knife and then saw a word engraved in the metal.

Sabatier.

CHAPTER 37

SUNDAY 20th September

It was 8am and Neil Ellroy was standing in front of the custody sergeant with his hands handcuffed in front of him by the time Ruth and Nick arrived. As the SIO on the case, it was Ruth's responsibility to transfer Neil to HMP Rhoswen where he was to be held on remand, and sign any necessary paperwork. She knew that, given the severity of the offence, he would probably be taken in front of a judge at Mold Crown Court the following morning when a date would be set for his trial.

The custody sergeant looked across at Neil and said, 'Neil Ellroy, you are charged with the murder of Geoff Williams contrary to common law. Do you have anything to say?'

Neil stared at the floor and shook his head.

A uniformed police officer led Neil out of the back entrance and down some steel steps into the rear car park where Nick had parked their car an hour ago. The torrential early morning rain had now stopped but the sky was still a dismal grey.

It was only a half hour journey to HMP Rhoswen where Neil would spend the next few months on remand before his trial.

Ruth and Nick followed him outside. Ruth was already starting to run through the paperwork she would need to prepare for the CPS in the lead-up to the trial. At least it meant she would be in her office for the next few weeks where she could stay dry and warm.

Suddenly, Neil smashed the uniformed officer in the face with his handcuffed fists and sprinted away across the car park towards the exit.

'Oh shit!' Ruth yelled.

'Bollocks,' Nick growled as they both broke into a run.

The officer groaned and sat up on the ground nursing a bloody nose.

'You okay, mate?' Nick shouted as he ran past him.

The officer nodded and said, 'Yeah, just don't let him escape.'

Ruth and Nick were sprinting after Neil.

'He can't get very far,' Nick said. 'He's wearing bloody handcuffs.'

'You'd be surprised,' said Ruth panting.

As they sped through the car park and reached the entrance, Nick grabbed his leg in extreme pain. 'Oh fuck!'

Ruth stopped in her tracks. 'What is it?'

'Hamstring,' Nick said, wincing and holding the back of his thigh.

'Christ, I thought I was out of shape,' Ruth said, already breathless. 'Don't worry, I've got this.'

Nick gave her a look. 'Be careful and don't do anything stupid. I'll call for back up, so keep your radio on.'

Ruth nodded and dashed away.

As she came out of the car park exit, she spotted Neil running ahead towards the main roundabout. Several pedestrians moved out of his way as he yelled at them. She was furious at herself that she and Nick had lost concentration and Neil had managed to escape so easily.

Setting off in pursuit, Ruth was trying to work out where he was going and how he thought he was going to get away. Maybe he didn't care?

There was the sound of an irate driver pumping their horn as Neil darted through the traffic. Up ahead was a three-floor multi-storey car park on Market Street.

Oh bollocks, he's going in there.

She watched as Neil ran past the automatic barrier at the car park entrance and then disappeared around the corner.

Thirty seconds later, Ruth arrived at the car park's ground floor. Sucking in breath, she stopped running and began to walk. Her chest was burning and her shoes were now rubbing the back of her feet.

Jesus, I'm unfit!

As she made her way inside, she continued trying to get her breath back as she noticed the drop in temperature from the outside. The car park was freezing cold and smelled of motor oil and urine.

Walking along slowly, Ruth gazed up at the low concrete roof and the long line of parked cars. The click of her shoes echoed noisily around the concrete walls.

Where the bloody hell has he gone?

Ruth clicked her Tetra radio. 'Three six to Control, over.'

'This is Control, go ahead three six.'

'I'm pursuing suspect Neil Ellroy who has escaped from custody. Suspect is now in the Market Street multi-storey car park, Llancastell, but I have lost visual contact. Request back-up, over,' she said as her breathing began to return to normal.

'Three six, received. Will advise, stand by, over and out.'

Ruth stopped, listened, and heard movement over by the door to the stairs. She jogged towards where she had heard the noise and saw that the door that led to the stairwell was open. As she went in, the stench of urine became overwhelming, and there were two syringes on the floor.

Lovely.

She began to walk up the stone steps and then heard, from higher up, the sound of someone running.

Where the hell is he going? And why is he going up to the top floor?

Picking up the pace, Ruth reached out and held onto the black handrail to keep her balance. Her head was swimming from the effort of chasing him.

The sound of movement and of doors opening came echoing from above.

Ruth yelled – her voice reverberating around the stairwell. 'Neil! Just stop. You're not going to get away.'

However, Ruth was beginning to feel uneasy. Maybe he had no intention of getting away. Perhaps he just couldn't face a long, emotionally-painful trial followed by twenty-five years in prison.

She started to take the steps two at a time, gasping for breath again as she went. The muscles in her thighs began to burn. She wasn't about to let her suspect throw himself off the top of a multi-storey car park.

The staircase ended and there was a door out to the top floor of the car park, which was open air. As she opened the door, a swirling gust of wind blew against her.

She clicked her radio. 'Three six to Control, I have pursued the suspect to the top floor of the Market Street multi-storey but still have no visual, over.'

'Control to three six, received. Backup is en route. ETA five minutes.'

There was a noise from the far side of the car park.

Ruth could see Neil climbing up onto a narrow perimeter wall.

Oh shit!

'Neil! Stop there. Please. I want you to talk to me!' she yelled.

As he glanced back at her, Neil continued climbing up onto the wall as best he could with his hands cuffed. It didn't look like he wanted to talk.

Ruth ran towards him, and she could feel the wind charging boisterously

around the cars. It howled and groaned as it swirled around her.

Getting to his feet, Neil glared at Ruth. 'Leave me alone!' he shouted as he balanced precariously on top of the wall.

Ruth yelled at him over the noise of the wind, 'Just stop whatever it is you're thinking of doing.'

Moving closer, Ruth could now see the road below. It was about a seventy or eighty foot drop. *He's not going to survive that.*

'Stay there!' Neil roared.

Ruth slowed her approach. 'Okay, but what about Louie and Rhian?'

Neil shook his head. 'They don't care about me. The person they really did care about is dead.'

Ruth shook her head and said, 'Don't you think they've been through enough?'

Neil gave an ironic laugh. '*I've* been through enough. With their mother, with Geoff, with Rhian.'

'This isn't the answer to anything, is it?'

'Do you really think I want to sit in a court with the faces of my wife and children full of hate, looking at me? And then sit for twenty years in prison for something I didn't do,' Neil shouted over at her.

Ruth moved closer. 'Don't you think now would be the time to actually admit that you killed Geoff?'

Neil's voice was filled with anger and resentment. 'Why would I? So you can wrap up your case nice and neatly. I don't think so.'

Ruth approached him cautiously and reached out. 'Come on, Neil. Just take my hand and come down. Please.'

Neil shook his head. 'No, I don't think so. I've got a three-second fall down there and then peace. That's a lot more appealing than what you're offering.'

Ruth leapt forward, grabbed the front of his jacket and pulled, getting her hands underneath his arms.

'What the hell are you doing?' Neil cried out as he struggled with her.

With an almighty heave, she tried to pull him off the wall.

For a second, she locked eyes with Neil before he gave her an almighty shove in the face, lost his balance, and then fell backwards and out of sight.

As Ruth raced to where he had fallen, she heard a piercing scream from the ground.

Neil's body lay in an awkward angle on the pavement below as passers-by stared in horror.

CHAPTER 38

48 HOURS LATER

Tuesday 22nd September

It had been a stressful few days and Ruth was now perched on a table at the front of IR1 going through the aftermath of Neil Ellroy's death with the CID team. It wouldn't be long before they began to pack up the scene board and return to the main CID offices.

'I've been informed this morning that there will be a full coroner's inquest into the events of two days ago, as well as an IOPC investigation. That means that everything we've done in this case up to this point is going to be open to scrutiny. I'm going to need all notes on interviews, telephone calls, and emails typed up and signed off on.'

'How do we approach investigating Geoff Williams' murder now, Boss?' asked French.

'Good question,' Ruth said. 'We carry on as if we were going to trial to convict Neil Ellroy of Geoff's murder. It doesn't matter that he's now dead. The CPS will want to see all the evidence that we've got. And if we find new evidence, or if we are still chasing leads or witnesses, then we continue with those, as we would do with any other murder case. Any questions?' Ruth looked at the team. 'Right, thank you everyone.'

As the CID detectives began to disperse, Ruth made her way back towards her office.

She spotted that Garrow was ploughing through more CCTV from the Shore Lane building site.

'Still going, Jim?' Ruth asked, looking over his shoulder.

'Living the dream, Boss,' Garrow said dryly. 'At the moment, there's no sign of Neil Ellroy going to hide the knife where it was discovered, which would be a clincher in terms of evidence.'

'Yeah, it would,' Ruth said, peering at the monitor. 'I'm trying to work out which part of the site we're looking at here?'

'This is the camera mounted on the opposite side to where you drive in. And this is where the knife was hidden and buried,' Garrow said pointing to a dark, shadowy area at the top of the screen. 'We see Neil coming in at 6pm, he fixes the fence and then he leaves at 7.15pm.'

'In his statement, he claimed to have left the family home just after five. And it's only a ten minute drive to Shore Lane, which gives him fifty minutes to go to Geoff's home, commit the murder and arrive here,' Ruth added.

'The only thing is, he never goes anywhere near this part of the site where the knife was buried,' Garrow explained.

'If he knew that we would be watching the CCTV to establish an alibi, then maybe he returned to the site at a later time to bury the knife,' Ruth said, thinking out loud. 'It could be worth having a look early the following morning. He might have used his arrival at work to cover him burying the murder weapon.'

'Yes, Boss,' Garrow said. 'I'll let you know how I get on.'

'Thanks, Jim.'

Ruth began to walk back to her office. She slowed down at the scene board and gazed at the faces of those who had been caught up in the tragedy of the last week. The Williams and Ellroy families. It was awful to think that, just over a week ago, those people were living relatively 'normal' lives. Going about their everyday business with no idea of what darkness was about to unfold. A horrifying week that would turn their lives upside down and see the untimely deaths of two men.

With this sobering thought, Ruth went into her office and saw Nick sitting at her desk.

'You sneaked in here without me seeing,' Ruth said with a smile. 'You okay?'

'Yeah, sort of,' came the reply.

'How's Amanda?'

'She's getting there,' Nick said. 'I need a favour.'

Ruth nodded. 'Of course. What is it?'

'Now that this case is coming to a close, I'd like to take some time off. Maybe a week. I'm going to take Amanda and Megan away and I've seen a beautiful place on Angelsey that we can rent. It's right on the beach.'

'That's a brilliant idea,' Ruth said with a smile. 'Take as much time as you need.'

'A month will do,' Nick joked.

Ruth laughed. 'Don't push your luck, buster.'

Nick looked at her with genuine warmth. 'Thank you.'

CHAPTER 39

THURSDAY 24th September

Zoe, Rhian, and Louie stood to one side of the cemetery at the church of St Joseph's and All Saints in Conwy. Built in the 14th and 15th centuries, it looked like many other churches in North Wales, with its grey and brown stone walls and squared-off steeple. As the wind picked up, it blew on Zoe's face and she gazed at the church spire as the grey clouds moved and gave way to sunshine.

It had been half an hour since they'd attended a very low-key funeral for Neil. Zoe had given Rhian and Louie the option of not attending given the events of the previous ten days, but they had decided it was the right thing to do.

'I'm going to wait in the car,' Louie mumbled and then walked away with his shoulders rounded, looking at the ground.

'I don't know what to say to him,' Zoe admitted.

'Give him time, I guess,' Rhian said.

Since Neil's death she, Rhian, and Louie had been in a total state of shock in the family home. For the first two days, there had been journalists and photographers outside their house. They had avoided reading or watching the news as what had happened was almost too much to bear. Zoe also had to battle for Neil to be buried in the family plot at St Joseph's. Even though the vicar hadn't said that he didn't want to carry out a

255

funeral for a murderer, the implication had been clear. Eventually, Zoe had agreed to a quick service and burial with just her, the children, and Neil's parents who had arrived and left again in virtual silence.

As two grave diggers ambled over to Neil's open grave and began to shovel earth into the hole, Zoe took a deep breath and began to cry.

'How has this happened?' she sobbed.

Rhian turned to her and they hugged. 'I don't know. I'm so sorry, Mum.'

As they faced each other, Zoe moved a strand of hair from her daughter's face. 'We used to come here every Sunday morning. The four of us.'

'Yeah, I know,' Rhian said with a grimace. 'I don't think me or Louie were very happy about it though.'

'You weren't. You kicked off every Sunday before we left home.' Zoe forced a smile and glanced back at the church. 'We got married here, you know?' she said, remembering the joyful day in June 1996. 'Your dad was so different back then. He was fun and a bit mad, but never boring or miserable.'

'What happened to him?' Rhian asked.

Zoe shook her head sadly. 'I just don't know.'

Rhian screwed up her face and began to sob. This time Zoe took her in her arms. 'Hey, it's okay.'

'It's not okay. This is all my fault,' Rhian whispered through the tears.

'You mustn't blame yourself, love. You didn't do anything wrong.'

Rhian moved back from her mother and wiped her face. ' did. I'm the reason that Dad's over there.'

Zoe shook her head. 'No. You can't blame yourself.'

'But it was me that ...'

'Rhian, listen to me. I won't have you living the rest of your life feeling guilty for what your father chose to do,' Zoe said sternly.

'But I am to blame.'

'No, you're not. You're not responsible for your father's actions. And you must never think that,' Zoe said with an earnest expression.

Rhian looked at Zoe directly with an expression that she couldn't quite read. 'Mum, you don't understand what I'm trying to tell you!'

'Okay, well tell me then.'

'It was me, Mum.'

Zoe looked at Rhian and frowned. 'What does that mean?'

'I did it.'

'I keep telling you not to blame yourself.'

Rhian raised her eyebrows and stared intently at her. 'No! I did it. I killed Geoff. It was me.'

For a few seconds, Zoe thought she had misheard her. She must have said something else.

'You didn't kill Geoff. Your dad did,' Zoe said. 'What are you talking about?'

Rhian didn't say anything but continued to stare at her. Zoe felt the pit of her stomach lurch as she froze.

Zoe moved a step forward and looked at her. 'You're scaring me, Rhian. What are you saying?'

CHAPTER 40

WALKING THROUGH THE doors of IR1, Ruth was pre-occupied with thoughts of Sarah -where she was and what might be happening to her. She tried hard not to let her imagination run away with her, but she knew it was likely that Sarah was being held somewhere in Paris, against her will, and that she was scared. It was horrible to feel so helpless, especially because as a police officer Ruth was used to resolving situations like this through being pro-active.

She made her way towards her desk, and noticed Georgie approaching.

'Boss, the pregnancy test that forensics found in the rubbish bin at Geoff Williams' home was positive. I don't think it has much bearing on the case now, but if Claire Williams was pregnant, I'm guessing that it would have been Paul Marlow's child.'

'Okay,' Ruth said, taking in the information. 'Thanks Georgie, but I think you're right. I don't think it matters now.'

Ruth went into her office and checked her emails. There was one from Stephen Flaherty which she opened immediately.

Hi Ruth

This morning I've spoken to the DGSE, which is Direction Générale De La Sécurité Extérieure (don't quote me!). It's the French version of MI5 apparently. They've been trying to track down Patrice Le Bon to question him about his involvement in international human trafficking between Paris and North Africa. They think they've found him hiding out on a five-hundred-acre farm close to the Forêt de Sénart, which is south of Paris. There is also intelligence that he is continuing to run Global Escorts out of the farm. So, the DGSE and Police National are now mounting a combined surveillance operation there today.

I'll keep you posted with any developments.

Best,

Stephen

Ruth immediately wondered whether Sarah was being kept on the farm in question. Maybe when the Global Escorts premises were raided, Le Bon took everyone living there with him to hide out in the middle of the French countryside?

There was a knock at the door and Nick peered in. 'Got five minutes?'

'For you, always,' Ruth said with a smile. Talking to Nick was a welcome distraction from worrying about Sarah.

Nick handed her the holiday forms that he needed her to sign. 'If you can scribble on these?'

'Of course,' Ruth said. 'When are you going?'

'End of the week,' Nick said. She could see that he had the sparkle back in his eyes that had been missing for a while now.

'You're going to have an amazing time. It's just what you guys need.'

Nick smiled at her. 'And we're going to set a date.'

Ruth's eyes widened. 'For the wedding?'

'Yeah.' Nick nodded. 'I haven't run it past Amanda yet, but I just think we should get married at Christmas.'

'Brilliant idea! Winter wedding,' Ruth exclaimed as she gave him a beaming smile. 'I don't do hats though.'

Nick laughed. 'Yeah, I didn't think you did, Boss.'

Garrow appeared at the door with a serious look on his face.

Ruth frowned. 'I always worry when you appear at my door looking like that, Jim. It's never good news.'

'I'm the Grim Reaper of CID,' Garrow said dryly and then pulled a face. 'But there is something you really need to see.'

Nick looked at Ruth. 'Doesn't sound good.'

Garrow came over with a memory stick. 'Okay if I show you on here?'

Ruth moved her chair back and nodded. 'Help yourself.'

Slotting the memory stick into Ruth's computer, Garrow used the mouse to find the right video file.

'What are we looking at?' Ruth asked.

'CCTV from the Shore Lane building site,' Garrow said as he found the file and brought it up onto Ruth's monitor.

'What's the problem?' Nick asked as he took a seat.

'I've been looking through the CCTV that Site Security sent over. I told you that I couldn't find any footage showing Neil Ellroy hiding the murder weapon where we found it buried in concrete,' Garrow said.

'Yeah,' Ruth confirmed. 'You were going to see if he came back at any point later or the next day to hide it.'

'Yes, I did that,' Garrow said.

'And did he?' Nick asked.

Garrow shook his head. 'No. So, just to check, I went back to 5pm on Sunday afternoon. I wondered if Neil had sneaked in to hide the weapon, gone out, and then reappeared at 6pm for the sake of anyone watching the CCTV to confirm his alibi. Bit of a longshot but ...'

Ruth gave him a quizzical look. 'And did he?'

'No,' Garrow said. 'But someone else did.'

Ruth's eye widened as she exchanged a look with Nick. 'What?'

'Someone else did. Watch.' Garrow began to play the CCTV. 'If you look in the shadows at the back here, there's a figure that comes onto the site, goes over to where we discovered the knife, partially buries it and then leaves.'

Ruth peered carefully at the screen. It was very difficult to make anything out as it was so dark. 'I can hardly see it.'

'Yeah, I completely missed it the first time I looked through it,' Garrow admitted.

'How do you know that's not Neil Ellroy though?' Nick asked.

Garrow pointed to the shadowy figure as they reached the gate. 'That person is a woman, Sarge. They're small ... and look at the person's shape.'

Ruth squinted at the screen. 'You're right. It's definitely not Neil Ellroy.'

What the hell is going on? Ruth thought.

'Have we got a better camera angle where we can see who it is?' Ruth asked, now worrying that there might be someone else involved in Geoff Williams' murder.

'Unfortunately, that's the only camera which covers that part of the site,' Garrows said.

Ruth's gaze moved from Garrow to Nick. 'Who the hell is it then?'

Nick shook his head. 'I don't understand. Neither Zoe or Rhian Ellroy would have helped Neil to kill Geoff and help bury the murder weapon, would they?'

'No, that doesn't make any sense.' Ruth's mind raced to try and work out what she had just seen. 'Maybe it's someone else?'

'There's a camera on the roof of the show home that covers not only the whole site, but also Shore Lane itself,' Garrow said as he searched the CCTV video files he had been sent. 'Maybe we could see our mystery person when they arrive.'

'That would be even further away than we are now, wouldn't it?' Nick asked.

Garrow found the file he was looking for, clicked it, and the high camera angle from the roof came up on Ruth's monitor. He whizzed the footage along to 5pm on Sunday afternoon, paused it, and pointed. 'There ...'

Ruth could see a dark figure in a hoodie scaling the wall beside the mesh iron entrance gates. 'I can't see anything more than that it's a person.'

Nick looked at them. 'Play it forward to when they leave the site, Jim.'

Garrow moved the footage forward until the figure came into shot again, scaled the wall, and walked down Shore Lane away from the site.

Ruth shrugged. 'Okay. I don't see how that helps us, Nick.'

Nick held up his hand as he peered intently at the screen. 'Just wait for a second. Keep it playing ...'

They all watched as the figure continued to walk down Shore Road until they reached a line of parked cars in the distance. Even though the figure was now tiny on the screen, Ruth could see that they had got into one of the cars.

'We're never going to be able to read a number plate at this distance,' Ruth said.

Nick looked at her. 'We might not need to.'

A few seconds later, there was the faint glow from the back-lights of the car as it pulled out from where it had been parked.

Nick pointed to the screen. 'That looks like a black Mini.'

'Jesus!' Ruth gasped.

She knew exactly who drove a black Mini.

'What the hell is Rhian doing?' she asked in shock.

For a few seconds, Ruth's mind started to race as she began to put the pieces together. Why would Rhian Ellroy be hiding the murder weapon at her father's building site? Then something occurred to her.

'Neil Ellroy didn't kill Geoff Williams,' Ruth muttered under her breath.

'What are you talking about, Boss?' Nick asked.

'The pregnancy test,' Ruth said.

Nick looked at Garrow – they didn't know what she was talking about.

'We found a pregnancy test loose in the bin at Geoff Williams' property. I assumed that it was Claire Williams. Georgie just told me forensics confirmed that it was positive.'

Nick looked at her and then nodded – he was now on the same page as her. 'But Claire Williams told us that she can't have children. So, why would she be taking a pregnancy test?'

'It's not her test,' Ruth responded. 'It's Rhian Ellroy's test. She's pregnant with Geoff Williams' baby.'

Garrow frowned. 'I'm totally lost now, Boss.'

'Rhian went around to Geoff's last Sunday afternoon. She thinks that she's pregnant, does the test in front of him, and tells Geoff that he's the father. Except Geoff's not interested,' Ruth said.

Nick continued. 'Geoff tells her to get rid of it and goes and has a shower.'

'Rhian has a pro-life poster in her bedroom. She was adopted from a very young mother who chose to have her rather than have an abortion. So, abortion is a highly emotive subject for Rhian,' Ruth said as the pieces started to fit together.

'Maybe Geoff said something flippant or even cruel about her getting an abortion and she just flipped?' Nick suggested.

Ruth got up from her seat and looked at Nick. 'We need to go and pick her up.'

'What about Neil Ellroy?' Garrow asked.

Ruth gave him a severe look. 'I think we might have got the wrong person.'

Nick glanced at his watch. 'It was Neil Ellroy's funeral today, Boss, so I know exactly where she'll be.'

CHAPTER 41

ZOE AND RHIAN SAT TOGETHER on a bench close to the black iron gates of the cemetery. Zoe was still in utter shock from what her daughter had just told her.

'I'm so, so sorry, Mum,' Rhian said, looking totally lost.

'What the hell happened?'

'I'm pregnant with Geoff's baby,' Rhian admitted.

'Oh my God,' Zoe groaned. It was all getting too much. 'Just tell me what happened.'

'When I told him that I was pregnant, he got really nasty. He said it was my fault even though I'd told him I wasn't on the pill.' Rhian began to cry. 'Then he told me to take a pregnancy test to prove it, as if I was lying.'

'What?' Zoe couldn't believe what she was hearing. 'That's vile. Why was he being like that?'

Rhian shook her head. 'I don't know. I've never seen him act like that before ... I did the test and showed him it was positive.'

'What did he say?'

'He shrugged and said it was nothing to do with him. He wasn't interested,' Rhian explained as the tears dripped down her face. 'He told me to get rid of it.'

'Oh love, I'm so sorry,' Zoe said, taking her daughter's hands.

'When I told him I wasn't going to do that ...' Rhian broke down and sobbed, '... he said that given my birth mother was a junkie whore, he didn't want his child sharing my genes.'

Zoe snapped and said, 'Oh my God! You told him you were adopted?'

'Yeah,' Rhian nodded. 'I never thought he'd use it against me. He said getting rid of it wasn't a big deal as it was just a few cells. Then he said he felt sorry for me as you were a whore as well.'

Zoe shook her head. 'I can't believe he said all that.'

'He said you were better in bed than me and I should ask you for some tips. And then he went to have a shower ... and I just lost it.'

'I'm so sorry.' Zoe had tears in her eyes as she looked at her daughter. 'Poor you. If I'd known he had said all that to you, I would have bloody killed him instead. Horrible prick.'

'What happens now, Mum?' Rhian asked desperately.

Before Zoe could answer her, there was a noise and movement over by the gates.

They glanced over, and saw that DI Ruth Hunter and DS Nick Evans had arrived.

Rhian stood up and looked at them. 'Have you come for me?'

Ruth nodded. 'Yes. We need to take you to the station, Rhian.'

Rhian looked at Zoe. 'I'd better go with them, Mum.'

'Yeah,' Zoe whispered and hugged her. 'I'll follow you up there, okay? Don't worry, we'll sort this.'

Rhian's voice broke with emotion. 'I love you, Mum.'

'I love you too, darling.' Zoe watched Rhian walk away from her and Ruth put her in cuffs.

CHAPTER 42

FRIDAY 25th September

Putting his finished paperwork into a neat pile, Nick pushed his chair back from his desk with a feeling of satisfaction. Tomorrow morning he, Amanda, and Megan were driving across to a cottage on Anglesey and he couldn't wait.

Llancastell CID had just got news that Rhian Ellroy's trial would take place in four months' time at Mold Crown Court. He couldn't ever remember working a murder case where it had been so incredibly difficult to identify the person responsible.

'I hear you're not in next week?' said a voice. It was Georgie.

Nick looked up at her. 'Yeah. We're going to a cottage on Anglesey for a week.'

'Oh right,' Georgie said as she raised an eyebrow. 'Sounds very cosy.'

Why has she made that sound like an insult?

Nick ignored her comment. 'Yeah, should be nice. Just the three of us. Right on the beach.'

'I bet Megan will love that,' Georgie said, sounding thoroughly disinterested. 'And Alison and you get a bit of time together.'

There's no way she's not doing that on purpose.

'It's Amanda,' Nick snapped. 'Her name is Amanda.'

Georgie frowned and put her hands up in mock defence. 'Amanda. Sorry.'

Nick bristled. 'Yeah, well I've told you that about a dozen times.'

'Okay, I'm sorry,' Georgie said and then took a few seconds before looking at him. 'Is everything all right, Sarge?'

Nick nodded. 'Yeah, of course. I'm about to go on holiday for a week with my family, so everything is absolutely fine.'

'It's just that it feels like you've been avoiding me?'

'I probably have,' Nick replied. He was happy to admit it.

Georgie gave him a playful tap on the arm and laughed. 'Oh, well that's nice. I thought we were friends?'

'Did you?' Nick asked.

'Am I missing something here?' Georgie sounded annoyed.

'Georgie, I'm happy for us to be friends,' Nick said. 'And it's my fault, but I also need to remember that I'm your DS in this department too. I've blurred the lines and that's not very professional.'

'What, and now you and me have to be all professional?' she laughed. 'I thought we were ... well, a bit more than just that.'

Nick shook his head. 'No, sorry. And I'm happy to admit to giving out mixed signals, but not anymore.'

'Oh ... right,' Georgie said, trying not to sound angry. 'Fair enough. Have a nice holiday then, Sarge. I'll see you when you get back.'

'Thanks, Georgie.' Nick felt a huge sense of relief as she turned and walked over to her desk.

CHAPTER 43

SATURDAY 26th September

It was Saturday afternoon and Ruth had just bought a ticket to visit Chirk Castle and its gardens. As she began to walk up the steep driveway towards the castle entrance, she looked out at the woods that stretched away to her right. It was ablaze with golds, oranges, and deep caramel browns. Taking a deep breath of cold air, she stopped for a moment about halfway up and turned to look up at the looming presence of Chirk Castle above her. The sky was a perfect blue with white cumulus clouds arranged like cotton wool in perfect symmetry. The double white lines of an aeroplane's contrail formed a neat curve between two clouds directly above her.

Leaning against the dark grey stone wall, she remembered the last time she had been to Chirk Castle. It was with Sian almost a year ago to the day. She had taken a photograph of Sian pulling a silly face in her purple knitted hat in the very spot where Ruth now stood. But now she was on her own. At the risk of feeling immense self pity, she wondered if she might find someone whom she could bring to Chirk Castle next year. What would the next twelve months bring?

The buzzing of her mobile phone broke her train of thought. The problem with being a Detective Inspector was that she was always technically on duty. Taking the phone from her pocket, she looked at it. The caller ID just read *International al Number Calling.* It could be anyone and, given her job, she never answered a call from any unidentified number. Putting the phone away, her hand touched her packet of cigarettes. She would have one when she got up to the gardens, she told herself.

As she continued to stride up the steep driveway, she spotted the huge, black wrought iron gates that had been built in the early 1700s. Gazing up at them, her eyes spotted the exquisite gold-painted highlights, the iron coronets, and the brightly-coloured coat of arms that lay at the gates' centre.

Her phone began to buzz again. It was the same international number, and part of her was tempted to answer and just demand to know what they wanted on a Saturday afternoon. Instead, she turned it off, returned it to her pocket, and took out the packet of cigarettes as she reached the entrance to the gardens.

Nick closed his eyes for a few seconds and took a deep breath of sea air. The autumnal sun warmed his face. He couldn't remember feeling this relaxed for a long time.

'Hey, I hope you're not going to sleep?' Amanda said with a playful tap on his shoulder.

Blinking open his eyes, Nick smiled at her. Her blonde tresses glimmered in the sunshine and her chestnut eyes looked big and beautiful. *Wow, she looks amazing,* he thought to himself. It was the same warm feeling he had got when he had first kissed her in a coffee shop in Llancastell.

They had been sitting on a blanket on the beach for nearly an hour and Nick couldn't think of anywhere he'd rather be.

'Are you okay?' Amanda asked with a frown.

'Yeah, I'm fine. I'm more than fine. Why?'

'You just had a funny expression.'

He smiled. 'Yeah, that's just my face.'

Megan wandered in the sand nearby with a bucket and spade collecting stones.

'Don't go too far, darling,' Amanda said as Megan toddled away.

Nick leaned in, kissed her and then stared at her. 'It's so good for us three to get away like this.'

'Yeah, it's lovely. Thank you so much.' Amanda touched his cheek with the side of her thumb, her lips forming a pensive grin. 'Just when I've decided you really are a twat, you do something like this to prove me wrong.'

'Aww, thanks. Happy to oblige,' Nick laughed. 'Do you remember when I proposed to you?'

'How could I forget?' Amanda said, shaking her head. 'You did that stupid thing with the metal detector.'

'I thought it was romantic,' Nick said taking mock offence. 'Bloody hell, it took me ages to come up with that. It was better than putting a ring in your pudding at a restaurant.'

'Yeah, it was certainly original. I'll give you that.'

'I want us to set a date for our wedding,' Nick said. 'After what happened last week, it just feels like we should ...' He was lost for the right words.

'... declare our undying love in front of our friends and family?' Amanda quipped.

'You're such a cynic.'

Amanda smiled. 'No, it sounds great. When?'

'December?'

'Ooh, a winter wedding!'

'Do you like the sound of that?' Nick asked.

Amanda gave him a knowing look. '*I do.*'

Nick laughed. 'Ah, I see what you did there. Very good. Well?'

'A winter wedding would be perfect.'

CHAPTER 44

SITTING OUT ON HER patio wrapped in a blanket, Ruth took a long swig of red wine as she watched the light of the day begin to fade. It was a Saturday night. For a moment, she thought of what Saturday nights used to be like when she was younger. It was a by-word for booze, drugs, and dancing until dawn. Twenty-five years ago she would have been at someone's flat in South London for pre-drinks. They wouldn't leave until gone ten, when they would head off to whichever club night they had selected. At first it was always the Ministry of Sound. Then The Cross, Bagley's or The End. The DJs she and her friends followed were like pop stars. Legendary names like Tony Humphries, Frankie Knuckles, and David Morales. It felt like a lifetime ago, and nights like that took 2-3 days to recover from even in her 20s.

Her mobile phone buzzed on the garden table. Picking it up, she saw it was an international number again. She pressed the red *Decline* button to end the call.

Reaching over to the table, Ruth opened her packet of cigarettes. Taking one, she picked up her lighter, lit the cigarette and took a long drag. She sat back on the padded garden recliner and blew a long plume of smoke up into the air, watching as it floated and rose in the still evening air.

The phone buzzed again. She grabbed it with a sense of annoyance, and prepared herself to tell whoever it was that she

wasn't interested in whatever goods or service they were trying
to sell her.'

'Hello?' she snapped in an irritated voice.

At the end of the line, there was white noise and then a series of bangs as if the phone had been dropped.

The line went dead.

Jesus! What was that all about?

Before she even had time to put the phone back on the
table, it rang again with the same *International Number Calling*
message on the screen.

She answered it.

'Hello? What do you want?' she growled down the phone.

'Ruth?' said a woman's voice which crackled on the broken
line.

'Who is this?' Ruth asked. She didn't recognise the voice
but she was definitely English.

The line broke up with a wave of white noise again.

'Ruth? It's Sarah ...'

Ruth dropped her cigarette and sat bolt upright.

'What?'

'It's Sarah.'

That's her voice!

'Sarah. Oh ... my God, I ...' Ruth stammered, feeling utterly
overwhelmed.

'I know. I can't believe I'm speaking to you,' Sarah said. Her
voice was now clear.

'Where are you?' Ruth asked, her hands trembling as she
held the phone.

'France. Somewhere near Paris, I think,' she said with a
sense of urgency.

'Is it a farm?' Ruth asked, thinking of the intel she'd been given.

'Yes, how did you know that? Oh my God, it's amazing to hear your voice.' Sarah sounded upset.

'I know. I feel like I'm dreaming,' Ruth said as tears came to her eyes. 'Are you okay?'

'Not really. I'm trapped here. But I'm not hurt ...' There was some noise from wherever Sarah was calling from. 'I've got to go, Ruth. I'll try and call again,' she said in a virtual whisper.

'I'm coming to get you.'

'I've got to go,' Sarah whispered. 'What did you just say?'

'Don't worry. I'm getting the first plane to Paris, okay?' Ruth said trying to get her breath. 'I'm coming to get you, Sarah.'

Enjoy this book?
Get the next book in the series
'The River Seine Killings' #Book 10[1]
on pre-order on Amazon
https://www.amazon.co.uk/dp/B096MTPJK7
https://www.amazon.com/dp/B096MTPJK7
Publication date August 2021

The River Seine Killings
A Ruth Hunter Crime Thriller #Book 10

Your FREE book is waiting for you now

Get your FREE copy of the prequel to
the DI Ruth Hunter Series NOW
http://www.simonmccleave.com/vip-email-club
and join my VIP Email Club

NEW RUTH HUNTER SERIES

LONDON, 1997. A SERIES of baffling murders. A web of political corruption. DC Ruth Hunter thinks she has the brutal killer in her sights, but there's one problem. He's a Serbian War criminal who died five years earlier and lies buried in Bosnia.

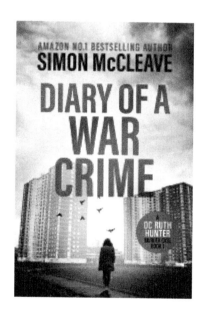

https://www.amazon.co.uk/dp/B08T654J73

https://www.amazon.com/dp/B08T654J73

AUTHOR'S NOTE

Although this book is very much a work of fiction, it is located in Snowdonia, a spectacular area of North Wales. It is steeped in history and folklore that spans over two thousand years. It is worth mentioning that Llancastell is a fictional town on the eastern edges of Snowdonia. I have made liberal use of artistic licence, names and places have been changed to enhance the pace and substance of the story.

Acknowledgements

I WILL ALWAYS BE INDEBTED to the people who have made this novel possible.

My mum, Pam, and my stronger half, Nicola, whose initial reaction, ideas and notes on my work I trust implicitly. And Dad, for his overwhelming enthusiasm.

Thanks also to Barry Asmus, former South London CID detective, for checking my work and explaining the complicated world of police procedure and investigation. My Editor Rebecca Millar, for pushing me to produce the best work I can. Carole Kendal for her acerbic humour, copy editing and meticulous proofreading. My designer Stuart Bache for yet another incredible cover design. My superb agent, Millie Hoskins at United Agents, and Dave Gaughran and Nick Erick for invaluable support and advice.

Printed in Great Britain
by Amazon